"Billerbeck has the most delightful voice I've ever read. I adore her stories, and she returns with an enchanting new novel, *The Theory of Happily Ever After*. I laughed, cried, and rejoiced with her wonderful characters and was sad when the story ended. Highly recommended!"

—**Colleen Coble**, *USA Today* bestselling author

"Kristin Billerbeck is back with a classic, witty chick lit. *The Theory of Happily Ever After* is a journey of self-discovery peppered with wisdom and truth. I loved Maggie Maguire, finding a little bit of myself in her. A must-read for lovers of chick lit."

—**Rachel Hauck**, *New York Times* bestselling author

"I absolutely adored *The Theory of Happily Ever After* from first page to last. Billerbeck's signature humor made me laugh again and again, and her memorable characters stole my heart. Don't miss this one!"

—**Robin Lee Hatcher**, Christy and RITA Award–winning author
of *You're Gonna Love Me*

"Billerbeck's latest, *The Theory of Happily Ever After*, is a fun romance with a multilayered main character you'll want to be friends with. This read does not disappoint in humor and romance. Highly recommend!"

—**Robin Caroll**, author of *Weaver's Needle*

the theory of
happily ever
after

the theory of happily ever after

KRISTIN BILLERBECK

Revell

a division of Baker Publishing Group
Grand Rapids, Michigan

Published by Revell
a division of Baker Publishing Group
PO Box 6287, Grand Rapids, MI 49516-6287
www.revellbooks.com

Printed in the United States of America

Library of Congress Cataloging-in-Publication Data
Names: Billerbeck, Kristin, author.
Title: The theory of happily ever after / Kristin Billerbeck.
Description: Grand Rapids, MI : Revell, a division of Baker Publishing Group,
    [2018]
Identifiers: LCCN 2017053996 | ISBN 9780800729448 (pbk. : alk. paper)
Subjects: | GSAFD: Love stories. | Christian fiction.
Classification: LCC PS3602.I44 T54 2018 | DDC 813/.6—dc23
LC record available at https://lccn.loc.gov/2017053996

Unless otherwise indicated, Scripture quotations are from the *Holy Bible*, New Living Translation, copyright © 1996, 2004, 2015 by Tyndale House Foundation. Used by permission of Tyndale House Publishers, Inc., Carol Stream, Illinois 60188. All rights reserved.

Scripture quotations marked NASB are from the New American Standard Bible®, copyright © 1960, 1962, 1963, 1968, 1971, 1972, 1973, 1975, 1977, 1995 by The Lockman Foundation. Used by permission. (www.Lockman.org)

18   19   20   21   22   23   24   7 6 5 4 3 2 1

This book is dedicated to the amazing people in my life who believed in me when I'd lost faith in myself. Sometimes God gives you friends to help you carry the load, but ultimately he has equipped you to handle what life throws at you. Words cannot express my gratitude for my fellow writers, who showered me with love and encouragement when I felt none: Colleen Coble, Denise Hunter, Nancy Toback, Cheryl Hodde, Jenny B. Jones, Christa Allan, Sibella Giorello, Kathleen Y'Barbo, and C. S. Lakin.

1

A harsh reality is better than a false fantasy. Life is not a fairy tale.

The Science of Bliss by Dr. Margaret K. Maguire

L IFE IS FILLED WITH IRONY. I mean, I wrote the book on bliss, and currently I am the most miserable person I know. Probably I'd be the most miserable person you know as well. Which is why I have been perfectly content to hole up in my tiny apartment for the past two months and binge-watch romance movies while simultaneously gorging on eggnog ice cream. There's the science of happiness, and then there's reality.

Unlike life, heartwarming television movies never let you down, and there is no unexpected twist in which the heroine looks like one big cosmic punch line. The hero in a TV movie never leaves our heroine for the mean girl—the mean girl actually gets shot down. There is no crisis too great that it cannot be overcome by true love. And everyone lives happily ever after. Isn't that how life should be? Truly blissful?

"In a Hallmark movie," I say to the cat, Neon, "your ex never tells you that his new girlfriend's hobby is aerial dance or that she's a professional trapeze artist. It just wouldn't happen."

Neon raises his head and looks at me questioningly. The cat generally stays near the door across the sparsely decorated apartment. It's as if he instinctively knows my failures might be contagious. My living room has a barren, college-dorm feel, which serves as a constant reminder that I didn't make the time to buy a condo with the royalty windfall from my book, that my hard-won title of doctor hasn't translated into practical motivation. The walls are a stark white, and there's a white processed-wood TV shelf against the wall by the door, a navy rocking chair my parents handed down to me, and the white vertical blinds that came with the place. Nothing screams home. It's like a lab experiment.

I set another Diet Coke bottle on the lonely IKEA coffee table. "Well, it wouldn't," I reiterate.

Neon meows. Even the cat is annoyed with me.

I scoop up a giant spoonful of ice cream and let it touch my tongue and linger momentarily, then devour it as though I haven't seen food for weeks. For one incredible moment, I feel only unadulterated joy, and Jake Stone's epic departure is not fresh on my mind. *Dirtbag.*

There is nothing more fantastic than the sappy, sugary-sweet love of a television movie followed by a creamy chaser of gelato. My life's work—the scientific study of how people find joy in life—isn't proper science. I see that my research is all unfounded now. Perhaps to find the secret of happiness, I should have studied miserable people and found out what they were missing. True bliss, it seems, is found in the avoidance of ugly truths and evading reality. Reality bites.

My phone trills and Jake's handsome face lights up the device. Argh. Why does he have to look so good? This would be so much easier if he were troll-like in appearance. I debate answering. Do I really want to hear anything he has to say?

Curiosity rules out.

"Hello," I say in a clipped business tone.

"Maggie, hi. I'm so glad you answered."

Silence. Inwardly, I'm congratulating myself on my self-control because I really want to resurrect my nana's barrage of Italian swear words.

"So, I know it's awkward that I didn't invite you to the wedding, but we didn't—"

"We?" I don't know why, but the word set me off. "There's no *we*, Jake. There's you and this ridiculous acrobat you've decided to marry on some wild whim or early-onset midlife crisis. *We* would be the couple who were engaged for one year, an appropriate, reasonable length of time to plan a wedding."

"You're still mad."

"I'm angry. Dogs get mad. People get angry. You made the university question my judgment. My chances of getting to work for Dr. Hamilton are nil." Dr. Hamilton is the renowned expert in the science of happiness at NYU. He takes on very few neuroscientists, and without my university's glowing recommendation, the chances of me going anywhere have evaporated, along with my dignity.

"So it's my fault you'll never work with the esteemed *Dr. Hamilton*?" Jake asks. "See, Maggie, you're so miserable to be around, and you take no responsibility for your own failures. It's comments like those that make me necessary in your work. You can't be Eeyore and go preaching about the science of happiness. We'll talk to the university together when I get back. We are fantastic together. *As a working couple.*"

"Is there a reason you called, Jake?" *Besides wanting to create a reason for justifiable homicide?*

"Maggie, you're a terrible speaker. You excel in your data gathering and research, but you need me to sell it. You always have. You're a scientist. Don't let your feelings cloud your judgment. If you ever want to get to NYU under Hamilton, you need me."

I pull the phone away, stare at it, and slap it back to my ear. "This is about your job?" I mean, one assumes when you dump your boss in front of the entire tenured faculty, you're going to accept that you must look elsewhere for work. Am I right?

"Think about those awkward speeches you've made on the speaker circuit. People were walking out in droves."

My TED Talk did okay without you. Half a million books sold in twenty different languages! I need you? The data tells a different story!

But I don't say any of this because some part of me—some icky, feeble part of me that I clearly need to shed along with the gelato weight—must think his version of the truth is genuine. He's rendered me a complete cliché. Kicked to the curb for a younger, hotter, more inane version of myself, and I never even saw it coming.

He doesn't stop here though. Apparently he hasn't completely destroyed me emotionally and professionally. "I'll be back from our honeymoon on the 27th. I'll see you in the lab on the 28th and we'll work on your presentation skills. Anichka is anxious to meet you. I think you'd be a great mentor to her."

Then he hangs up on me. *He hangs up on me!* I'm left shaking with rage, obsessing over everything I should have said.

I clamp my eyes shut and mumble some divinely inspired mantra to get his voice out of my head.

I am enough.

I am worthy of love and respect.

I choose success.

I forgive Jake as a gift to myself.

But it's no use. The murderous thoughts don't stop coming, and I'm pretty certain that my Lord Jesus along with all decent people would frown upon that. Without looking, I press the volume button on the television until the sickly-sweet movie channel, and not the positive thought mantras, quiets the phone call.

It isn't five minutes until my peace is once again shattered. My front door slams against the wall with a loud crash, and a framed photograph falls from the top of the TV. Ironically, the picture in the silver frame is of my two best friends, and they are now standing across my living room by the open front door. A flash of blinding sunlight forces me to shut my eyes again, but there's no mistaking their distinctive forms. When I open my eyes the tall, muscular outline of Kathleen and the petite, girlish figure of Haley begin to take shape in shadows.

"Go away," I moan.

"Enough of this." Kathleen's bark is like a drill sergeant's. "Get up!" She's pushy like that. A personal trainer by day, she gives marching orders as if protests are not allowed. Usually Haley and I follow blindly, but not today. Today I want one more bite of gelato and to finish my movie.

As I lift the spoon toward my mouth, Kathleen yanks it away, and ice cream splatters onto the dingy brown carpet. Neon is there to lick it up.

"You're in my way," I say, trying to see the television screen. I try to watch around her, but Kathleen has a booty and fills out her yoga pants well, so I can't see around her Nicki Minaj impression.

I love my friends. They're amazing for being here and trying to rouse me from my binge-watching stupor, but I'm not ready yet. It's not time.

"I'm blocking the screen on purpose," Kathleen says, too loudly through my sugar hangover. "We've given you more than enough time to wallow. It's time to get up. Jake's moved on, and you've got no choice but to move on too."

I point at the television. "The hero just found that dog. Look how sweet. It just appeared like that, and there's no one to take care of it. He's going to take care of it because there's no one else to do it. Where are the men like him?"

"Are you crying?" Haley asks. She has the sweetest voice to match her tiny, pixie figure, and I wish I possessed an ounce of her honeyed charm. Maybe Jake would still be here. Maybe he wouldn't have been out scouting the circus talent that had come to town. "Maggie, this is insanity! This TV hero wouldn't take care of the dog if it wasn't scripted that he had to take care of the dog. Let's go."

13

Kathleen moves my legs onto the floor and scares the cat in the process. I do my best to ignore her, thinking she will eventually give up and leave me be. I try to explain the importance of the moment—the dog, the hero . . .

"The hero is going to fall in love with the heroine because of the dog. Isn't that the sweetest thing? I mean, who doesn't love a dog?"

"You're going to get bedsores from that sofa," Haley warns, bending over me with her long strawberry-blonde hair that I've coveted since childhood. She pets Neon. "Maggie, whose cat is this?"

I shrug, but my eyes widen.

"You stole that little old lady's cat from outside, didn't you?" Kathleen's face settles into incredulous accusation.

"I didn't *steal* it. He meowed at me, and he wanted some attention, so I left the door open and he wandered in. There's raccoons and stuff out there. Maybe even a bobcat or two." Orange County, though in the heart of Southern California, was still very rural in places.

"There is a little old lady outside on a walker looking for that cat." Haley picks up Neon, opens the front door, and gently deposits him on the porch.

"That was mean," I tell her. I call to Neon, but he ignores me and shoots out of sight.

"Don't bother talking to her." Kathleen shakes her head and sighs. "She's gone. She stole a cat. What sane person does that?" She pulls my slippers off. "Just go get her packed. I'll force her into the shower."

"Shower?" I sit up quickly. "I don't want a shower! Oh." I zone back into the screen and try to block out the chaos around me. "Look at the dog. Who could give up a dog like that?"

"No one," Kathleen says gruffly. "That's a two-thousand-dollar dog. Only a TV movie thinks we will believe that a two-thousand-dollar designer dog is a mutt running loose in town needing to be rescued. This is fantasy, Maggie. Reality is better than fantasy. You said it yourself. Page 218." She points to my book on the shelf. "I looked it up."

"That thing," I tell Kathleen, nodding at the book. "What a bunch of drivel. I can't believe people bought that book. The science is wrong. My premise was based on the falsehood that Jake was a decent man, that if you live your life right, God will reward you. The lie that there are any decent men outside of romantic heroes paid to play their part on the romance movie channel. Really, some people get Job's luck. No rhyme or reason to it."

"That drivel, as you call it, is paying your bills, and the science isn't wrong. You simply applied it incorrectly to your own life. Common scientist mistake, from what I understand. Operator error. But if your readers find out the truth of how you've been living? That money is going to dry up faster than a bottle of Evian dripped on an LA sidewalk."

I scrunch up my face. My friends have way too much energy. "You need to go. Really. I'm happy here."

"What are you eating?" Haley takes my ice cream and sniffs it. "Is this gelato?"

"Maybe."

"Do you know how many calories are in gelato?"

"I know that I don't care how many calories are in gelato. Have you ever had eggnog gelato on homemade banana bread? Because I'm here to tell you there is nothing outside of this house that compares with that kind of bliss. I have no current plans to leave this heaven that I've created."

"This heaven, as you call it, smells like soured bacon. This is no paradise. This is a precursor to a *Hoarders* episode. You are one movie away from a fridge full of expired meat and cat bones under a pile of old newspapers."

"Maggie," Haley says more gently, "you need to take a shower because our flight leaves in three hours." She leaves the room, and soon, to my dismay, I hear water running. I'd make a break for it, but like a linebacker poised, Kathleen is ready for me by the front door.

"Our flight?" My heart starts to pound as I realize my friends really might make me leave. I straighten my shoulders. "I can't go anywhere.

I have to see how this movie ends. It premiered last night." I lean in toward Kathleen. "That means it's new."

Kathleen rolls her eyes. "It ends like they all end. The couple falls in love, they keep the dog and any orphaned, unloved children they happened to pick up along the way. Oh, and if there's a real Santa in the mix? He will mysteriously disappear on Christmas Eve. The end. Let's go."

"Fun sucker."

Haley comes back in the room. "Come get in the shower. We really have to get moving, Maggie. What should I pack for her?" she asks Kathleen.

"She needs at least a couple of suits and one fun, sexy dress." Kathleen laughs. "We both know she doesn't have one of those. Just get her fanciest dress. I'm sure she wore something to one of her nerd events. Oh, and find her some shorts if she has any."

My jaw drops. "Really?" At the same time, Kathleen's totally right. The last dress I wore was for the global summit on happiness science. "Sexy is all about intellect. The brain is the sexiest part of the body."

"Sure it is, Maggie. That's why the men are lined up outside the science departments trolling for hot chicks."

"I'm not going anywhere." I burrow into my sofa and flop the throw blanket over my feet.

"We're going to have fun if it kills you!" Haley claps her hands together like she's playing a princess at Disneyland. "It's a 'New Year, New You' cruise."

"For singles," Kathleen adds.

"A singles' cruise? Ugh. It's even worse than I thought. You expect me to go from bingeing on romance to a singles' cruise with no warning?"

My friends are wonderfully devoted, but this time they're expecting far too much from me. It's not just the breakup. It's the reality that all of my work may be completely inaccurate. My unrelenting pursuit to the secret of life—and happiness—has been fruitless, and I've been walking in a great scholarly circle.

"We are going to have a blast," Haley sings in her typical cheerleader voice. "You've been a hermit long enough, and it's time to move forward." She twists a red tendril around her finger and stares at me. "Jake is moving forward," she says softly.

"Well," Kathleen says, "technically Jake moved forward before they broke up, but that's another story. It's no reflection on you, Maggie."

"But it sort of is, isn't it? I mean, he's getting married this weekend and has managed to convince my entire department that he's the resident expert." I stuff another shameful spoonful of ice cream into my mouth.

"They'll see through him eventually, but you've got to fight, Maggie. You can't just let him win." Haley puts her hand on my shoulder. "That's not the Maggie we know."

He already has won. He's happy and I'm miserable. Doesn't take much data to figure that one out.

"His joke of a wedding," Kathleen says, "is the reason we're not going to be anywhere near this town this weekend. You're not going to be near a cell phone, a computer—anything that allows you to stalk him on Instagram, Facebook, Snapchat, or any other form of social media. Our queen of effervescent bliss will return home triumphantly, and we are here to make sure we have a front row seat for it. Living well is the best revenge, and this"—Kathleen waves a judgmental hand around the room—"is not living well."

I seriously love how my friends believe in me and my hackneyed science that probably has a million statistics wrong with it, and they still love me. Logically, I know that a guy who would drop me for someone barely out of her teenage years who hangs on silk scarves and twirls, deserves her. I don't think she deserves him, but that's hardly my problem. I need my heart to catch up with my head, that's all. So far the only remedy—which I could probably not prove scientifically—is more fattening desserts and sugar-coated dialogue.

If someone must investigate the science of gelato and romantic movies, I volunteer as tribute.

"He deleted me from Snapchat," I tell them. "Such a humiliation."

"Good," Kathleen says.

"Incidentally, I don't want to stalk him. I don't even really care that he's getting married." I'm a little shocked to find that it's the truth. "I just want my life to look pretty again. Hopeful again. I want the data in my book about the science of bliss to be true. And it doesn't seem to be true. It can't be or cheaters and thieves wouldn't always win. I'm the first to admit, I may be naive in the ways of dating, but really, did I deserve this?"

"We'll see about your data being true, Maggie," Kathleen says. "You don't have perspective. You've got to get out of this house. It's depressing. As your own book told the world, 'You can't change your life without changing your view.' And your view can't be from over the top of a bucket o' gelato because that just screams desperation."

My stomach rolls. "Oh man, did I really say that? In print? What did you two do? Memorize quotes before you came over here? You both sound like a high school guidance counselor's poster collection."

"There are memes on Instagram with your quotes, Maggie. You forget—you inspired people. Your work changed people's lives."

I smack my palm to my forehead and groan. "You can never take it back when it's in print. How will I ever face the world again? Like I had some kind of key to happiness. Look at me and what a fraud I am."

"You're not a fraud. Stop saying that. We'll prove it to you this week. Give us one week and we will prove 'the science of bliss' works for its writer and anyone else who wants to put it into play."

Haley had disappeared into my bedroom and now reappears holding up a pair of ratty beige panties. "Seriously? We're stopping at Target before we leave. Look what she's wearing! Anyone would be depressed putting these on. These are basically for a homeless grandma."

I jump up and yank my underwear from her hands. "Do you mind? Do you two have no boundaries whatsoever?"

"She's up! Let's move out—a body in motion tends to stay in motion," Kathleen says, and swipes the gelato from my hands. "Come on."

"Curse your body physics, let me be," I wail.

She pushes me roughly down the hallway to my bedroom. "We're going to the shower. Either you can wash yourself or I can do it for you. Take your pick."

Kathleen is not simply a personal trainer. She's the scary type who screams at people until they do ten more pull-ups than they thought themselves capable of because they're fearful she'll kill them otherwise. It's pointless to resist her. She's like a Marine drill instructor on a bad day.

"Fine, I'll take a shower," I tell her, while I'm wondering if I can fit through that small window in the shower and actually escape this harebrained idea of my restoration.

"Where's your swimsuit?" Haley asks while rummaging through my drawers.

"I bought a bikini for the honeymoon, but I'll never wear it."

"You will," Kathleen says. "Because you told women they needed to own their bodies and be grateful for the working, beautiful machine God gave them."

I groan. "No more quotes. I think I just threw up a little." As I grab my fluffy bathrobe and head for the bathroom, it occurs to me I'm really being forced from my happy place, and I don't want to go. I know my friends mean well, but I'm not ready. "You're not really taking me on a cruise. Where are we going? If you two signed me up for some kind of boot camp—"

"We're going on a cruise," Haley reiterates.

"There's a new movie on tonight. Can I at least set my DVR? It's a premiere."

Kathleen frowns. "Oh, honey. We're taking you to find real bliss because clearly neither love with the lying, cheating Jake Stone nor a successful writing career was the answer for you. Like that infernal GPS in my car, we have to recalculate."

"I can't go out there, Kathleen. My reputation as a scientist is blown once I do."

"Mexico," Haley says. "We're going to gather new data in Mexico on the love boat for singles. Stop being so all-or-nothing. We're human. We make mistakes. Jake was a mistake. Why do you seem to think you're the only one who will never overcome a mistake?"

"That's easy. I was never allowed to make a mistake."

"Man, your parents did a number on you," Kathleen says.

"Mexico. Hmm." I start to imagine a world where no one cares about the science of happiness. Where no one knows me or my failure. "No one will know me in Mexico."

"Right. Where's your passport?" Kathleen asks. "I probably shouldn't mention that the passengers on the boat will be coming from America. I suppose that's obvious to a scientist like yourself."

I pout. "You see? See how out of it I am? I didn't even think of that."

"It's in her bottom drawer," Haley says, and I suddenly realize I've been betrayed by my best friend and publicist.

I look straight at her. "Haley, you traitor! I thought this was all Kathleen, but now I know that you must have signed me up for this cruise with my own credentials."

Haley shrugs. "Maybe. I could have used the credentials to cancel your cable, did you ever think of that?"

"I'm revoking your signing privileges for me. From here on out, I see every calendar engagement that comes across my desk. Even vacations."

She shrugs again. "Whatever. Like you've ever taken a vacation." She pulls out my passport along with my hibernating bikini.

Bikini. As if I'm ever getting into that thing. I'll be the one on the beach in jeans and flip-flops. Two months of gelato is not swimsuit friendly, and as the consummate expert on bliss, at least for now, I can hardly steal others' joy by making them stare at my cellulite.

Meanwhile, Jake seems to have found his bliss without me, and that has to mean my research on happiness is flawed and I'm a fraud.

And like poor James Frey who got a verbal lashing on *Oprah*, I'll hear about it soon when readers want their money back. I'll be in eternal debt to my publishing company. I'll have no career, no husband, and two pushy friends. I'm washed up at the ripe old age of thirty-one. How do I dig myself out of that?

At least Jake's aerial dancer has found her passion in life and knows where she belongs. When she's twirling from the ceiling in that slinky-piece-of-nothing leotard, she is true to her calling. Granted, she's also a moron, but she's a happy moron, so she's ahead of me in the race toward bliss.

2

Trial by fire is often the only practice run we get or that
we need. Blissful people understand the value of trials
inherently. They look at obstacles as stepping-stones to
the next level.

The Science of Bliss by Dr. Margaret K. Maguire

THE FOLLOWING DAY THE CRUISE SETS SAIL out of Galveston,
Texas. As we line up to board the *Empress of the Seas*, the world
looks new again and I'm feeling hopeful, as if I can recover from
Jake's betrayal. Most people probably had their first broken heart
somewhere between seventh grade and college, but I'd never had
time to date. I saved up all my junior high boyfriend insecurities for
the first suitor I took seriously. While my parents prepared me for
the Mensa test, they may have left me extremely emotionally stunted
in their quest to make me the perfect child.

"Maybe I've been too much of a drama queen about all this," I say.

"You think?" Kathleen replies, then softens her tone. "You're entitled to a breakdown after a lifetime of living at your frenetic pace,
Maggie. But it's time now. There's nothing wrong with your data. Go

back to the university and be straight about what happened. I promise you, this too shall pass."

I shake my head and the memories come flooding back. "They love Jake. I'm sure they're convinced I can't do my job without him."

"Then you'll have to convince them otherwise, which you're not going to do from your sofa." Haley presses me forward in the line.

The ship seems to sparkle in the distance and offers me a glimmer of hope. For the moment, I've forgotten my comfy robe and my blissful, albeit fattening, existence. The vast size of the ship reminds me that there's a future filled with hope and new journeys in front of me. There's a slight sulfur smell in the air, so it's not quite paradise. Anytime the air reminds me of when my apartment's sewer line backed up, there's cause for concern.

"It means a lot to me that you two loved me enough to spring for a cruise. I would have never thought of this. I can't remember the last time I took a vacation." I turn to give them both hugs, but Kathleen stiffens at my embrace. "No, really. Thank you for grabbing me off the couch. I know I wasn't on board originally, but now I see it. I get that I need a new perspective. The singles thing is a bit much, but I'm sure I'll be fine with a book out on deck."

"I'm so grateful, Maggie. We were really worried." Haley hugs me back.

I stare at my two best friends with all the gratitude I can muster. Good friends are so much better to have around than bad boyfriends. How long will it take me to learn this simple lesson? This is like that show *Intervention*, without the deep, life-scarring, emotional letters. Well, and the drugs—and trust me, I'm fine with that. This is my "trip-ervention." The point is, they care.

"You didn't tell her?" Kathleen frowns as we wait on the windy walkway behind a bevy of unfortunate Hawaiian shirts. The swirling scent of sulfur becomes more intense.

"Tell me what?" I ask with trepidation. Since I'm not much of an adventurer, I worry that Haley has booked us on some kind of four-wheel-drive tour, or perhaps we'll be snorkeling in the choppy waters off the lawless coast of Mexico.

Haley lifts her tiny shoulders. "I'll tell her now. No time like the present." She turns to me, and I brace myself for whatever exciting "surprise" they're holding for me now—as if shoving me in the shower, onto a plane, and into a Motel 6 for the night wasn't enough excitement for two days. "So, the good news is that your trip is paid for in full." She raises her spindly arms to the sky. "This beautiful gulf cruise is going to cost you—us, actually—nothing whatsoever." She flips her hair in the wind. "Who has her client's back?" She cocks her head to the side and puts a hand to her heart.

Haley is my publicist. Well, she *was* my publicist before this fiasco—I'm not sure a failed neuroscientist needs a publicist. For such a demure little thing, Haley sure can be pushy. Which is fine when it's working for you and all wrong when it's not.

"Paid for in full? That is good news." I cock my brow. "And the bad news?"

"Nothing's ever truly free, is it, Maggie?" Kathleen asks. "I mean, you can't eat everything at the buffet without working it off in the gym."

Haley glares at her. "Must everything be an exercise reference?" Kathleen smirks at me.

"I feel it's necessary to create anticipation for your next book release," Haley continues in her soft business voice. "Publish or perish in your academic world, right? *This opportunity* . . ."

I've been warned. This sugary-sweet valley girl voice means I'm on my own. I'm not floating aimlessly in the Gulf of Mexico. I have a distinct destination.

"We need to push the reset button on your life. Sitting on your sofa watching kitschy movies wasn't going to make that happen." She brushes an imaginary dust particle off her shoulder and fiddles with her Louis Vuitton suitcase.

"Can't we be done with the sofa shaming already? Not being able to button up my pants is enough shame for anyone. What is going on? If you two don't tell me now, I'm off this gangplank to find myself a hotel."

Kathleen traces a finger down her cheek to mimic crying.

"Empathy is not your strong suit, Kathleen. Has anyone ever told you that?"

"Every. Single. Day." She grins. "I can't wait to see what the running track looks like on board."

It occurs to me that maybe my friends are the problem and I should invest in fellow couch potatoes. Kathleen finds her passion in her sadistic love of the denial of good food and the impending doom of exercise. I mean, did I expect to find my bliss with her along for the ride? She's the most regulated of us, and veering from her schedule probably causes her to break out in hives. She spends hours in her Bible every week and attends nearly every event the church coordinates. The girl loves a schedule, and I don't mean the one found on *TV Guide*.

Then there's Haley. Everyone loves her. Men fall at her feet and she takes no notice of them. She leaves a trail of wilting suitors behind like a flower girl who has dropped her petals. How can I rise up when she's beside me with a sparkling crown atop her head? Someday she will tap the right Prince Charming with her scepter, but for now she proves that she's stronger than she appears and ready, willing, and able to go it alone.

I look at them both—Kathleen with her gym-perfected body and Haley with her spellbinding aura—and decide we're a strange threesome. An athlete, a princess, and a brain with a stunted emotional quotient.

"The best way to create anticipation for your next book," Haley says, flipping her coveted red hair, as is her habit—to remind us plebs that we will never possess her natural charisma—"is to promote your current release with a speech reminding people of your contribution to the world. We'll up your fan base with these book events. This is just the beginning."

A speech? My contribution? "Wait just a minute!"

"You've been hibernating, but I totally believe the best is yet to come from this detour!" Haley says.

"Haley, are you delirious? There's no next book!" I panic. "I haven't written one chapter! I haven't checked any of the research, I—"

"Relax," Haley says. "There *is* a next book because your contract with the publisher states there is a next book, and you've already cashed the advance check. No doubt spent a healthy portion of it on ice cream and your cable bill."

"I can pay it back," I lie.

"You can't pay it back," Kathleen interjects. "Haley is trying to save your career here, because contrary to what you might think, lazing around in your bathrobe, which smells like old bacon, is not actually a profession. Last time I checked anyway."

"Please let me deal with my career," I plead with Kathleen. "You need to go and find a place to run. Exercising makes you human."

Kathleen sighs heavily. "I'm here for you, aren't I? I canceled a week full of clients to be here for you, and that wasn't cheap. Haley got you this gig because cruises are always looking for educational opportunities. No one else is going to tell you what you need to hear. They're too nice. Telling you the truth is *our* job, and it's not pretty being your friend right now." She hikes her gym bag over her shoulder. "This is the perfect event to restart your speaking career. You've got your statistical knowledge on the science of happiness, and this cruise is brimming with a crap ton of people who want to be happy. Do the math."

"A crap ton of people? For someone who spends so much time at church, your language could use some improvement."

"I make grown men cry every day. That's what makes them stronger! Pain is weakness leaving the body."

"Okay, Stonewall."

"It's just a little speech." Haley emphasizes her words with her thumb and forefinger close together. "A minuscule speech. Maggie, *please*. My parents are already telling me that changing my career was a lesson in failure. I need to succeed in this publicity business, and I know it's selfish, but you're my best hope. I have a *New York Times* bestselling author on my roster, and that helps me get other clients."

I inhale deeply, knowing I can't let Haley fall. She hasn't done anything to deserve this.

"A little speech about finding bliss after setbacks," Kathleen explains. "Easy-peasy. Besides, look at the bright side—your audience will probably be plied with alcohol and extremely happy regardless of what you have to say."

"That's comforting, thank you, Kathleen. Haley, the only research I have on finding bliss after setbacks is in a quart-sized carton of gelato. Something tells me they'll be looking for more . . . I don't know . . . substance."

The line crawls forward closer to the ship.

"They're not looking for substance. Look at this crowd. Looks like they cleaned out Grandpa's closet before coming on the cruise."

"Why are the men so old?" I whisper. "Is this a senior singles' cruise?"

"You're not here for that anyway. Look at it this way—they can afford to buy your book." Haley lets go of her Louis Vuitton and grasps my hands in hers. "You're on your way to the coast of Mexico and vacation. *This* is recovery after a setback. What other research do you need?"

"I can't write a book on the science of happiness and say, 'Yeah, take a cruise, you'll feel better. Sorry about the twenty dollars you just wasted on this book, but you have to shell out a little more for a luxury cruise.'" I spin around to get off the gangplank, thinking it's my last shot to escape, but there's a swath of people in line behind us. Besides, Kathleen is like a human wall when she wants to be. My stomach plummets as I realize there's no way out of this other than going through it.

This is going to happen whether I'm ready or not. No aesthetically pleasing, clean-cut romantic hero is coming to rescue me near a fake Christmas tree while the snow crunches pleasantly under our feet. I'm going on a singles' cruise—with lots of men who appear to have raided my father's vacation wardrobe.

3

....

Life without tension doesn't create happiness. Rather, life must be filled with struggle and striving or flow— forward motion.

The Science of Bliss by Dr. Margaret K. Maguire

....

WE ENTER THE GLASS-ENVELOPED GANGPLANK, where we are met by an official-looking faux sailor in a white suit with crisp creases in his slacks and bright silver buttons on his lapel. "Welcome to the *Empress of the Seas*. Please stay with your designated party and be prepared to present your travel documents to guest services. What name will you be traveling under?"

Haley steps forward. "Dr. Margaret K. Maguire and Associates." She turns around toward us and giggles. "We sound so official!"

As we step onto the hull of the ship, I tell myself it's a tiny speech. Worst-case scenario, I can read from my book and make my way to the buffet before there are any questions. Maybe even fake a hypoglycemic episode. I'm all right with that misleading and decidedly un-Christian scenario until we step into the cavernous lobby and I'm assaulted by an oversized, movie-like poster of my face. Once we're in the lobby, the loudspeaker announces our arrival as if we're royalty.

"Please welcome onto the ship Dr. Margaret K. Maguire and her associates!" A few paid lackeys in sailor suits clap for us. I offer them my best *I'm sorry* smile.

"Finding Your Bliss after Life's Setbacks, with Dr. Margaret K. Maguire" is printed across the top of my airbrushed author photo, alongside an image of my first book—which has nothing to do with bouncing back from trials. *It's science!* I want to shout. *Measurable data, people!* Then again, I'm trying to get a grant to gather more data, but it's nowhere near ready. Normally I wouldn't rest until I'd proved its necessity to the pursuit of science and happiness. However, judging by my recent work ethic, I'm probably not first on anyone's list when they're handing out grant money.

I cringe at the poster—I swear it's getting bigger as I stand beneath the thing. It's like an IMAX movie screen. Is there anything worse than an author photo? Publishers believe introverted bookworms who never leave the house—or in my case, the lab—will magically turn into supermodels simply because they wrote something. It's crazy! And it's why authors usually have that deer-in-the-headlights look that book publishers try so hard to Photoshop away. If I looked at my author photo and then ran into the real me, I'd be sorely disappointed. It's why I've avoided online dating, if I'm honest—who knows what mad photo-editing skills the bachelors of today have?

Haley pipes up, all business. "I had two cases of your books shipped to the boat. They're going to be selling them in the cruise bookstore, so you'll probably have to sign a few after your speech."

I sigh. "Aren't you Miss Efficiency?"

"Look, it's either sell them or lug them home. Take your pick," Kathleen says. "And I'm not helping."

I stare at my oversized photo again. It reminds me that all of these strangers expect my public self—the one who studies statistics—to come up with factual conclusions. Not the romance addict with dairy treats, but the businessperson who wears a suit with a lab coat and dons professional makeup. *That Dr. Maguire really looks like she has it all together.*

"I don't even know that person," I say.

"You *are* that person," Haley reminds me. "You watch what happens. You'll slip on your heels and that brilliant left brain will force her way to the surface, spouting all her facts and data. You'll have people bored out of their minds within ten minutes."

"Spouting facts and data? You make me sound like a human computer." Seriously. "Even *I* wouldn't want me. No wonder Jake ran for the hills."

I wish I was able to explain to Kathleen and Haley that it isn't Jake's leaving that ripped the proverbial wind from my sails. It was the loss of purpose, the halting of forward motion and flow toward something. In my lifetime, when I accomplished one goal, it was on to the next. When Jake left, that momentum all but stopped—no wedding to plan, no study to continue. I had nowhere to go. The light at the end of the tunnel had faded and I was stumbling around in the darkness. It sounds overly dramatic as I think about it, but what can I say? I was lost, looking for what was next.

"Stop!" Kathleen roars so that it echoes. "You can't move forward as long as you're obsessing about the past."

"Kathleen, hush!" Haley says in her sweet drawl. I swear she sounds Southern when she's trying to calm us, but she's as Californian as both Kathleen and me.

"No." Kathleen shakes her head. "I deal with excuses every day, Haley. She needs some tough love." She turns to me. "Maggie, yesterday we found you lounging in a ratty robe, smelling sour pork, and stealing cats. We need our Maggie back. The world needs that Maggie back. Besides, those gelato and cable bills aren't going to pay for themselves. Enough of the science of depression. Back to the science of happiness. No man is going to bring that to you, and you know as well as we do that you're better off without Jake in your life. He had you question every move you made—like some Stepford wife.

I know your parents may have stunted your romantic ideals, but it's time to grow up, honey. It's time to lose that obsession with Prince Charming fixing everything and get back to work."

She had me there.

"Hmm. There's a science to happiness?" A deep voice slides over my shoulder like a silky scarf, and I turn around slowly, secretly hoping the face matches the voice.

My Prince Charming fantasy isn't dead yet. Apparently I'm not completely out of my rom-com coma, which I know is a bad thing.

I'm catapulted back into reality when I'm insanely aware of my complete lack of makeup and a hairstyle that resembles something like a human Brillo pad. The smooth, robust voice, which sounds like good espresso tastes, belongs to a man who is much taller than Kathleen, so I'd say about six feet four, give or take a few centimeters. He has intense, stare-through-you, deep brown eyes and an authoritative nature that makes me feel as if I've fallen off my heels in the swimsuit competition, and he, being the Russian judge, has given me a score of 2.4.

Naturally, I'm desperately attracted to him. He's got all the arrogance and dark intensity that I seem to covet in a man—right up until the moment he breaks my heart and I realize these characteristics are what neurotypicals, aka normal people, would call "red flags." My next thought is that I can save us both some time and trouble by completely ignoring him. Besides, until I fix the mess I've made, I've got no business even thinking about romantic heroes—unless it's on a tiny screen with a familiar logo flashing across the bottom.

But this heavenly-looking being is speaking, and I'm sidetracked by the warmth in his eyes—and his hot looks, which I realize is shallow, but whatever. I'm so fixated on him that I have no idea what he's saying, only that the way he's saying it looks so good. Utterly mesmerizing.

Kathleen taps my shoulder. "Maggie, he's asked you a question." She reaches out and shakes the man's hand, and I watch as his long fingers clasp hers tightly. "Yes, that's her on the poster. This is Dr. Maggie Maguire. You've read her book, I'm assuming?"

He shakes his head. Once. "I'm afraid not. Not big on junk science. No offense, of course."

I can't help but laugh out loud at his response. Just like Jake, he boasts all the same social skills in polite conversation. "Why would I take offense to you calling my life's work 'junk science'?" *Even if it happens to be true.*

Still can't keep my eyes off his. *Why would someone with all the warmth of a lizard have such kind eyes?* the devil on my shoulder asks.

"I'm only saying, this kind of study can't be replicated in a lab. It depends upon subjective data, and if you ask me, that's questionable science at best. Don't get me wrong, I know the masses eat it up. I've heard about your success."

"Actually, I didn't ask you." I surprise myself saying this aloud. Could it be I'm over the Neanderthals and ready to move on to normal men? Neurotypicals? "But you're entitled to your opinion, of course. Have a lovely trip, won't you?" I force myself to turn toward the front desk, proud that I've made progress and can see past the visual perfection that this striking hunk of masculinity is. It's a facade. A well-wrapped package says nothing about what's on the inside where it matters. Have I learned nothing from Jake?

Haley stares me down. "Maggie," she says through her teeth in a hissing whisper. "Defend yourself with the science."

"He hasn't read your book, though trust me, I've tried to get him to. He did see your TED Talk." A spritely woman with short hair and the same deep eyes comes beside him. She has a manic energy about her and no doubt was a cheerleader in her former years, and maybe class president. She was definitely a sorority girl.

The hot Neanderthal raises a single brow. "My sister is correct. I did see your TED Talk. They forced us to watch it as part of a team-building day at my office. But I'm afraid it didn't really resonate with me."

Gee, I wonder why. Could it be the storm cloud that follows you around?

I size him up again. He couldn't be a romantic hero—despite the small Bible he's carrying alongside his passport. It makes me wonder if he's some kind of pastor, but if that were the case, would he really need a "New Year, New You" cruise? Of course, I'm here and I'm certainly in need of a new me, so I probably shouldn't judge. Besides, he's much too dark and brooding for a pastor. He doesn't have that sweet-natured, virtuous look that I've obsessed over the last couple months. I'm definitely holding out for that innocent type, like the drop-dead gorgeous preacher who, although his pews are filled every week in the movie, is inexplicably single without prospects.

This man's eyes, though, are exceptionally kind. They're throwing me off, so I can't quite figure him out. His eyes contradict his surly disposition and what comes out of his mouth. I'm intrigued by the mystery of this inconsistency, but I've learned my lesson. I'm not going to ignore that first impression, despite the Bible—which, let's face it, could be a prop to collect women on this singles' cruise. Maybe it's his way of getting women to let their guard down. I narrow my eyes and clutch my laptop case close to my body. I'm ready to walk away when he speaks again.

"I hope I haven't offended you. It's just that I question some of your research. Firstly, that happiness is a quantifiable emotion." As cold as his words are, they don't contain any venom, but rather curiosity. He doesn't take his warm gaze from my eyes, and it feels as if we're having an alternate conversation. I'm lost in the language of his eyes, virtually ignoring his caustic review of my work. His words are nothing I haven't said to myself in the last two months, which is why they sting all the more.

"It is quantifiable, I assure you. Numerous studies support happiness psychology, including my own. It can be measured objectively. I'd direct you to both Stanford and Harvard, which currently have happiness psychology. Martin Seligman defines the equation as happiness = S + C + V." Even as I say this, my Spidey sense is telling me to shut it down.

The expressive eyes before me have glazed over. And thus demonstrates my life experience with men. I begin talking, they start looking like students in a ninth grade science lecture. I should have known Jake was up to something by the mere fact he seemed interested in what I had to say.

"What?" The man shakes his head.

I, being me, decide to make matters even worse. "S represents our happiness set point, C is life circumstances, and V is voluntary or intentional activities. Like with your choice of careers, you set an objective. Or being on this cruise. It was intentional."

"Not on my part, I can assure you. The cruise notwithstanding, this all sounds subjective to me, but if you'd like to discuss it over coffee this afternoon, I'm more than willing to hear you out."

Ignoring his polite brush-off, I continue. Sometimes I'm like a dog with a bone and I cannot let things go. "It's subjective like an eye appointment is subjective. You tell the eye doctor what you see, which is subjective, but it's based on the objective parameters of good eyesight. When the black fuzzy shapes morph into letters, you can tell the doctor you're seeing better. When more of what makes your life fulfilling and purpose filled is part of your daily routine, you're happier."

He glares at me and frowns, as though he's disappointed in my answer. "Does that explanation mean you're not interested in coffee? I can tell you from my own valuable research that coffee definitely evokes happiness. I mean, there has to be before-and-after evidence with Frappuccinos littering Instagram, am I right?"

Haley steps in front of me. "I'd love to have coffee with you, Mr. . . ."

"Sam." He thrusts his hand toward me rather than Haley and clasps mine in his own gently. "Sam Wellington."

"You two should go have coffee." The petite blonde with a pixie cut and cheekbones to die for slaps his shoulder. "He's here to have fun. Aren't you, Sam? The first day of the rest of your life and all that."

Sam remains unmoved by his happy-go-lucky sibling and, if possible, seems more miserable than ever. I want to tell him, *I feel ya, dude. Happy people suck when you want to be left alone.*

"I'd be happy to explain Dr. Maguire's work in detail, Mr. Wellington." Haley steps in front of me again, and Kathleen's eyes are wide as if to tell her to back off. It seems Mr. Wellington is immune to Haley's charms and Kathleen is fascinated by this strange upset in the nature of things. I'm still uber-focused on legitimizing my work, which is progress at this point.

"It's my contention, Dr. Maguire, that smart women—educated, intellectual women—are incapable of true happiness," Sam continues, to his sister's obvious dismay. "They will overanalyze and destroy any hope of it. I thought perhaps—" Sam stops when his sister grinds her stiletto heel into the top of his foot. "What? It's the truth."

"All right, and that's enough discussion for the day." She pulls him away from us, but his words have woken me from my stupor.

"Mr. Wellington." I follow him. "What did you say about intelligent women?" He couldn't have said what I think he just said. No one is that clueless, and if they are, I may as well start writing my pickuplines book as we speak.

Sam breaks free of his sister's grip. "What I mean to say is, has your research taken IQ into account?" He speaks over his sister, who is still trying to drag him away from me. His magical eyes are focused directly upon me, and there's a desperation in his gaze that makes me take his question seriously. Until I realize I'm probably just Mowgli, hypnotized by the manipulative snake—just like when Jake challenged me at the start of our relationship.

"Everyone is taught to get his or her education and keep moving forward," Sam continues, "but what about when that doesn't bring happiness? All I'm asking is, can you prove to me that intelligent women are capable of happiness?"

All the warm, bubbly feelings I've been registering erupt like a live volcano and dissipate into the air around me. Sam Wellington said exactly what Jake said to me—that intelligent women can't be happy.

His words would mean nothing if they didn't feel true. After all, Jake specifically told me that he needed a woman who was more fun in life. He needed that and, apparently, the research he stole as his own, but that's another kettle of fish. His words were stunningly similar: "You overthink everything, Maggie. That's why you're miserable and you'll never be happy. Don't you ever want to sit back and down a brew or watch a ball game?"

No, I didn't actually want to sit and watch a ball game, nor did I want to down a brew. But suddenly I'm imagining my glamour-shot author pic next to the dictionary word *buzzkill*.

"Of course she has taken intellect into account," Haley, in full publicist mode, says. "Tell him, Maggie."

But I've lost all spirit to go into battle. What does it matter if I can prove him wrong? He's not wrong. About me, anyway.

"Sam," his sister chastises. "You've got three gorgeous women in front of you and that's what you're going to go with? A rant on smart women?" She lets out an extended sigh. "I didn't introduce myself. I'm Jules Jensen from New York, and this is my brother. He's from Silicon Valley in case you couldn't tell." Jules rolls her eyes. "I can assure you he doesn't believe anything he's spewing. He's just angry that I made him take a vacation. Give him a few days. He's quite charming, actually."

"Really?" Kathleen raises her eyebrows, then she whispers in my ear, "I think she means give him a few days and lots and lots of alcohol."

For me, the words of proof won't come. I could cite any of the studies that show smart people are happier because of good health and a lack of concern over basic needs. However, I say nothing because Sam's words sting like a jellyfish. Maybe I am incapable of true happiness, and numbing myself with the romance channel is as close as it gets.

There's little doubt that Jake's soaring, Lycra-wearing Tinkerbell sprinkled pixie dust in her wake and left him feeling as if he too could fly, while a scientific downer like me spread nothing but Spock-like facts and despair—covering a room with a dark, dingy feeling similar to volcanic ash.

This gorgeous stranger with his spellbinding gaze is onto me and my "junk science." If he gets it, how much more the scientific community? I should be at home, checking to see if Taco Bell is hiring. *Yo quiero Taco Bell.*

I grab Kathleen by the hand. "This trip has disaster written all over it."

Naturally, she has no mercy. "Since when are you a ball of nerves who acts on her feelings? That's Haley's MO. You're one of the most analytical people I know, and you're here on this cruise for a reason! Think about it and stop letting Jake or this random dude get into your head! You've been utterly reprogrammed. It's like you've been stuck in a cult."

My body shudders unconsciously. Kathleen is right. She has to be. Happiness is ahead of me, not behind me. Stepping out of my misery is something only I can do. If for no other reason than to prove to men like Jake and Sam that they're wrong about women like me. I'm anxious to get to my room and find every study on record that proves Sam's theory about intelligent women is absolute hogwash.

"Dr. Maguire?" A young woman with a musical accent reads off a clipboard. "You and your entourage will be staying on the Luxe promenade deck. We have you and your party for the early dinner seating, is that correct?"

I stare at her, blinking rapidly. *How would I know? I'm clearly a passenger in my own life at this point.*

Sam's eyes plead with me, as if he needs an answer, but I force my view to the wildly decorated blue carpet rather than be caught off guard again. This is not my battle.

The gal with the lilting voice is still speaking in her beautiful, singsong way. "Since it's a singles' cruise, most tables are mingling and changing every night. Your party requested to stay at the same table, is that correct?"

That probably sounded like a good idea at the time, but no doubt with my luck, Quasimodo and his brothers will be seated at our table and looking for love.

"You can always eat in any of the ship's restaurants if the early seating doesn't work for you on a particular night. Someone will meet you at your stateroom one hour before your speaking engagement and bring you to the proper room. One last thing—the final night is the 'New Year, New You' gala. It's a formal event, and we encourage all passengers to find a date for the ball."

I stare openmouthed. "Seriously? I have to relive my prom rejection all over again?"

"Aren't you funny," she says. "Is there anything else we can help you with?"

I shake my head and take one last look behind me toward the handsome Sam Wellington, who I thought had disappeared. But he stands behind me in all of his arrogant glory. Like me, he probably looks really great on paper and has a résumé that would make Oprah swoon. In essence, Sam Wellington has Jake Stone written all over him. Like the rest of the men in my history, he's probably searching for someone bubbly who will cheer him on for simple acts of heroism, like putting the toilet seat down.

I am not that woman.

4

OUR SUITE IS LUXURIOUS AND EXPANSIVE. Taupe walls, a
swirly-textured beige carpet, and an L-shaped sofa that resembles a gently roasted marshmallow make the suite cozier than my
own apartment. There's a shiny wooden console with a television set
separating the living space from the king-size bed and the two smaller
bedrooms. While this suite must be twice the size of my apartment,
after I've been holed up in my own space for so long, the walls feel
as if they're closing in on me and I must escape. I grab my e-reader
from my laptop bag.

"I'm going to discover the ship," I tell my friends.

Translation: *I'm going to discover a tacky, lighthearted beach read
and forget why I'm on this floating barge of desperate fools.* I know
my friends mean well, but a singles' cruise? The last thing I want to
be reminded of is my relationship status. I'm not ready to admit to
being single yet, much less tag my Facebook picture with "It's complicated." It makes it all too real that I can't live up to my parents'
expectations for a successful life.

"We'll go with you," Kathleen says, but one look at my darkened brow and she backs off.

"I'm fine, Kathleen. I'm not going to jump ship. I simply need time to prepare my talk and get into my head. It's been a long time since I've had to be Dr. Margaret K. Maguire."

Kathleen tries to understand my loss, but she has no desire to get married in this lifetime, and she certainly can't understand my grieving over the loss of Jake. She never liked him. And after her parents' tumultuous divorce, her dad remarried, and the new wife is about to give birth to Kathleen's little brother or sister. Nothing like a thirty-year age gap to forge the bond of siblings. Kathleen now devotes herself to eating the perfect diet and shaping other people's lives into a structured place of order. She loves a schedule and a hamburger bun that tastes like sawdust. Some part of her believes if she sticks to a proper order of doing things—God's way, she would most likely say—she won't fall victim to her father's weak-willed nature. *Mistakes were made*, she'd say. *Lord forbid mistakes be made!*

In contrast to Kathleen's drama-laced parents, my parents are boring, pseudo–happily married tenured professors at UCLA—who constantly remind me how far behind their schedule I am. Conversations tend to fall into depressing comparisons to their own accomplishments.

"I was married for six years and had you by the age of thirty-one."

"Yes, Mother."

"The average age for tenure for scientists is younger, Margaret. Most scientists have it by your age. Perhaps you should change your field of study."

"Yes, Dad."

"I suppose it would help if I actually wanted tenure," I say aloud, and my friends stare at me as if I've lost it.

"What?" Haley asks.

"Nothing."

While Kathleen tries to convince the world they need to be in better shape and I analyze why certain people are happy, Haley collects monthly marriage proposals like Victorian dance cards. I suppose you could say that she has to beat them off with a stick. Men generally take one look at her and believe they've met their soul mate, but Haley isn't interested in a husband just yet. She believes the right one will come along the day and moment she's ready—and the truth is, she's probably right. She looks in a guy's direction and he's instantly smitten. If I truly wanted romance in my life, I'd study Haley.

Meanwhile, Jake was the first and only man who pursued me. The only one to ask me for my hand in marriage. Maybe I got flustered and worried another offer wouldn't come along, but I don't think that was it. I think I genuinely loved a man who was only pretending to love me. What can I say? He was a good actor and being in love felt amazing. I finally had my parents' approval.

"We thought it would never happen!" my mom had squealed. My mother is not the squealing type.

"I didn't even have to pay this guy. Remember that with her prom date, Carol?" My dad laughed and pumped Jake's hand, as if they were in collusion while signing over the pink slip on me.

Even my parents thought Jake was too good for me. And I didn't go to prom. My dad gave my homecoming date gas money—maybe he slipped him more that I didn't know about. Some questions are better left unasked. I know the pain behind my parents' fears for my future, but it didn't make things easier.

"You're going to find love," Kathleen says as I grab the doorknob.

I should mention that Kathleen believes she has the slightest gift of prophecy. Randomly she says things out loud with this ethereal, low voice. They're usually things you want to believe, so you go with it. In the moment, you let her believe she's gifted. However, Kathleen never warned me about Jake, so her prophetess status is questionable at best.

"Be nice to everyone," Haley warns as I open the door to our cabin. "Your new publisher is on board this ship and I have no idea who it is."

"How is that possible?" I ask. "They've hired a new publisher. I would think that's public-domain information—you know, for stock-holders."

"Apparently it's an interim thing, hiring from within. They have to prove themselves before the announcement is public, so it appears that your book is going to be crucial to the new publisher's success."

"Peachy."

"I must admit, I wondered if it was that tall guy who said smart women can't be happy. Maybe it was a test. You know, to see if you could defend your work?"

"That guy is not for you, Haley," Kathleen says in her ominous prophetess voice. "I saw the way you stared at him. I'm going to say no to that right here, right now."

"Oh, Kathleen, you don't know everything."

"I'll be nice to everyone," I grumble as I escape into the hall.

Haley calls after me, "Don't forget. We have that icebreaker before dinner!" She hands me an itinerary and I shove it into my bag.

"I won't forget." I snake my way through the labyrinth of claustro-phobic hallways to elegant corridors with twinkle bulbs and bronze rails. Our suite overlooks an indoor mall, which resembles an old-time downtown city block from a bygone era. It's ridiculous, but who am I to judge? I've been living in stained sweatpants for two months.

I finally reach an outdoor exit and push against the wind to reveal gray, cold skies typical of a blustery January afternoon. I'm on the exclusive concierge-level deck, and it's empty except for a small bar tucked away against the wind. The city of Galveston is below, and I can see the snaking traffic with passengers still making their way toward the ship. Haley knew what she was doing having us board early.

I climb onto one of the barstools when a commanding voice startles me from my perch. "We're closed."

The slippery wood stool seems to have spouted oil and ejects me with a thud. The cold teak floor greets my backside, and air escapes my lungs from the impact. A strikingly handsome face stares down at me from over the bar. It's one of those awful moments in which you need a friend beside you to laugh it off. My isolated ways have made me too bold—I wasn't ready to surface in society alone. I bounce from the floor as if attached to a mighty rubber band.

The bartender has dark, spiked hair and rounded, inflated muscles emerging from a blue tank top with the ship's name emblazoned across it. "Did you just fall off that stool?" he asks me, leaning on the shiny bar to emphasize his bulging bicep. "The bar isn't even open."

"I didn't think anyone was here. You startled me. I thought I'd have the place to myself."

He laughs in an "I feel you" way, and his blue eyes light from within. He's like every handsome hero I've ever loved rolled into one amazing, buff, clean-cut, clean-shaven package—except he's missing the stray dog. I check the back of the bar to see if it's there, but nope. No canine wingman. There is an air of danger about him, a little edge not normally seen in my films. He's a bartender, after all. Considering I don't drink and my mother would never approve of his vocation, it's as good as a face tattoo or a motorcycle in my world.

I force myself to keep from staring. He puts out a hand and I reach for it. The romance fantasy will always be my undoing. In my overly analytical world, it's my one weakness.

"Brent Spoils," he says, and I feel the electricity coming off him. "You're famous." He points to yet another sign featuring my overly optimistic author picture.

"Oh my goodness, did they mass-produce that photo?" I settle onto the stool. "I've written a book. I'm here to talk about it."

"Cool. You wrote a book, huh?"

I sit up a little straighter and try to capture some of the joy that I felt when I first learned I'd be published. "I did."

"So you're smart too. You don't often get the full package—smart and beautiful."

44

It's a pickup line, probably one he's used successfully a thousand times, but I hardly care. I'm in no place to be particular about false compliments. Why I picked today to go au naturel with my makeup confounds me, but I suppose I did because it's been a few months since I *didn't* go au naturel.

The wattage of his smile increases. "I can't open the bar until we set sail. You can go inside if you need a drink, but I hope you'll stay out here and visit."

"Can I have a sparkling water? Or is that contraband too?"

He looks around like a secret agent. "For you, anything." He grins. "Seems like you may need something stronger. Recent breakup?"

My face starts to pucker, and before I can answer, he cups his hand on mine. "Don't worry. It's not obvious. I'm a professional. No one sees more brokenhearted people than a therapist or a bartender. In fact, some would say we're one and the same."

I grab my e-reader, which now has a cracked screen. "It's broken," I say. I knew I wasn't ready to face the world. "Thanks for the offer, but I'm going to go back to my stateroom."

"Wait a minute," he says, pressing his hand to mine again. "I can't let a beautiful woman go when she's got the secret to happiness. Isn't that what your book says? *The Science of Bliss*? That's some title, Dr. Margaret K. Maguire," he says, reading the sign.

"Call me Maggie, and heck if I know what happiness is. I thought it was gelato and sappy movies, but my friends informed me that I was wrong." I look up at his handsome face and can't even fake it. "Do I look happy to you?"

He shakes his head. "Not particularly. You look fresh though, and after a breakup, trust me, that's no easy task. I think you should cut yourself a break. No one's happy all the time—unless they're on something."

"I bet you say that to all the girls who mope at your bar."

"Not too many women moping at this bar. People are on vacation. They're happy to be away from the office."

I shrug. Proof that everyone inherently has this mystical emotion called happiness that I've been trying to pin down for years.

Brent mystifies me. Alcohol is so foreign in my life, and he seems so very normal for being a bartender. That would probably sound ignorant if I said it out loud, but my parents simply never associated with people who drank, and without acknowledging that way of life, I instinctively inherited it.

"Everyone's had their heart broken, Maggie." He says my name softly and with intimacy. Brent really has a magical way about him. It's obvious he says these lines to women all the time, but he's so handsome that I'm still giggly and stupid, wanting to believe I'm special.

"So who broke your heart?" I ask him to get the attention off myself.

"My former fiancée. Whitney Gaspar."

"That's a terrible last name. It sounds like a balloon expelling air or something."

"Right?" He laughs. "It is a terrible name, but I figured I could rescue her from that. Thought I'd be her hero. She'd be Whitney Spoils and I'd spoil her rotten."

"You weren't her hero?"

"We were young. I met her in college." He wipes the counter in front of me and places a Perrier on the bar. "She was stunning, full of life, and studying psychology."

"Oh."

"Why do you say that? Aren't you some kind of psychology expert?"

"My dad wouldn't let me study psychology. He said only crazy girls did that, in his opinion as a college professor. Granted, I was still crazy enough. I just don't have the degree to go with the personality."

"Well, she *was* crazy. That, and she didn't want to marry a restaurateur. Thought she could do better with a hedge fund manager." He wiped the top of a plastic wine glass. "The truth is, she probably could. We both would have been miserable if she hadn't broken it off. That's why, Dr. Maguire, you need to count your blessings. Sometimes, getting your heart broken is the best thing that can happen to you."

"A restaurateur? This isn't your regular job?"

"Nah. I own a restaurant in Texas. I do this once a year to get away. Tomorrow I'll teach a mixology class, work here for a few shifts, and then I can do whatever I please, all expenses paid. Having a purpose on board somehow makes it easier to book a vacation."

"Ah, another workaholic."

"Maybe."

I laugh in a flirtatious way that makes me sound ridiculous. Women like me can't get away with the whole coquettish giggle. It sounds like a goose honk coming out of a baby chick.

When I turn in my barstool, I spy Sam Wellington, the man from the foyer, sitting in a lounge chair beside a glass wall overlooking Galveston. We lock eyes before I quickly turn back to Brent. Maybe Haley is right. Maybe Sam is my new publisher.

I venture one more glance, and I'm ashamed to admit that for a brief moment in time, I wish I'd been born sweet and brainless. I suppose an argument could be made for the latter after my two months of binge-watching happily-ever-after movies, but I'm plagued by a brain that never shuts down. Meanwhile, Tinkerbell climbs on a silk scarf and writhes all her problems away. I have trouble believing that's the kind of woman real men want; sweet and weak-natured.

I'm drawn to Sam, who is across the long, winding deck, rather than the gorgeous bartender with the brilliant blue eyes in front of me. Sam's presence is hard to ignore and I wonder why. Maybe because I'm a glutton for punishment, but I can literally feel his presence. I feel . . . dare I even think it? *Tingly.*

"You know him?" Brent asks.

I shrug and try to act casual. "I met him when we checked in. He's here with his sister." *Oh, and he essentially called me a spinster. Other than that, he's great.*

My eyes linger across the empty deck. Sam is straight out of a J.Crew catalog with khakis, a crisp white T-shirt stretched across his muscular chest, a black blazer thrown haphazardly over the outfit, and suede oxfords without socks. He types into his laptop, and I notice he's got great hands with long, animated fingers. I'm taken by how he wears casual in an inherently uncomfortable manner. He's not exactly the poster child for a party girl's boyfriend, so he may have to get over the brilliant woman who apparently dumped him and find another.

In essence, he's complicated. The antithesis of what I need in my life—even for the duration of a cruise. I need fun . . . playfulness . . . the vacation equivalent of a Hallmark movie.

I stare at Brent the bartender with his winning smile and sparkling eyes. Brent is simple, a guy's guy who might be able to show me how to have fun again in life if I could follow his lead this week. The mystery of him and his life fascinates me—I mean, what is it like to be Brent and provide a good time for his customers? Maybe I can pick up some of that lightheartedness. Then I'd go back to my university job refreshed and maybe slightly more sorority-like. Maybe that would help me get noticed by the eminent Dr. Hamilton at NYU. Maybe my résumé hasn't resonated with my idol because it's too serious—too void of actual happiness. My dream is to work with Dr. Hamilton and to be a part of the cutting edge of happiness science. Maybe Brent can teach me a thing or two.

I lean on my elbow and try to focus on friendly banter, but my elbow slides off the edge of the bar. As I nearly fall out of my barstool again, my e-reader hits the floor with a sharp crack and lands in three jagged pieces.

"No!" I shout.

Sam jolts up in his chair to help, but one wilting look from me and he leans back. It's clear I inherited one trait from my mother.

"I'd say someone is trying to tell you something about reading," Brent says. "Maybe you need a break from studying and it's time to have fun."

I don't mention the many beach reads I've got loaded—or *had* loaded—onto my reader.

"He seems more interested in you than being with his sister."
Brent grins. "Smitten, I'd say."

"Trust me, he's not interested in me." *Or any woman with a brain.*
He's Jake 2.0. Likes them dumb and willing. I am neither.

I turn back toward the sexy bartender, who's been watching me,
and avoid my fascination with the complicated Sam Wellington. It's
best to change the subject. "Smart woman or dumb?"

"Is that a trick question? Am I being recorded for some podcast?"

"No, no. You said I was beautiful and smart—and even if that was
a total line, I'm asking you, is that a good thing? Do guys like you
want to be with a smart woman, or is dumb okay?" I shake my head.
"I don't mean dumb—that's a terrible way to describe someone. I'm
asking this: if you had a choice between a woman who didn't make it
through high school or an executive, who would you choose?"

"Whoever I liked more." He shrugs a shoulder. "Maybe the girl
who dropped out of high school took care of her sick mother after
school, so she had to drop out, you know? She wouldn't be described
as educated, would she?"

"No," I say, taking a swig of my bottled water. "Who do you think
is happier?"

"Ah, this is a trick question. You're practicing your speech on me.
I'm going to end up as an illustration."

"No, I'm legitimately asking. If you had to guess who was happier,
who would you guess?"

"That's easy. The person who is closest to who they were meant
to be." He unlocks a cabinet and starts lining up bottles. "If bartend-
ing has taught me anything, it's that everybody has a purpose on this
earth. Some embrace their vision early on, and some people spend
their whole lives searching for it. So I'd pick the girl who knew her
place in the world. She's more settled. Kind is more important than
being either smart or ignorant."

So, not the girl who sat on the sofa for two months trying to figure
out her purpose.

"What's the matter? You look sad. That the wrong answer?"

I glance over at Sam with his laptop, who obviously can't stop work long enough to take a vacation. Then I stare back at Brent, who always seems to be on vacation. He lines up the bottles so straight against the mirrored wall, it's like an art form.

Finally, my gaze settles on the oversized poster of me in the lighted brass frame on the wall, looking every bit the successful author and doctor. *Wow*, I think. *That chick really looks like she has it all together. The irony.* And regardless of what Brent has to say, men aren't picking her—ahem, *me*.

Sam Wellington may be missing a filter, but his words are far closer to the truth than I'd care for them to be. In the poster that's plastered everywhere, I'm wearing my lab coat. I look more like I work at the Lancôme counter at Macy's than the university. Maybe that's my true calling. Maybe then I wouldn't get caught without makeup when it's necessary. I'm thinking most women would know intrinsically to brush some powder over their blotchy skin before stepping foot on a singles' cruise. Even if they didn't know they were going on a singles' cruise.

Along with "fun," I'm going to add "common sense" to my to-accomplish-in-this-lifetime list.

5

....

Happy people give themselves permission to play. They
make time for fun.

The Science of Bliss by Dr. Margaret K. Maguire

....

LEAVING MY BROKEN E-READER ON THE BAR, I amble to the
edge of the deck where the city of Galveston can be seen in the
distance. This elite top deck that apparently came with our room offers amazing views of Galveston and the long, thin line of cars trying
to get to the ship.

"It's so peaceful up here," I say to Brent.

"It won't be soon. People come up here to watch us set sail. Of
course, you'll have the safety drill before that happens."

"Safety drill? I'm not on the *Titanic*, am I?" I hold my hair in place
to keep it from whipping my face.

"Mandatory. It's out on deck. You don't have to bring your life
jacket any longer."

"Life jacket?" I squeal, looking over the edge and the long drop
down to the sea.

Sam chuckles loudly enough that I hear him.

"Is something funny, Mr. Wellington?"

He raises a palm. "No. I've learned my lesson when it comes to questioning your opinion on matters, Dr. Maguire. But incidentally, how many times have you watched *Titanic*?"

"Once. It's too sad. Plus I have a hard time believing that when the ship is going down, her ex would be worried about chasing them with a gun!" I shout over the wind. If I'm trying to prove I'm not one of the intellectual women he abhors, I'm doing an excellent job.

It's not lost on me that the most successful romantic movie of my era doesn't work for me because of plausibility issues. Yet I'm completely okay with snow that's spongy in a Christmas movie and expensive purebred dogs being passed off as lovable mutts.

Sam laughs again, and I can see by the small creases beside his eyes that he's not without mirth. He's obviously spent a great deal of his life smiling in the sun, and my mind wanders to an image of him in the California sunshine. I realize this theory is more of my projecting my Prince Charming imagery on a man who may simply be naturally aging. Maybe he's never been in the sun or surfed or sailed or even laughed. I remind myself that it doesn't matter why this complete stranger seems stilted and cold. Imagining his past is a dangerous road and I'm not going to take it—I'm searching for the alternative route.

Recalculating. As Kathleen instructed me to do when I got lost in my fantasy world.

I saunter up to the bar again and hang on to the stool while I plant myself on it. "So Brent, what's your musical guilty pleasure?"

"My what?" he asks, leaving two bottles out of place on the counter.

"You know, that band or singer you listen to when no one's home. The music makes you deliriously happy, but you'd be mortified if anyone found out you actually listen to it when you're alone."

He shrugs and offers a cocky smile. "I'm into classic rock."

I roll my eyes. "That's not a guilty pleasure. That's just the music you like, and it makes anyone sound cool to say they're into classic rock." I shake my head. "Let's try this again."

"Is this another test?"

"Maybe." I guess my question is a test. Everything with me is a test on some level, which is the most likely reason I'm still single. I'm like an eternal four-year-old, always trying to figure out what makes people tick and asking "Why?" instead of just letting them be.

He leans over the glossy wooden bar as if he's got a great secret to tell. As he leans on his elbows, I can't help but notice again that the man has some healthy biceps. I stare back into his blue eyes.

"Probably Taylor Swift. But if you tell anyone, I'll have to kill you," he growls.

"Not scared. I'm a scientist, remember? Your secret is safe with me. This is strictly professional."

"If this goes in a book, I'll need you to guarantee me anonymity."

"I'd just tell you to shake it off."

He grins. "I see what you did there. 'Shake It Off' is one of my favorites. Hard to stay still with that if it comes on in the restaurant."

There's something delightful about being perched atop this incredible ship with two of the handsomest men I've ever met in my lifetime. It's like God whispering in my ear that there's hope in the world and I will figure it out. Like here's an appetizer sampler to practice my feminine wiles on for a week before going back into the real world.

"So tell me, why the interest in musical guilty pleasures?" Brent asks as he dusts off the top of a counter.

"My data shows that men who immediately admit their musical guilty pleasure are more honest in general. They're less likely to be harboring a dark side."

"So the longer it takes for a guy to say 'Taylor Swift,' the more dishonest he is?" Brent raises a brow. "Sounds legit." Then he laughs. "Do you have anything to back up this study?"

"Of course not. It's utterly ridiculous, but it's a good conversation starter, wouldn't you say?"

"So you're basically trolling me with a pickup line, is that what I'm hearing?" He shakes his head slowly. "The poor men who fall under your spell in the name of science."

I will myself not to flirt. Whenever I do, it only comes off as awkward and humiliating, and even though I'm never going to see this hot dude after this week, why risk it. Now is the time to practice real people social skills away from academia.

"My data—"

"Your data?" he drawls.

"*Data* might be stretching it." Naturally, I can't prove this in any professional manner—nor would I want to, as my professional reputation is already in shreds. Attach One Direction or Lady Gaga to my data and put a fork in me, I'm done. "It's just something I've noticed," I add.

"I play Taylor Swift in the restaurant. The female patrons are an easy excuse. Besides, who doesn't love Taylor?"

"So you're dishonest about your listening guilty pleasure. Blaming others for your own listening pleasure. Hmm."

"Is that bad? I thought it was pretty brilliant myself. What does that say about me, Dr. Freud?"

"I'm certain it has something to do with your mother, but I can't put my finger on it quite yet," I quip. The way he looks at me expectantly with his sumptuous eyes, I want to answer whatever would make him happy. "What do I know? The research on guilty pleasures is still out."

Jake never confessed to any guilty pleasure band, but I heard him crooning like a rooster at dawn to Barry Manilow. *Barry Manilow!* The ultimate guilty pleasure for any straight male, but Jake was too proud to own up to it. I should have broken it off then and there! Admitting he knew the words to "Mandy" would have only made me love him more, because Barry was his mother's favorite, but he just wouldn't confess to being a Fanilow.

"Maybe the Spice Girls too," Brent adds. "How I loved Posh Spice." He breaks into song about what he "really, really wants," and I start to laugh. "Attagirl," he says. "I knew you had another giggle in there somewhere. No one who studies happiness can be all doom and gloom. It's not in your nature."

If he only knew. Lately my picture would look more appropriate in a Prozac ad than on my book jacket on the road to bliss.

My cell phone trills from my back pocket. "There's cell service on the ship?"

"Only until we set sail. Then, depending on your carrier, it will cost you a small fortune. Best to turn it off."

I nod, but then I nearly fall out of my seat again when I look down at the name flashing. It's Jake. My stomach does a feverish flip because it hasn't caught up with my brain. I'll let it slide this once.

"It's my ex." I look into the well-worn smile lines beside Brent's amazing eyes, wondering why he doesn't tempt me. Too nice, maybe? Too much fun? Not complicated? Normal, that's it. He's normal—a neurotypical.

"Want me to answer it?" He flexes his arm and lowers his voice. "I'll make it intimidating."

I force a smile. "He's supposed to be getting married today." I stare at Jake's name flashing before me, paralyzed by the sight of something I never thought I'd see again.

"Then why don't you ignore that call and let him get married."

"Great advice." I nod. But everything within me wants some closure with Jake. Or to know if he's changed his mind. Has he realized that it was me he really loved and Lycra Girl was only a passing fancy?

I drop my head to the bar. "I've been ruined by romantic movies." Which is an understatement.

"Pardon me?" the poor innocent bystander asks. He probably doesn't even have the Hallmark Channel. I'll bet his television never moves from ESPN.

"As a scientist, I have recently come to the conclusion that feelings must give us more momentum than facts. It's bothersome. Facts are easily dealt with while emotions are not, and yet we act on feelings. Why?"

He stares at me awkwardly. "Give me that phone." He grabs it from me. "You need a drink."

Another thing Jake used to say to me. "I don't actually drink. It doesn't agree with me. My church never allowed it when I was younger, and I just never started."

"Well, we need you to have a good time, so the first rule is no talking to the ex on his wedding day. That is not how you start to have a good time on a cruise. That is how you go backwards in life. Do you want to go backwards?"

I shake my head. "I do not want to go backwards. I have only one direction in life, and that is forward."

Brent holds the phone close to me. "If I give this back, do you promise not to answer it?" He puts it down. "Hey, mate, you need a drink? I can't serve you until we start up, but there's a bar right inside that set of doors there."

When I swivel on my barstool, Sam Wellington is standing directly in front of me. His eyes are dark and oozing with softness like melting chocolate, and just as tempting to me right now. It must be the residual Jake effect. The thrill is short-lived, because those soulful eyes harbor the man who told me, in essence, that he's searching for a flying ditz of his own. I must secretly desire rejection as a way of life.

He reaches his arm toward me and I nearly take it. "It's almost time for the mandatory safety drill," Sam says without taking his chocolate eyes from mine.

I blink a few times, trying to figure out what he's telling me. *Aaannd?*

"May I escort you to your stateroom? You'll need your flotation device."

"Not anymore. Right, Brent?"

"Correct," Brent says from below the counter as he preps the bar. "No more flotation devices. How long has it been since you were on a cruise?"

"My parents took me in high school," Sam says. There is something so delicious in his innocence. He's strikingly handsome and has this grizzled wisdom that comes across despite his youthful appearance.

"Brent, meet Sam Wellington."

Brent stands and the two men size each other up, then shake hands brusquely. I'd like to think this is about me, but it's clearly more of a dominant male thing that has nothing to do with me or my broken e-reader beneath them.

Sam clears his throat and turns back to me. His gaze is intense, and something tells me that he's not used to hearing the word *no*. "Dr. Maguire, I'd like to make up for my rudeness in the lobby. I don't know what came over me." He seems sincere, but what do I know? Jake seemed sincere too right before he told me he was getting married to someone else. Clearly I'm not as observant or as discerning as I think I am.

"May I remind you that my IQ is slightly above that of the flotation device in my room?"

He appears stung by my comment, and I regret my words immediately. Was that really necessary? The man apologized! It wasn't his fault I had baggage about being the nerdy librarian girl to Jake's scarf princess. The flying Anichka would have never said such a thing. She would smile and accept his apology like a lady.

One thing I now know for certain: being educated doesn't necessarily make me smarter.

Brent, meanwhile, laughs out loud, but straightens up when Sam glares at him.

"I spoke out of turn earlier," Sam says, his arm still outstretched. "I owe you an apology and I'd like to make it up to you."

There's something disingenuous about his confession, and I wait for a punch line. Lord help me, I can't stop myself from challenging him. "But you do actually believe women of a certain intellect can't be happy." Granted, I may be miserable, but I'm hardly the poster child for intelligence at the moment. I will, however, learn from my mistakes and let this conversation with Jake the Second go no further. Even if his words are as smooth as butter and he makes a young Johnny Depp look average.

"Let's just say in my experience, that's proven to be the case. I'm sure there are exceptions." Sam rakes a hand through his dark, floppy hair. "Listen, I'm trying to extend an olive branch. For my sister's sake."

I notice he's still got the small Bible stuffed in his jacket pocket. "Do you carry that with you everywhere so you look more innocent?"

He looks down at his pocket and laughs. "No, I'm writing a Bible study for my men's group. We take turns and I'm in charge next time."

This feels like God's not-so-subtle reminder that I need to get back to church to meet a decent man.

"Will you accompany me to the safety drill?" Sam asks again. "It's mandatory and we have to go anyway. I thought it might give me the opportunity to explain myself better."

"It's mandatory that I go with you, or that I attend the safety drill?" *Ugh. Why must I keep challenging him? Just move on!* If Sam *is* my new book publisher, I'm in serious trouble with Haley—not to mention the Big Guy Upstairs regarding how I treat fellow believers. Jake's probably right about me. Otherwise, why am I making this completely innocent man pay for Jake's mistakes?

Brent interrupts. "Mate, you best go on and find your sister. They'll have you line up by stateroom with your party. This little filly will find her roommates."

Little filly? Only a guy as good-looking as Brent could pull that off—comparing a woman to a horse. It comes off with all the bravado of an old John Wayne movie.

Sam ignores Brent's comments and cocks an eyebrow toward me, awaiting my answer. I have to say, it's kind of sexy in that romantic come-hither way. If only I could will myself to lower my walls and take him at his word.

"I'm not staying with my sister. Thanks for your concern though, *mate*." He grins at me, and those melty brown eyes spellbind me in a way that makes me want to forget his stinging words. But that's exactly what got me where I am. Ignoring obvious truths. This one being that Sam Wellington is looking for the silent, sweet type who'll applaud him for his brilliance, regardless of whatever harebrained move he makes. I steel myself against his seductive stare and turn my attention toward Brent. Nice, friendly Brent. The patron saint of mopey women.

Brent is like the golden retriever of men—eternally happy, always looking for people to wag alongside. Perhaps he's been sent here by some cosmic force to make sure I've learned my lesson and can leave complicated men in my past. Just because I'm in academia doesn't mean I have to surround myself with malcontents. Brent probably likes baseball, apple pies, maybe a little country music. He probably drives a truck and does the two-step. His brand of fun is exactly what I need this week as I crawl out of my self-imposed hermit months. Mindless, soul-stirring fun.

Both handsome men stare at me expectantly. Rather than replying with something charming, brilliant, or witty, I smile numbly, collect my broken reader, and jaunt like a scared rabbit to my stateroom. Alone. Maybe I'm not as smart as I think I am. The data is certainly beginning to take shape. I may be the wrong person to represent intelligent women in Sam's "too smart to be happy" scenario.

6

....

We are happiest when engaged with others. The amount
of time spent socializing has a direct correlation to one's
happiness.

The Science of Bliss by Dr. Margaret K. Maguire

....

D O WE HAVE TO GO TO SPEED DATING?" I don't know why
I bother asking the question. The whole point of this trip is to
get me out of my comfort zone. I can be thankful my friends are not
depositing me on some barstool for the duration of the cruise. "Can't
we just go straight to dinner?"

"No," Haley says. "We're committed and they're counting us in
their numbers." She points at me. "Great research!"

I'm certain that we will never add speed dating in one of my
chapters as a scientifically proven means to happiness. Essentially, it
is an avenue to get rejected at a much quicker pace and without the
beautiful anonymity of a finger swipe on one's smartphone. I'm here
because, like all bad ideas, it started with Kathleen saying, "Come
on, it will be fun!"

The women, i.e., casualties, all take seats around the room at
individual tables for two in a closed-down-for-the-night burger bar.

For decorations, the room has a single white candle in the middle of each table. I'm assuming this is to represent our sad loneliness. It's all very suspect. Is this supposed to be romantic? The room could double as a séance setup for a coven in a horror movie.

"Can I suddenly become a drinker?" I ask. "This seems like it would be easier with alcohol."

"Stop being funny," Haley says. "Men don't like funny women."

"Or smart women. I know, I've been told. Why am I here again?"

From what I've gathered, what's about to happen is that for four minutes, timed by a bell, some bloke will sit at our table. We will try desperately to impress each other with small talk and random facts about ourselves. Kathleen is seated on the left side of me and Haley the right. They're both fidgeting in their seats, far too excited about this entire process.

"I've never seen a speed-dating round as part of a story that included happily ever after," I say. "You'd never see this on the Hallmark Channel."

"Live a little. I love meeting new people," Kathleen says with glee. "What a stellar way to meet the maximum amount of people in a short time. People are on this ship from all over the world. This is going to be fun." She gives us a seal clap.

"You know what would be fun, Kathleen? If we got to see you use your black belt skills on some of the more vile participants. I would enjoy that. Kind of like a speed-dating-meets-*Fight-Club* scenario. I'd pay to see that. I bet a lot of people would." I nod. "Yeah, I'd enjoy that."

The dating process and me clearly don't mesh. This could be why I'm desperately single. The bigger question is why, after Jake, being single makes me feel so unworthy.

"Now who's the buzzkill?" Haley asks. "You make Eeyore sound like he has the gift of encouragement. Honestly, what's gotten into you?"

"Haley, look around." I put my hand on hers. "You don't feel like you're at a meat counter waiting to be ogled by hungry carnivores?" I squeeze her hand. "You know how in those nice, fancy steak restaurants, they parade the meat platter out and tell you all about the marbling and the aging process on the slabs of beef? That's us. Meat on a plate, and they will come out and judge our marbling and aging process. And we signed up for it. We're here by choice."

"You *are* a buzzkill," Haley says, yanking her hand away. She taps her name badge with her dating number: 16. "How do you suggest we meet people? Hide out in your lab and hope some focus group will bring us all underwear models posing as lawyers?"

"I wouldn't marry a lawyer," I say.

"Is there a lawyer who wants to marry you?" Kathleen asks. "Then I fail to see your point. This is great research for your books. You should want to be here more than either of us. If you think of bachelor number one as study number one, maybe you can identify what he needs in his life to be happy."

"Your picture isn't plastered all over the ship. If I get weird stalking emails after this, I'm holding you two accountable."

"Now she's worried she's going to get stalked," Kathleen says to Haley. "She must have switched over to the Lifetime channel once in a while when she was couch surfing."

There's an overly excited MC in the middle of the tables. This cruise seems to have a run on these animated types—the game show industry must be missing a few wannabes. The MC tells us exactly what's going to happen and not to get too flustered.

"Just have fun with it!" he shouts. "Here we go! Round one! Gentlemen, take your seats."

The first guy who sits down in my chair is Ed, #52, which could very well be his age, but I'm not asking. He's wearing a lumberjack red-and-black flannel shirt—on a cruise ship to Mexico. *Okay then.* He is big and boisterous with a lot of male energy. I'm going to suggest he finds showering regularly an unnecessary activity.

"Ed," he says as he thrusts his hand toward me.

"Maggie." I shake his hand and he pumps my arm as if it's going to suddenly spew water.

"You hunt, Maggie?"

"Um, no. I live in a city in California."

"Up in Alaska, living off the land is the right way to go. I don't believe in killing it if I'm not eating it, so don't think I'm just one of those people who loves to kill. No sir. They say you live longer the closer you are to your food source. I'll tell you right now, I'm very close to my food source."

So whoever picks him has a long coupling before her. Fair enough.

"Is that so?" I try to sound encouraging, but it comes off as disinterested. Small talk is not my forte.

"You're not one of them vegans, are you? They say California is the land of all them fruits and nuts."

"I'm not a vegan. I enjoy a good steak. I don't hunt for it though. I go to Vons."

"Well, you can't just shoot a cow, now, Maggie. I mean, cattle take a lot of land, you know that? It takes about two acres of land to support one cow." He holds up his forefinger. "One single bovine. I don't have me that kind of space on my property. That's the trouble with you women. You want it all."

"I want it all?" What does me liking steak have to do with the price of acreage in Alaska? Suddenly I'm a gold-digging man-eater with a necklace of filet mignons strung around my neck. Maybe it's me. Maybe I'm giving off a negative vibe. I change my attitude. "Now, no offense meant, Ed. Do you fish too?"

"Everyone fishes. A man who doesn't fish is not to be trusted."

Four minutes is truly an eternity. An eternity!

I lean over to Kathleen and whisper, "I know who I nominate for the black belt recipient." I turn back to Ed. "I don't want it all, Ed. Not all women want it all." I lean over the table. "Why exactly are you on a 'New Year, New You' cruise?"

"Bear season is over. What else did I have to do?"

My unrequited love for Jake is starting to make more sense to me. *Please let the options get better than this. Mountain man needs to find himself a female copy. Sort of a female bigfoot.*

After an excruciatingly detailed lecture on the intricacies of bear hunting, Ed is on to Kathleen's table. Is it wrong that I want her to arm-wrestle him and take him down and show him not all city women are frail damsels in distress, waiting for our man to bring us some meat tied on top of the truck?

I fidget with my collar as I wait for Haley's last date to get recycled to me.

"Hi," says my next victim, I mean date. "Brandon. You are?"

"Maggie," I say, using my finger to underline my name badge. "#31."

"Is that your age or your IQ?" He laughs. "Nah, nah. I'm kidding. This is awkward, isn't it?"

"It is my age, actually."

He cursed. "No kidding. Well, for an older gal, I'd give you a solid six. Seven or eight if you let that hair grow out. I like a lady with long hair. It's more feminine."

Instinctively, I pat the back of my head. "Do you now? Duly noted."

"Where are you from?"

"California. Los Angeles area."

"That explains it. You could use some meat on your bones. You appear frail."

I rub my hands down my sides. This is not the easiest exercise on the ego. But it is a good excuse for more gelato. "Thank you?"

"Do you know any movie stars?" Brandon asks.

"No, I don't, but I saw Gwen Stefani at Whole Foods once."

"Who?"

"It's not important. Where are you from, Brandon?"

I'm not listening to his answer. I'm terrible at this, not because I'm not a good listener—I'm generally an incredible listener—but this is not for me. I'm so out of my element, and knowing people on a casual level seems like a waste of time. Everything about my personality is "slow and steady wins the race." Speed dating is just that—speedy. Efficient. Somehow, efficient dating is missing the entire point of knowing someone on a deeper level. I understand it's only the introduction, but I'll be darned if I want to tell my grandchildren that I met their grandpa on a singles' cruise and got his number in a speed-dating round.

"Hi." A nice-looking blond with kind blue eyes sits across from me. "I'm Steve from Dallas."

"Hi, Steve, I'm Maggie from California."

"You're the happiness doctor on all the posters."

"I am. Don't hold that against me and I won't use you in any books. I promise."

"Neither will I. I'm an aspiring science fiction author." He then proceeds to tell me the entire plot of his novel and asks if I know any agents.

I repeat this painful exercise eighteen more times before I'm released into the wilds of the cruise mainstream. Sam didn't come to the speed dating, and surprisingly, neither did Brent. Because they're both smart? Perhaps not desperate?

"What did we learn from this?" Kathleen asks as we huddle together.

"I think we learned that 'happily ever after' is one big hoax. I'm ready to snuggle up with a good Christmas movie and abandon the dating scene altogether," Haley says. "Maybe Maggie didn't get everything wrong."

I sigh. "How many phone numbers did you get, Haley?"

"That's not the point."

"It sort of is. How many?"

"Six, maybe? They just handed me their numbers. Oh, and one room key. As if."

"You, Kathleen?"

"Two."

I hold up my fingers and thumb in the shape of an O. Not even the bear lover looking for bigfoot was tempted by my feminine wiles.

But let's be honest, I wasn't really trying. Until I restore my heart to the position of grateful, I know that I'll continue to attract the negative energy I'm exuding. God wants to restore my heart, but I need to let go of my anger at Jake and forgive him. Jake didn't do anything other than be himself. It's unfair to blame a snake for being a snake, isn't it? At the very least, it's naive.

"Now, Maggie," Haley says as she straightens my curls with a flat iron before dinner, "remember, you don't get a second chance to make a first impression." She taps the tip of the appliance against a copy of my book. "No one knows that you've dropped out of sight for two months. This is a chance for a fresh start to build anticipation for your next book."

"What was speed dating for then?"

"Forget about speed dating. That was just to give you some quick practice on social etiquette."

It's probably best not to tell her about my run-in with the Bible-toting Sam Wellington at the bar just yet. I'm not sure if he saw me fall off the stool the first time, but he definitely saw it the second time, and I did not exactly accept his apology graciously. If I see him again, maybe the third impression will go over better, but I won't hold my breath.

"Did you hear me? The next book . . ." Haley's voice trails off as I start to ruminate. *Again.*

I feel as if I'm having an out-of-body experience. *The next book.* I can't even string a sentence together at the moment. "There's no next book," I tell my publicist, who should know this. Granted, according to my contract, there is a next book, but I'm partial to ignoring that fact at the moment. The current fantasy is far more conducive to my current way of living than my normal factual data.

"You're a career scientist at the top of her game," Haley says in her resident cheerleader tone, trying to hype me up like a football coach to his losing team. "You exude confidence." She ratchets her enthusiasm down. "Fake it if you have to, because that new publisher at BrainLit Books is going to be scrutinizing you to make sure that their predecessor made a smart investment. You're currently their lead author now that Malcolm Gladwell has left, but since the former publisher was fired, I assume they'll be checking the contracts carefully."

"No pressure in that." I can't even sit on a barstool properly and Haley expects me to impress some fancy New York publisher? *It's Sam Wellington. It has to be.* With my luck, it couldn't be anyone else.

Haley puts down the iron and unplugs it. "This is my biggest client, Maggie," she reminds me. As if I need more pressure. "If you can't behave yourself for your future, do it for me. Do it for Dr. Hamilton—he can't ignore the work of a two-time bestselling author on happiness science. No one reads about science for pleasure. You make it accessible."

I nod. "I want to get back to work, Haley. I really do. If today on deck taught me anything, it's that I need to focus on where I can find success in life, and that's my work. Because it certainly isn't picking up random men at a bar when there is literally no competition."

"That's the spirit."

But it's short-lived.

"My only fear is that Jake might be right and I'll lead people down the wrong path. What if my research needs more data and people are making bad life choices due to what they've read in my book?"

"They have personal responsibility, Maggie. If they quit their job without thought to the consequences, that won't be your fault. This cult of Jake mind control you've got going on needs to end already."

I try to explain myself one last time. "All this data told me that Jake and I had shared interests, that we supported each other's dreams . . . The data did not account for someone lying to me, nor that betrayal would leave me in a pit of despair. I didn't lose a fiancé. I lost my working partner as well. I collected the information. He shared it in speeches. You should have seen him in the corporate world. CEOs and human resources departments ate him up! I can't do that. I don't have that natural charisma."

She stares at me as if she just saw the biggest bug crawl out from under the bed. "That's why you're burying yourself in a fantasy Cinderella world? You think you need Jake to do this job?"

"That's not all of it, of course, but so many people depended on this book and the prestige it brought the university. Jake had his job because of this book. You've had yours as a big-name publicist on a book no one in marketing believed in at the time. Our sociology department is up for more grants because of the success of this book. That's a lot of pressure, and if Jake is gone, it's all on me."

"So don't write another study to be published in a journal ever again. Stay at home and watch television. Let Jake do it. Oh wait, he can't because all he knows how to do is read a teleprompter and read your work aloud."

"He would improvise too."

Haley's face turns a crimson color close to the hue of her hair. "Every career has setbacks. The data isn't flawed, and the only person you're leading down the wrong path is yourself. You don't have to be perfect. I'm not asking you for the perfect book. I'm asking you to translate the data into meaningful works for a typical audience."

She makes it sound so simple. Trusting has never been a simple exercise for me. Not since God took the only person who ever loved me, flaws and all.

I shake off the thought. "My parents aren't a typical audience," I remind her. "They use my book to show up their friends at the country club, and so far it's worked. If I'm a fluke . . . if the book is illegitimate and my audience is all pseudo-intellectuals, this is all going to collapse like a house of cards." My voice wobbles and I swallow down the panic. Normally I'd run to my flat screen and be enveloped in sweetness and light, but Haley and Kathleen aren't about to let me escape this time. This time I really have to face the wall in front of me. "I've been researching jobs at other universities—"

Haley flings my book on the bed and sits beside me, taking my hands. "First off, Jake can find another job. He never should have had that one, and we'll never know if he targeted you from the start. You owe Jake Stone nothing. He manipulated you so that he could give the speeches and make himself look good." Haley smooths her curls. "He told you he was better at speeches so many times that you actually believe it."

I did believe it. Because it was true. Jake didn't have those hard voices reminding him of how he didn't measure up. He didn't have parents who were left heartbroken with only one child—the not-as-bright child—to fulfill all their expectations.

I wasn't allowed to speak of the loss of my sister at home, and somehow I'd been programmed never to speak of the loss out in the world either. Even Haley and Kathleen had no idea my parents had an heir and a spare. Amy was supposed to be the heir. I was the spare, and I'd simply snapped from the pressure because I wasn't like her. Life hadn't come easily to me like it had to her. I didn't spread sunshine and light behind me like Amy had. Nor did I attract people to me as though I was a human magnet. In essence, I wasn't a unicorn. Amy was a unicorn among wild mustangs.

"Does Jake have a TED Talk?"

"Well, no. But he doesn't have a degree in—"

"Secondly, no matter what you do, your parents will always expect more, so you can't let their reaction motivate you. Finally, this book isn't a fluke and it isn't garbage. I believe in it and I believe in you, and if you can't believe in yourself, you're just going to have to let Kathleen and me do it for you. You're not just a television movie addict who steals cats."

"Borrows." I hold up my forefinger. "I borrowed the cat."

"Fine. Borrows cats. Tonight is important, Maggie. I already tweeted out to your followers something positive about starting over and the power of resilience. You can use Jake's dumping you as a springboard for success. Everyone's been dumped. People will identify with your vulnerability. I mean, who doesn't love a Rocky story of overcoming?"

I start shaking my head before she gets the last word out. "I'm not talking about my breakup. Haley, that's not what I do. I'm not a self-help guru, I'm a scientist. I relay factual information to neurotypicals."

"Stop using that word. It makes you sound like a weirdo."

"Well, I am a weirdo. Remember in college when you went to the football games and I went to the library? My social skills haven't really improved since then. Learning comes easily. Small talk? Not so much."

She sighs. "You're a bestselling author because of how you make science accessible to the average joe, not because of the actual science. The science is just reporting data. A monkey could do that."

"Thank you. I'm glad my life's work is so important to you. Monkeys aren't great at small talk either. I'm just saying."

Haley laughs. "You know what I mean. People want to connect with you. Connection makes the science come to life."

Haley's bright red, full lips mesmerize me for a minute. They're like men's kryptonite. No wonder she collects suitors like a child collects seashells. Her copper-hued hair waterfalls down her back in long, bouncy curls, and she always appears crisp and clean, as if a stylist follows her around. Even to the gym.

Let's just say that if I were an overflowing canvas duffle bag, Haley would be a perfectly packed Louis Vuitton travel case. She always has the right statement piece for her outfits and a fresh, crisp collar. Her accessories always coordinate with her outfits perfectly, and the result always looks effortless. In her free time, Haley surfs, skis, refinishes antique furniture, and runs her own successful company. If I hadn't been forced upon her as her first college roommate, we'd probably never be friends. She took pity on me and tried to clear my closet of Gap sweatpants and replace them with Juicy Couture tracksuits, but I could never get used to the idea of having *Juicy* plastered across my bum.

"I know you mean well, Haley, this being a singles' cruise and everything, but no one wants to hear about my nerdy self getting dumped for a pretty airhead. That's not news. It's life! It starts in junior high school when you come home with all A's on your report card, and your cheerleader cousin comes home with a boyfriend."

"There's science on overcoming adversity, that's what I'm talking about. You touch on it in your current book. You've applied for a new grant on the subject. It's all in the neuroscience, right? This positive psychology? All I'm asking you to do is what you do naturally—write about the science. Make the connections."

"Sure," I tell her. "Instead of *Eat, Pray, Love*, we'll call it *Eat, Binge-Watch TV, Buy Bigger Sweatpants*. Think of it—all the pleasure centers in the brain lighting up. No human contact necessary, and definitely no flooding by that pesky love hormone, oxytocin."

"I give up," Haley says. "Kathleen!" she yells at the bathroom door. "You talk to her."

Kathleen comes out of the bathroom wearing an electric-blue sheath dress that shows off her cut arms while managing to make her look wholly feminine. She takes one glance at me and shrugs her muscular shoulders. "She'll be fine. She can only feel sorry for herself for so long, and then she has to earn an actual living. She's too practical not to have figured that out by now." She shakes out her blonde locks. "Let's go. I'm starving. No one should ever be starving on a cruise ship. It's like a natural law of the universe."

I stare at my reflection in the mirror and try to delay my fate. I'm wearing a beautiful cocktail dress in cream-colored lace, with a black lace overlay at the scalloped neck and skirt. It's innocent and elegant, but lacking in finesse. My dress is cute. Not sophisticated. Not grown-up. I might never have noticed had Jake not left me for a chick in tights.

"I look cute," I say dejectedly.

"Isn't that the point?" Kathleen asks, while smoothing her sophisticated bodycon dress and knowing she will turn every head on board.

"Maybe when you're sixteen, but you and Haley look sexy. *Worldly.* I look sweet, as if I were having a quinceañera."

"Because you're an innocent-movie freak. That's how they dress. Turn on some Bravo, girl!"

"She needs Lifetime. Maybe if she watches a few women take out their straying exes, she'll stop feeling sorry for Jake."

When it appears that I can stall my friends no further, I decide to let the last secret of my lifestyle breakdown dribble out. "There's one more thing I need to tell you girls before I go tomorrow and spew happiness advice."

"If we hear you out, do you promise to head to the dining room with no more whining?" Kathleen asks. "We know you're stalling."

"Absolutely. The thing is, I haven't told my parents yet about Jake. Or the job, if I'm being honest. It never seemed like the right time, and before I knew it, it was too late. Way too late to tell them casually."

Haley and Kathleen both sit back down on the bed with their mouths agape. It takes something to shock my friends, who know me inside and out, but I've obviously succeeded.

"You haven't told your parents that you haven't been to work for two months?" Haley asks.

"And that I'm not actually getting married."

"That's why you didn't change your Facebook status!" Kathleen says. "I thought that was weird."

"How did you keep it from them? You don't so much as belch without your mother knowing about it," Haley says.

"When my mother called, I told her I was too busy at work to help with the wedding plans. She'd ask white or ivory, peach or pink. I'd give her an offhand answer and be back to my show in under a minute. The gelato didn't even have time to melt. Before I knew it, weeks had passed and Jake's real wedding was upon us, and then it became clear that the problem was bigger than when I'd started lying by omission."

"Lying by omission?" Kathleen raises a single brow in that judgmental way. "That's what we're calling this?"

"You know it's not like me to lie. Even by omission. I've been a good girl all my life."

"Maybe that's your problem. Maybe it's time to stop being a girl and become the woman you're supposed to be. Regardless of how your parents feel."

"I'm sure you're right. The problem is, this whole thing snowballed and now it feels too overwhelming to tell them. I have no idea where to start. I mean, I knew that eventually I would have to come out of my apartment and face the music, but with all those happily ever afters I watched, I thought something magical would happen and it would all get fixed by the time it was over."

My friends' mouths are still open, their eyes huge with astonishment.

"Maggie, that's terrible," Kathleen says. "Your mom is still planning the wedding?"

"I know." I drop my face into my hands. "I'm a terrible person! But what can I say? This is what a nervous breakdown looks like. It's not pretty. There are casualties. Collateral damage. Don't make me feel worse."

"It would be worse if your mother wasn't your mother," Haley says. "I do hope I'm there when you tell her. Something about seeing that woman *not* get her way brings me a distinct amount of joy." Her plump red lips form a wide oval. "You're telling us that your mother is still planning this wedding at her country club, and she has absolutely no idea that Jake supposedly married someone else today?"

I nod.

"Maggie, the invitations will be sent soon." Haley is ever worried about proper etiquette.

"Like I said, I was going to tell them eventually."

"When?"

"In my defense, would you want to tell my parents bad news? Bad news of any kind?"

"Well, no," Kathleen says. "But when were you planning on telling them any of this?"

"I was thinking about the rehearsal dinner. When Jake doesn't show up, I'll just say—"

"The night before the supposed wedding? You cannot be serious."

"I thought I'd have their sympathy then, at least. I was going to tell them I was caught up in my deadline and—"

"The deadline for the book you haven't started, you mean? Maggie, who are you? When did you become a pathological liar?"

"That's easy. When my parents asked me anything about my dating life. What sane man would want to marry into my family?"

My friends' faces say it all. There is no excuse for what I've done. None at all, and my excuses don't hold water.

"Did you ever think what might happen if Jake's wedding announcement gets put in the newspaper before you tell your parents?" Haley asks.

"Well, not until now!" I wail. "Besides, he's not that organized, and you know Tinkerbell isn't," I say emphatically. "I believe shotgun weddings don't usually have formal announcements in the society page, but I could be wrong in this one instance. Jake does like the spotlight."

Jake and Anichka weren't getting married in a shotgun wedding. In fact, they were getting married at my church. Well, what used to be my church until Jake came in and charmed the pastor into believing he was the next missionary to the scientific world. This was the church I'd been at since my junior high years. I'd brought Jake there and introduced him to everyone, and soon he was leading the men's ministries at the midweek studies. The long and short of it is, in the breakup, Jake got the church and our wedding plans.

My pastor told me it was selfish of me to keep them from getting married in my church and that I'd misunderstood the gospel in terms of God's plan for marriage. Apparently somewhere in his Bible it says that men can do whatever they like and women should be subservient and step aside. Especially if the man in our story falls in love with someone younger and prettier. I think that betrayal hurt worse than Jake's, if I'm honest. The pastor's misinterpretation of Scripture was soul damaging.

"You can't let the invitations go out, Maggie. It's fraud, and you're in enough trouble at work. You've got to clear this up. Your fiancé will have been married to someone else by the time those invitations are sent. There will be no hiding the fact that you lied to your parents, and it can harm your credibility at the university."

"Details," I stammer. "I'm not running for office. I simply got dumped and then lost in my research. I didn't *lie*. I just never told them that the wedding was off and that my engagement ring was now an expensive paperweight. Details, schmetails."

Haley looks stunned, and the shame I feel with the way she glares at me is palpable. "As long as I've known you, Maggie, you've never so much as had a late library book. How is it you've managed to screw up your entire life in two short months?"

"She is a perfectionist," Kathleen interjects. "Maggie never did anything halfway. If she's going to screw it up, she's going to screw it up big-time."

Judging by my friends' reactions, it is as bad as I thought. It occurs to me that I could simply get off this ship of fools at the next stop and disappear into the Mexican jungle. That would solve everything.

"After your speech, we're calling your parents and telling them there's no wedding in March," Haley says. "Tomorrow we're fixing your career, and this entire debacle will be nothing more than a forgotten detour, you got it?"

"If this were a Hallmark movie," I say enthusiastically, "I could meet someone. They would fall madly in love with me and we'd be married in March as scheduled. I could just say there was a typo on the invitation and that I'd misspelled the groom's name."

Kathleen gives me a death stare. "Sure, Maggie, that could happen."

"Please be nice to everyone tonight," Haley says. "No more of those pointless arguments like you had with that poor guy at check-in."

"Sam," I remind her. "His name is Sam Wellington. I met him again on deck. He's what we in happiness science know as the archetype for the nihilist—he's anti-happiness. No joy in the present, lost all hope for joy in the future. Like he walks around with a rain cloud following him."

"See?" Haley says. "That's exactly what I'm talking about. Why do you have to judge that poor guy? You know nothing about him and you're calling him a nihilist? Incapable of happiness? That's a tad harsh. Didn't you notice the way he looked at you? He asked you to coffee! I stood there while he asked you right over the top of my head. And I'll tell you, if you're not into him, I totally call dibs."

"He's a buzzkill at the very least. I was just starting to feel enthusiastic, then he has to go picking on smart women. You can't just stereotype all women with a certain IQ like that. Some smart women are happy." Just not me at the moment, and I'm certain my intellectual capabilities are being questioned by a lot of folks at this point. "Do you think he's sadistic?"

"Maybe he's analytical like you and hands out facts like candy." Kathleen turns to the door. "And in his defense, we, who know you best, questioned your intellect the entire time you were dating Jake."

7

Avoiding negative emotions does not make one happier.
Dealing with negative emotions is essential to mental
health.

The Science of Bliss by Dr. Margaret K. Maguire

THE SHIP'S DINING ROOM IS EXTRAVAGANT and three floors high—it reminds me of the library scene in the animated *Beauty and the Beast*, and I want to dance through the tables and sing. Spirals of staircases and filigreed wrought-iron rails wind their way up elegantly to the different heights and give the impression of a grand castle or a French cathedral. Stately Roman columns connect the elegant levels. Our table is located on the first level underneath a colossal cut-crystal chandelier. Around the table are six royal violet velvet chairs. There are only three of us.

This is not your sweatpants kind of place.

Haley sits at our table, and I ask, "I have to be social?" My recent vow to be more fun—more interesting and eccentric—suddenly feels highly implausible, considering the sight of three extra chairs sends me into a panic.

"Just talk about your speech tomorrow," Haley says without an ounce of empathy. "Please don't discuss your neighbor's cat or the best gelato flavor. You'll be fine."

Social butterflies never understand the introvert.

"At least she can't reach Jake out here," Kathleen says.

That's true. I can't reach Jake. I know this because I frantically tried returning his phone call after the safety drill. By then, there was no cell service and that was probably a sign. I may or may not have kept trying incessantly until caught by Kathleen, though I'll never own up to it. Jake is probably on his honeymoon as we speak, and the hope for any closure has evaporated like a small puddle on deck.

We settle into our purple chairs as if we've suddenly become royalty. The sight of everyone dressed to the nines in the cavernous room makes me long for the quiet of my sofa and my neighbor's cat. "I wonder what's on television tonight."

After a long, rambling autobiographical introduction by our waiter, Phillipe, I order an iced tea. Simple enough, but when it comes, it has alcohol in it. A lot of alcohol. And I don't drink. Rather than risk embarrassment and my burgeoning reputation for being the life of the party, I say nothing about this faux pas. That's my first mistake.

I'm tempted to devour the whole glass. I could use a little liquid courage as we await three strangers, but the liquid would no doubt be like burning magma crawling down my teetotaling throat, so I stay thirsty. This is like when I was in college and went to the one party I was invited to. I got a red Solo cup, filled it with 7 Up, and walked around the party like I was so cool.

Instead of drinking anything, I stuff a piece of bread in my mouth when Sam Wellington and his sister approach the table. *He looks so good in a suit, it should be illegal.* When I notice they're sharing our table, I swallow . . . and the bread lodges tightly in my throat. I panic as I struggle for air. I grab for my throat as Sam tries to shake my hand. I make a horrifying wheezing sound, and Sam in all his GQ glory comes behind me while I gasp for breath. *Really, just let me choke.* I'm mortified, and there's no coming back from this.

Kathleen's and Haley's eyes appear as if they're going to pop out of their heads, and while I realize the severity of my situation, the reality of the nihilist saving my life is too much for me. When Sam's arms come around me, I grasp his wrists as they pummel into my solar plexus—once, twice, then three times. Until the bread dislodges from my throat and lands with a clink on Haley's bread plate.

Remember how Ananias and Sapphira died instantly in the Bible? If only . . .

"Thanks," Haley says. "I'll get myself a fresh slice." She laughs to lessen the awkwardness of the situation. As if that's going to happen. If this guy Sam is in my presence, it seems I'm going to be at my worst. I don't know how I expect to prove to him that intelligent women can be happy if I'm an idiot every time I'm around him.

Sam is still behind me, arms clamped tightly around my middle. I'm reminded of the gelato baby I'm carrying and the sad loss of my waist. He sets his chin gently on my shoulder and whispers in my ear, "You look beautiful tonight."

He drops his arms and pulls my chair out for me. His eyes meet mine, and I'm hypnotized while he helps me back into my seat as if we're all dignified here. I've just choked on a crust of bread—it's not as if I haven't been eating for three decades—and he acts as if it's never happened and I haven't made a scene. Nor does he seem to notice the entire three-level restaurant looking in our direction.

He motions for the waiter and asks him to bring me water and a regular iced tea. When I sit down, my hand flinches and I accidentally knock over the Long Island Iced Tea glass. It clanks against the dish and splatters across everyone gathered around the table—even Sam's sister, who hasn't even had a chance to sit down because of all my antics. A team of waiters rushes the table. One collects up the plates, another the silverware, another the glasses. They regroup like a team of skilled surgeons and whisk away the tablecloth, then replace it with a fresh one.

For what feels like an eternity, our entire table is displaced and everyone stands around trying not to engage me, lest the luck I'm having be passed onto them like the curse I seem to be. Once the table settings are replaced and it looks like I've never stepped foot in the room, I stare up at the multiple levels of diners. I am clearly still the center of attention. The floor show, you might say.

Tomorrow's speech where I'm the authority on happiness ought to be a blast. "Hey, aren't you that chick who couldn't handle eating solid food last night?"

We all sit down—Haley, Kathleen, Sam, Sam's sister, a new guy, and myself.

"Thank you," I finally manage to croak to Sam, my voice scratchy.

"Forget it," he says. "You remember my sister, Jules, and I'm not sure you've met her husband, Kyle."

"They allow married folks on the singles' cruise?"

"Only if we behave ourselves," Jules says. "They require us to sell the joys of marriage to be here." She laughs at her own jokes, and I like her. She's nerdy and owns it.

"You're sitting at *this* table?" I ask. I thought being on a cruise was all about meeting new people, not the same ones I've managed to make a fool of myself in front of. I'm hoping for a new audience to share my wealth of antics with.

"All week," Jules says.

Stellar.

Introductions conclude, and Jules and Kathleen discuss the benefits of yoga compared to weight lifting. Sam, who is now sitting beside me, begins to poke the bear that is my last nerve. "So tell me, Dr. Maguire, is there ever a physical reason—an objective reason—that some people can't find happiness? Or is it all in the mind, this positive psychology stuff?"

"Sam, leave her alone," his sister says. "We just got here. Maggie, Kyle is the one who introduced me to your work. It's partly why I took my new job."

I smile at her, then turn to her brother and tell him a pointed fact. "Some men can't be happy due to low hormone levels." I take a sip of water. "Testosterone, to be specific."

Now it's Sam who chokes on his water.

His sister's jaw drops while Kyle laughs out loud. "Not a problem in our house then."

"Maggie." Haley stares me down as if she's ready to kill me. "I haven't properly introduced you to Sam's sister. Ms. Jules Jensen has just introduced herself to me as the new president and publisher at BrainLit Books. When she says she took the job partly because of your work, it's because your upcoming book will be the first published under her tenure."

I swallow over the lump in my throat. "So, *my* publisher?" As if I need one more way to be a failure. *This* is why I stay home or in the lab. The person who hired me to write these books has been relieved of his duties, so I imagine Ms. Jules Jensen is questioning the worth of my contract. We have that in common, I guess.

At the very least, my friends now recognize the terrible error of their ways by pulling me away from my lonely apartment life. They should have let me rot there in my melted glory.

Sam just gazes at me with those deep, dark eyes and makes me feel like the principal used to in my elitist private school: *guilty*. The sting of tears is forming, as everything I ever feared happening when I left the comfort of my couch is coming true. Even though my friends are beside me, I've never felt so alone.

Brent Spoils, the bartender with the blazing blue eyes, walks by our table toward the exit. He's what experts call a hedonist—the person who searches out pleasure at the expense of everything else, not giving a thought to the future or its consequences. Right now, Brent is the only shot at bliss I can imagine, and I want to chase after him like a runaway kite.

"Excuse me, won't you?" I stand and drop the linen napkin onto the table.

"Maggie, we're just about to order," Haley says, reminding me Jules is essentially my new employer.

"My sleeve is wet. I think it would be best if I went back to the room and changed. I think I'll get something at the buffet. Nice to have met you all," I say as I make a break for the exit. "Jules, I'm so looking forward to discussing what's next for us." I throw that in just to remind everyone that I'm not completely nuts. But I'm close.

I venture a look back at the table as I go, and Sam's intense scrutiny almost makes me turn around and forget my soggy sleeve. *Almost.* Until I remember what he said—the same thing Jake said. *Smart women can't be happy.* That's code for *I'm looking for a good-time girl who is always blissfully rapturous without the added weight of being a genuine person.* That way, they can forget their own misery by never having to face it. Red flag.

Just as I'm about to exit, Sam mouths, *I'm sorry.*

I pause before remembering just how dangerous a man like Sam is to me. How warm and sensuous his words were before he turned on me and called me out on my science in the next sentence.

How many times did Jake say he was sorry? But he never was. Romance couldn't save me then, and it can't save me now. It's not the answer. I'm not the kind of woman men fall in love with, like Haley is. I'm here to search for answers to life's bigger questions. I know I can't run from my problems forever, but for just one more night, will anyone truly care? Someday I'll be able to act normal again when confronted with hard truths, but that day is not today.

This will all be over in a week and I'll never have to see any of these people again anyway. Granted, they may see me, considering my mug shot is all over this ship, but I won't have to see them.

8

Being able to laugh at yourself is critical to your health and
well-being. Laughter is associated with a longer life span.

The Science of Bliss by Dr. Margaret K. Maguire

B RENT SPOILS HAS AN UNRELENTING SMILE—it's etched
into his face as if by permanent marker. Not like the Joker in
a creepy, masked way, but in this hypnotizing way that offers you a
portion of his amiable manner, if only you're willing to reach for it.
Since everything else I've reached for has led to disaster, why not a
week learning from a fun person how to have fun? Brent seems to be
that man-child who loves a good time with his bros, but commitment
makes him weak in the knees.

Brent is a safe target for this week's excursion into rampant escapism that doesn't consist of sappy movies. He doesn't take life
seriously enough to be a suitable partner for anyone, except his bar,
but currently he possesses the one thing I'm missing: an exuberant
zest for life.

I follow him out of the dining room like a zombie, never giving
a thought to what the people I've left might think, except for that

quick glance back to the dangerous enigma who saved my life while also dissing my life's work.

This complete lack of self-awareness seems to be a recurring theme with me lately. The truth is, I'll have to face my new publishing boss—and her brother—soon enough, but for one last night, I don't want to worry about consequences. I want to have fun and remember who I was before I ever met Jake Stone and his charming but manipulative ways. If only I could regain that innocence on how I viewed people. Tonight I want to ignore why Jake's breaking up with me sent my life into a complete tailspin and why I've lost the ability to trust myself. Brent is the Band-Aid I need.

"Brent!" I call after the muscular bartender, ignoring my damp arm. He turns and offers his thousand-watt smile. His teeth are perfect, like he's been waiting for his close-up on a nighttime drama.

"If it isn't She Blinded Me with Science!"

I don't let it bother me that he doesn't remember my name. The fact that he remembers who I am is enough for me. Though there are posters to remind him throughout the ship.

He touches my chin ever so gently. "Maggie," he growls in a seductive manner, "you've escaped the intellectual crowd and their pompous arrogance. Does that mean you're ready to have some fun?"

I hardly remember the last time I had fun. "Yes!"

"Awesome! I thought you might be one of those who hide behind work for all their natural-born days and let the fun play out for others."

"Me? Never," I say with far more assurance than I feel. The truth is, my comfort zone is back inside with colleagues and the friends who rescued me from my stupor. It's exactly why I have to break out.

The night air is brisk but refreshing, and I let the wind whip through my hair—taking my career-appropriate coif with it. I start to shiver, but rather than worry about my dress, I focus on having fun. Would Kylie Jenner let a damp dress ruin her night? "Let's run before my friends come looking for me."

"Oh, a mad escape. The night is filled with potential!" Brent takes both of my hands and stretches away from me. He drinks in my appearance like a thirsty man in the desert. "You're a vision in that dress."

"My friends say I dress like a librarian."

"No librarian I've ever met—though I haven't spent a lot of time in libraries either. Have they gotten hotter since grade school?" He twirls me around and brings me in close with his arm cinched tightly around my waist. "I think we should go dancing. You're dressed for it. Then, maybe after our courses are taught, we'll go skydiving."

Maybe I'm overestimating myself. "Skydiving in Mexico?" I stammer. "That doesn't sound sketchy to you?"

"Nah, it's incredible. The bluest sky, pristine aqua water below. It's just what you need to clear the palate after a breakup. After you've jumped from a plane and into the abyss, you'll know you can accomplish anything you set your mind to, and that loser will be nothing more than a mist of a forgotten memory."

My heart hammers at the mere thought of jumping out of a perfectly good airplane. *I've gone too far. Too much too fast.* Wearing a dress is one thing, but turning into Adventure Girl when the statistics go against it might be too much for me to take. I second-guess myself when I look into Brent's reassuring eyes. If I run now, I'll hide behind fear for the rest of my life.

"Why not?" I say, while thinking of a million good reasons why not.

"Forget skydiving for now. If you think about it too much, you'll chicken out. Tomorrow, since we're all day at sea, you'll have huge success with your talk. I'll teach on mixology and you'll let me handle the plans in Mexico. Just trust me. We don't want to do anything the ship offers—too expensive and too many forms to sign. I know this guy . . ."

"How many bad ideas start with that sentence?"

"Mm-mm, a pretty face like that needs to smile more. That's my specialty."

I'm starting to panic already, but I try to breathe in deeply and focus my attention elsewhere. *Fun.* This is a new experience. Of course it's going to feel unnatural. "If you don't mind my asking, what exactly is mixology?"

"Specialty drinks. It's one of the few classes they charge for on this barge. They charge to cover all the alcohol and probably my room, which is a dank cellar in the bottom of the ship. Remember the third-class passengers on the *Titanic*? My room is slightly better—as in, I don't think there are any cages on my level, so I could make a swim for it if we went down. I suppose they treat your kind better than that."

"My kind?"

"The doctors, stockbrokers, artists . . . people who make the high-end clientele able to write this trip off. I'm in charge of the partiers, and on a singles' cruise, there are plenty. The people they want to keep reined in—cattle on the south forty of the ranch. Though they probably spend the most money on the ship. We may be classless, but we spend wads of cash."

"Hmm." His words give me pause as to the disparity between us. Like the time I got kicked out of a high school party when I questioned the underage drinking. I was being *responsible*. They used the word *narc* and a few other choice cuss words before expelling me from the party. Shockingly, I was never invited to another one. Brent seems like the kind of guy who would have thrown those parties and never looked at me twice in high school.

He pulls me to the edge of the ship and leans over the rail. He stares into the darkness, and I can hear the gulf below lapping up against the ship. Brent's bulges from his muscles ripple the back of his shirt, and it's apparent that when he's not behind the bar he's in the gym. He's probably never seen a chick flick in his life—unless the gym was playing the Hallmark Channel in between UFC fights.

As I stare up into the night sky dotted with sparkling jewels of stars, my senses are awakened as if they've been in a deep slumber. The cool breeze in my hair, the salty tang of the gulf air on my tongue, the low hum of the ship. It's magical.

Brent reaches for me. "Come here."

I take his hand, and he pulls me close and wraps his arm around my waist in one swift move. "So you've said what makes your ex happy. What makes you happy?"

I face Brent in an uncomfortably close manner. I tell myself this is better than a romantic movie, but it's extremely awkward. Being in the sights of a guy like Brent, someone so easy and unflappable, makes me realize how surly and finicky Jake could be. I never felt at peace in his presence, like he was too good for me and I was always reaching and struggling to please him. It doesn't take a psychologist to figure out where that came from.

I force myself to relax and rest my head on Brent's shoulder. He casually touches the side of my arm, but it feels intimate. Accepting . . . and maybe a tad forced.

I step back and grab the railing. "The stars are incredible out here. Who knew there were so many?"

"That's right, you're a city girl. Texas has a few stars. You ought to spend more time in the Lone Star State."

A blanket of stars in the night sky makes me feel like a speck—as if my troubles are nothing in the scheme of things. I imagine they are, but I don't want to be judged on my accomplishments alone any longer. The pressure never lets up. Everyone should be entitled to a bad day here and there—even a happiness researcher.

I study Brent in the pale moonlight. He truly is a walking bag of sunshine. He seems to glow and creates an aura around him, and I want to be enveloped in it and leave behind my shadowy self. *This feels like the answer.*

"People think money brings happiness," I tell him, gazing out over the waters illuminated by the ship. "Statistically, it doesn't." I look into his eyes. "What's your secret? Why are you so happy, do you think?"

"No degrees necessary for that truth about money not buying happiness. A night in my bar would teach you that much." He twirls me until I'm facing the water again and he's got his arms around me, pointing to the stars. "Some of the richest people I know are the most miserable. Too much pressure in life."

I think he's making a move, but rather than address this, I spout some facts—my go-to chastity belt. "Happiness comes from having meaning in your life—a purpose," I continue, as if he's asked me.

Brent knows his purpose. In his little corner of the world, he serves up drinks and probably bad advice by the glassful. He gives people a place to go, and while I've never hung out in a bar in this lifetime, I covet his easy purpose: making people happy with food and drink.

I can't help but wonder if my path might have been easier if I didn't have my parents' voices and their goals for me in my head. What would it be like to be okay with myself if I were a secretary or a cashier, or even a garbage collector? The world can live without another happiness researcher, but can it really live without a garbage collector? Brent's at peace with himself, even as a guy who takes working vacations, and I covet that. He probably doesn't hear the rules spouted in his head all day long. He must hear something more like Luke Bryan crooning.

"The mood out here," he says. "Getting a bit dark for me." I take this to mean that reality is getting in the way of Brent skating through life, untouched by human suffering. The researcher in me can't help but wonder if Brent's eternal happiness is due to a lack of dealing with anything he doesn't want to deal with in life.

"Can you swing?" Brent asks.

"Swing?"

"Swing dance. Can you swing dance? That dress you're in looks made for it, and there are swing lessons tonight, so even if you can't, we could learn together. I'm more of a line dancer myself. Swing dancing would be a welcome break from the two-step in boots."

I couldn't even make it through dinner when starving. How on earth can I expect to dance? I suck in a deep breath. It's time to feel the fear and do it anyway.

I allow Brent to take my hand, and we glide across the deck like two skaters ready to collect our gold medals. I'm carefree and light, as if I have wings and am about to take flight, when I'm stopped in my tracks by Kathleen and Haley. Haley actually looks as if she has murder on her mind, and for once I fear her death stare more intently than Kathleen's.

"We're going dancing," I say breathlessly.

"I thought you were changing your dress." Kathleen has taken her linebacker stance. "You don't think you should rest up for your speech tomorrow? Maybe prepare a little?"

"It will be easy. I'm going to talk about road mapping. We'll hand out pencils and paper, and everyone can create their own road map to happiness. A few questions and then done. We can spend the rest of the cruise collecting real-world happiness data."

Brent greets my friends. "How are you? The name is Brent." He stretches out his hand, and Haley just stares at it as though it's covered in bacteria. "I'm taking your beautiful friend swing dancing. Come along, the more the merrier! Judging by the number of guys on this cruise who probably remember when swing dancing was fresh, I think there will be partners for everyone."

His joke falls flat with a solid thud. I stare at my friends with a pleading look on my face. This is the only thing I've wanted in months, and just to desire something feels like progress. "Come with us," I say. "We'll dance."

Haley comes toward me, her sea-green eyes brimming with tears. "I'll lose my job, Maggie. BrainLit Books is my biggest client right now. I know it wasn't fair to do to you, to put more pressure on you, but I swear my motive was good. I love you and I hate seeing you like this, broken by a man who wasn't worthy of you in the first place. You told us you were changing your dress. Sam was worried he upset you and wanted to check on you, but we promised to do it for him. Now this."

"Brent out," he says. "Catch you girls later." He turns and walks off.

"Solid, respectable guy you found there, Maggie. What are you thinking? Wandering off with a stranger on a cruise ship is no less dangerous than the city. Honestly, I'm starting to really worry about your state of mind."

Well, that makes two of us.

My temporary joy falls away like water off a swan's back. In that one gaze from Haley, I see how utterly selfish and childish I've been for months. I lied to my parents—through omission, but lied nonetheless. I abandoned my friends for an extended pity party, and I took a work sabbatical without a genuine explanation to my boss. Now, in Haley's tears, I see that there are consequences to my actions and everyone else has felt them. Just because my chances of working for the great Dr. Hamilton are dashed doesn't give me the right to destroy Haley's chance at a bright future.

I dash after Brent. "Hey, I'm sorry. It appears I have work to do."

He nods and winks in that oh-so-sexy, cocky way of his—like I won't be missed at all and he'll find my replacement within the next five minutes. "Meet me at the dance floor if you can get away," he says nonchalantly, and plants a kiss on my cheek. "We'll talk later about skydiving." Then he wags his finger at me. "Your problem is your friends. You need to ditch them and find someone who knows how to have a good time."

As I watch him walk away, I feel like my chance of ever having fun in this lifetime goes with him. Some people are the serious sort and get all the work in life done. That's who I am. Haley's eyes jolt me back to reality.

"I'll fix it," I say to her. "I'll fix everything."

She hands me a slip of paper. "This is Sam Wellington's room number. I suggest you start with an apology to him before you discuss the next steps with BrainLit Books and your new title. No testosterone—really, Maggie?"

I snatch the sheet of paper. "He's sitting in his room waiting for my apology?" I roll my eyes. "Pathetic. I stand behind my comment. This"—I wave the paper—"just proves my point."

"Just keep your thoughts on his hormone levels to yourself. You shouldn't be talking anyway. How much estrogen did you gain by the sheer number of chick flicks you watched? Or ice cream you ate?" Kathleen is supporting Haley, so I give up without further battle. They both seem so *disappointed* in me. They may as well be my parents.

I make one final plea. "Don't you two understand that I *would* be the old Maggie if I were capable?"

"That's just it," Haley says. "We think you are capable, and you can start proving it to yourself by apologizing to Jules's brother. What Jake did to you was callous and cruel, but you have to get back up, Maggie. There are no other options in life. You're not responsible for Jake. You're only responsible for you. Now get to it!"

I nod. I know they're right. Broken hearts are a tale as old as time, and mine is no different. I wave the scrap of paper again. "He's in his room already? Why does that not surprise me? Is he playing online chess for a night of laughs? Or maybe he's breaking the big guns out and playing Sudoku."

"You're only proving his point by being so miserable. Show him some of that happy you're selling and maybe he'll believe that smart women are capable of true happiness."

"I don't care what he believes."

"We know you don't. More importantly, show him some humility so we don't lose that contract you so desperately need. At the very least, the guy saved your life tonight, and he said nothing about you projectile vomiting bread across the table toward his sister. What does it take to impress you, Maggie?"

"I'm in a bad mood, all right?" I sulk off toward the room of this sorry sap who got his feelings hurt. Let's be honest. He should be apologizing to *me*. If for nothing else than ruining a public night of fun with a genuine live human being and no gelato in sight. And maybe for saving my life.

9

Authentic direction in your life is necessary to happiness. Be honest with yourself about your true desires and passions.

The Science of Bliss by Dr. Margaret K. Maguire

S AD SACK'S ROOM IS ON THE UPPER LEVEL. I call him that name in my head just to prepare myself for his handsome face. I don't want to be swayed by his looks or his charm. I've learned that lesson already. I knock lightly on the double doors and turn to scamper away when the door opens. "Dr. Maguire," he says in a low, bored tone, as if he's been expecting my falsely contrite self. This man saved my life, so why can't I muster up some proper humility? Something is clearly wrong with me.

I wish I could wipe the smirk from his face. "I came to apologize."

"How very humble of you. Won't you come in?" He opens the door wider to his suite, which makes the one I'm sharing with my friends look like a closet.

"Holy cow! This is all for you?" I stare at him. Not having a verbal filter must pay well.

The room is surrounded by windows. There's a warm ecru on the walls and stunning red carpet on the floor. The well-appointed lighting makes it all seem like a decorator's addition, and I'm drawn to the wall of windows and the vast darkness behind them. "This must offer some fantastic view when the sun is up."

"You'll have to come by and see during the day."

Yeah, that's not going to happen.

"Anyway . . ." I turn to face him so I seem sincere. "I'm sorry I implied that your hormone levels might be subpar. I am not a medical doctor and should not have made any reference to your medical history, nor provided an unprofessional, armchair diagnosis."

He actually throws his head back in laughter, then cocks that expressive brow of his. "That's my apology?"

I cross my arms. "What was wrong with it?"

"It's anemic."

"Anemic?"

He shrugs his wide shoulders. "Anemic. Not substantial. Did you run that by your lawyer before you came by?"

"I know what it means. What did you expect me to do, come up here and grovel?"

"Yes, please. I did save you from choking. I figure it's the least you could do. I also ordered you a regular iced tea since you clearly can't handle your alcohol, and I made sure you stayed sober in front of your new boss. Personally, at this point, I think groveling a little couldn't hurt. I've been Superman tonight."

"I wasn't going to choke—"

"Don't you have anything about being grateful in that book of yours on happiness? I mean, all the happy people I've ever met are extremely thankful people." He crosses his arms across his expansive chest. "You know . . . they're *gracious.*"

The word hits my last nerve. "Do you know how hard it was to come up here? You basically said I'm destined to be alone for the rest of my life and seemed to enjoy it. You are such an incredible, life-size jerk! Has anyone ever told you that?"

"Surprisingly, no. But then, I believe that most people are equipped with some kind of a filter. A smidgen of tact."

"That's the pot calling the kettle black. Didn't you tell me smart women can't be happy? Before you actually introduced yourself? I mean, those are some mad charm-school skills you've got there. Is that what they taught you in prep school?"

"Ah, so you think I went to prep school and was handed my money, along with estimating my level of masculinity. But I'm the judgmental one, is that right? And here Haley told me Kathleen was the prophetic one in your group."

"Maybe I attacked your masculinity because you attacked my femininity, did you ever think of that?" My head drops in shame as I realize what I actually said to him and how true it is. He hit my soft spot—one that I didn't even know existed.

"No, I never did think of that," he says, his voice a whisper. "I have my own history with intelligent women, and I imagine my conclusions might be skewed. I'm sorry you bore the brunt of that."

My whole body seems to soften at his admission, and I want to call a truce. For his sister's sake. "There's nothing wrong with your masculinity," I blurt out. Mostly because it's the truth and it was his masculine self saying the torturous words that was the problem in the first place. "I want you to know, though, that some man out there might be challenged by a woman with a few degrees behind her. Maybe not you, but certainly someone." I look up.

He brushes my hair behind my shoulder, which should feel forward and far too intimate for our casual acquaintance. But it doesn't. It seems innocent and natural. As if he's the bigger person, able to show kindness when someone truly doesn't deserve it. "You're right. Any man would be lucky to have you, and I'm ashamed to have implied otherwise. I'm sorry." He picks up a leather folder from the table and hands it to me. "Do you want something from room service? Or did you get to the buffet while you were avoiding me by changing your dress?" He stares at the same dress I left the dining room in, as if waiting for an explanation.

I'm starving. There are pictures on the menu—like it's a high-class Denny's—and my flesh is weak. I swallow the lump in my throat and straighten my shoulders. "Don't flatter yourself, Mr. Wellington. I wasn't avoiding you. I simply wanted to have some fun, so I left what seemed to me a table of corpses." As soon as I say the words, I shudder at their impact. "I'm sorry. I haven't eaten. I think I'm hangry. Feed me or I'm like one of those monsters after midnight."

"A gremlin."

"Yes, a gremlin," I admit.

"You must be starving. Everyone gets grumpy when they're hungry. Sit down and eat." He turns to his butler, who is standing stoic and unconcerned in the corner like a zombie statue. When he moves, I nearly jump out of my skin. "Marcus, would you bring in the meal I ordered for Miss—*Dr.* Maguire?"

Marcus nods. "I'll get it from the kitchen." He leaves the two of us alone in the expansive room by exiting through a different door.

"You have a kitchen in the suite?"

"Just a small one," Sam says. Which is like someone telling me they have the lower-end Porsche.

It's so homey in the suite, and the idea of there being a magical kitchen behind the door makes me feel as if I'm in a fairy tale.

"You already ordered dinner for me?" I pull out the chair at the small table and wilt into it. "That's presumptuous, isn't it?" Why did I say that? Why can't I tell him how absolutely famished I am and that he couldn't have done anything sweeter for me, especially since my behavior hardly warrants any favors?

"Is it? I felt it was common courtesy. You've had a long, emotional couple days. Your friends told us that you didn't plan to be here and that they surprised you yesterday. I can certainly identify with that." He pushes my chair closer to the table. "You seemed rather in a hurry to get away. I figured you might not have eaten after you left the table."

Not since this morning and that stale muffin at the motel. It was not worth Kathleen's sermon on empty calories. My stomach groans as a reminder.

Sam's eyes have a depth to them that brings out the scientist in me. I want to explore them, scan them for data, and discover the basis for his attitude against smart women. He might offer the key for why all men seem to want something other than me. I narrow my eyes and look into his to see if the answer is in there.

"Everything okay?" he asks.

I sit up taller in the chair. "Everything is great," I say in my best chipper voice.

Sam's small, heroic act of ordering me dinner makes me want to cry and I have no idea why. I suppose I'm exhausted and my stoic nature has given way to my sappy side. The sting of tears begins and I blink them away, wondering if my Prince Charming fantasies have ruined me forever. Unfortunately, Sam notices.

He presses his hand softly to mine. "Put your armor away for one minute. I can't possibly harm you with Marcus coming back shortly. He's only gone to make sure your food is warm. Let's call a truce, maybe? At least until you're done eating and have your strength back. Then you can go right back to telling me why I'm a—what was it you said? A life-size jerk."

"I don't want to fight you, Mr. Wellington. You make it sound like I'm in kindergarten." If I thought having my book quotes parroted back to me was trying, it was nothing next to my unfiltered self with Sam Wellington. "Why are you being so nice to me?"

"Why are you so suspicious?" He grins, and my eyes are drawn to the stubble of growth on his jawline. It wasn't there this morning, and I'm reminded that perhaps my previous view of his hormone level might be tainted by my feelings about him and his vast similarities to Jake. *Will I forever blame men for Jake's failings? Is that what I'm doing?* If so, it only proves my point that I don't belong in science any longer. I used to be such an excellent student of people, hunting patterns and deciphering scientific markings from others' thoughts and behaviors. My sabbatical has left me soft.

"Truce," I tell him. "I wasn't on my best behavior at dinner."

"You think?"

"It's been a long week. I probably don't need to explain that social settings aren't my strong suit."

He cocks that infernal brow.

"I assure you, tomorrow I'll perform like a dancing monkey for your sister's publishing house." I rap my fingernails on the table.

"A simple, professional speech is all we ask. No dancing necessary."

"I am a professional, though I realize I haven't given you any indication of this."

I want to blame it on him and tell him that it's his fault for putting me on the defensive with his comments, but that's hardly fair. Or Christian, for that matter. I need to take responsibility for my own garbage or I'm . . . I'm just like Jake. Did St. Paul whine about being in jail? Or why he wasn't out preaching? He did not. He wrote letters of encouragement from jail! Why can't I be productive like that in my misery? All I did was write a romantic screenplay that will probably never see the light of day.

Sam shakes his head subtly. "You seem to think I'm always judging you in a harsh capacity."

"Aren't you?"

Sam's other stinking eyebrow raises! I am ready to shave them both off at this point.

It takes every ounce of energy I have to maintain my seat and not run from everything I'm feeling. "What is going on in that head of yours then? You seem to expect me to understand you when I have no idea what you're thinking."

"Trust me, there's not nearly as much going on in my mind as you're thinking." He laughs. "I'm not worried about your speech." Sam sits beside me in a cushy, sea foam–colored recliner. He smells divine. Earthy and woodsy like he'd just stepped out of the room where my gramps kept his pipe. Sam dwarfs the chair and leans forward, coming closer to me. His eyes meet mine with an intimacy I haven't felt in ages, and I catch my breath. Reality strikes me that Jake never looked at me like that. Not even once.

He wraps his hand around mine. "Let's start again. I'm sorry I offended you earlier. I mean that sincerely, and there are no additional dark thoughts muddling around in my brain, if that's what you're thinking."

I avert my eyes rather than face the stirrings within me. I see a cut-glass railing on a spiral staircase, similar to the one in the dining room, and my mind wanders as to where it leads and if there are actually two floors in this suite.

"I wasn't myself after being dragged on a cruise," he claims. "I've been told I can be abrupt at times."

"Dragged on a cruise?" I laugh. "You and I are possibly the only two people who view a cruise as some kind of condemning punishment."

"You mean it's not?" Sam grins playfully. "It's not all bad. I got owned by a *New York Times* bestselling author."

I want to escape his charm, and yet I find myself leaning into it. I clamp my eyes shut. I need to escape his cozy love nest before I let any of his charm get under my skin. I breathe in deeply and search for the tough weed of a woman my parents raised me to be.

"You have a staircase?" I ask to avoid letting this conversation plummet the depths of my tentative emotions.

"Up to the bedroom. You really should go see it, and no, that's not a pickup line. I'll wait down here while you check it out. It has a circular bank of windows all in front of the bed, so when you wake up, it's a captain's view."

"It's not really!"

"Go and see, I don't mind."

I can't help my curiosity. I'm not generally impressed by fancy spaces, but engineering a two-story suite into a ship? That's something I have to see for myself. I climb up the spiral staircase as if I'm wearing glass slippers and slip into the expansive room. The entire crescent-shaped space is a wall of windows framed by the white steel of the edge of the ship. There's a television hung on the middle frame of the windows. It stands directly in front of the king-size bed so the view surrounds the television. Naturally, I can't help but think of how magnificent it would be to hole up here and watch chick flicks until this infernal cruise is over.

"Holy cow, can you imagine a movie marathon from here? With a butler? You'd never have to move except to go to the bathroom!"

"Did you say something?" Sam calls from below.

"Uh, no. Nothing. Just oohing and aahing my approval."

I stand at the bank of windows and question the study that says money doesn't make you happy. It may not, but this suite could certainly prolong a lack of misery.

"What do you think?" Sam is standing a safe distance away on the landing. His feet are crossed at the ankles as he awaits my answer.

"I think my friends and I could all fit into this bed and you should switch rooms with us. Although it might be more difficult to get me to make an appearance at my speech. I might get lost in here."

"You and your friends are welcome to hang out here. Did you see the deck below? I suppose you didn't—it's dark. But I imagine I'll spend most of my time there getting some work done."

"You're going to work in this room? Sam! This is amazing. Why didn't you bring someone to enjoy it with you?" As I ask the question, I regret it immediately. I mean, why didn't I bring someone?

He smiles. "My sister seems to think a week on a singles' cruise will fix all that." He scoffs at the notion.

"I'm sorry." And this time I mean it. "I didn't mean to pry."

"You and I aren't exactly winning any awards for social graces in the near future."

"You don't think we should start up our own charm school?" I say to lighten the mood. "What would we call it? Friends without Filters Charm School?"

Sam grins. "My sister means well, dragging me on a singles' cruise, but she doesn't understand that I'm happy working. I'm fulfilled."

I nod. "In my research, some people *are* happy working, without intimate relationships in their lives."

His mouth drops.

"Not that you're one of them, of course. For all I know, you could have a long-term girlfriend . . . or maybe a wife." I'm making it so much worse. *Shut up already!*

"If I did, do you think my sister would force me on a singles' cruise?"

"Oh, right. Probably not."

Sam steps toward me, and we stand side by side staring out at the vast, dark sea in front of us, with only a small light from the ship to guide us. Then he turns and stares into my eyes as if he can read my mind. I scramble for anything to say to avoid the intimacy . . . and the desire I'm feeling for his proximity.

"Look, I know your sister is my new boss, but I've made a terrible error in my data and I want to ensure that it's correct before I release another book. I'm trying to protect her, don't you see? She's only just become president of BrainLit, and I'm not sure . . ." My voice trails off.

Sam says nothing. He simply keeps gazing into my eyes as if I hold the secret to the universe.

"I—I've made an error in my calculations," I say again. "Did you hear me?"

"Yes, I heard you." He's so close I can feel his breath graze my lower lip.

"When I originally signed the publishing contract—years ago, incidentally, for a two-book deal—I saw potential in the science of happiness and my role in that science. I'm trying to be honest here. I don't want your sister to lose credibility. I'm waiting on grant money for the study on resilience, and there's no guarantee it's going to happen." I keep talking, hoping to increase the space between us but not having the will to do so. "What I've collected right now, it just isn't enough for an entire book. I may not have anything to say in the new book, don't you see?"

He nods, but it's clear he's not thinking about his sister's business. Every cell in my being wants to reach up and kiss him. This man who offended me and all women like me. I'm currently an insult to women everywhere, but his draw is powerful. Magnetic.

I step backwards and begin to pace in front of the window. "It's important that a woman has stepped into that role as publisher, and I want her to have the best outcome possible. I don't want her to be the laughingstock at the booksellers' association. She needs to find a different scientist. I can help her. I know everyone in the field."

"You're worried about my sister, is that it?"

"I am," I say breathlessly. *And I'm worried that I'm going to kiss a complete stranger.*

"The science of happiness is a burgeoning field." He actually makes these words sound sexy. I've watched way too many romantic movies. "Doctors who previously studied depression have started to look into the science of happiness for the cure. The cost of depression on employers is into the billions and rising. This research will have a direct correlation to the economy if it provides the answer."

I can't tell if he's toying with me. "You seem to know a great deal about my field."

"I know a lot about business. You're a maverick. Maybe you're not comfortable in that position and are passing it off to the next doctor of happiness. Is that truly wise? The work is going to happen with or without you because it means money in the pocket. You're willing to give that up over this obsession you have with your past data? Data becomes outdated, no? So find the new data."

I clench my hand and dig my fingernails into my palm. "Money to find new data is hard to come by. Have you ever written a grant?"

"Forget the grant. All you need is a corporate sponsor. Done. What are you so afraid of? You're not happy, so you think you're a fraud. Do you think all cardiologists have healthy hearts?"

I look directly at him. For once someone understands, and he's hit at the raw, tender nerve of my truth. I feel exposed. Sam actually gets it, and I'm filled with revived hope, but it's quickly dashed by his next sentence.

"Fashion designers are some of the worst-dressed people in the world."

"What is your point?" This comes out sounding much ruder than I meant it to.

"You don't have to be Tigger to study happiness. It's just data that you're analyzing, not your own life. But it's data that matters. Employers are losing billions because people aren't happy, and this book will shed light on that, so it's important to the business community as well as the science community. You want grant money? I'll find you grant money."

His belief in me scares me. He sounds like my friends, and I wonder why so many have so much faith in my work. "I don't want grant money to support corporate greed. There's no trust in that kind of study. Do you remember when cigarette companies paid 'scientists' to tell us smoking was good for us? Science isn't science if you're not willing to read the data truthfully."

"I see it now." He nods knowingly, like he's a doctor ready to make a dire diagnosis. "You're one of those science snobs. It can't be used to help anyone. It's for knowledge only. To better the world somehow."

I'd protest, but realizing he's under my skin yet again, I don't feel the need to defend myself. I realize that he doesn't mean anything demeaning by his words. He's clarifying for himself. Perhaps that's the worst outcome of my career dive. I seem incapable of hearing something rationally. It all seems to go through a questioning filter, as if everyone is out to get me.

As I tear my gaze from his, I think he must be a very decent man to invest in his sister's career so heavily. He clearly takes loyalty to a new level, so he can't be all bad. No matter what my current black-and-white thinking tells me.

My cell phone beeps downstairs. "I thought we didn't get service on board." I clamber down the steps, anxious to get away from his inquisitive nature and his prying eyes.

At the dining table, I scramble through my small handbag to get my phone. Sam stands calmly behind me.

"It's intermittent. I notice I hear from my assistant at random intervals. We must be close to shore if you're getting a call."

I shrug. "It's probably Kathleen ensuring that I've actually apologized to you so she doesn't have to rough me up when I get back to my room. You caused me a world of trouble today."

He gives a sideways grin. "I'm glad to hear it. Here I thought I failed to make an impression."

If you only knew. Inexplicably, I feel at home with him, and for a brief moment, gone is the unrelenting ache that gnaws at my stomach on a daily basis. Dare I say it? I feel *happy* in his presence.

10

Empathy allows connection. Feeling sad with someone else connects us relationally, but so does feeling others' happiness.

The Science of Bliss by Dr. Margaret K. Maguire

RIFFLING THROUGH MY HANDBAG for my phone allows me to focus on something other than Sam's magnetic presence behind me. The ringing continues in the form of my favorite song, "Humble and Kind," and I'm thankful for the diversion. Why would I react so easily to a man who feels the way he does?

Marcus's presence is welcome as a chaperone as my emotions are overflowing. "Do you need some help, miss?"

"No." I shake my head. "Thank you, Marcus. It's right here!" I lift my phone in triumph.

"Shall I bring in your dinner?"

Sam shakes his head. "Not just yet, Marcus."

To my horror, a text picture of Jake and his new bride lights up on my phone. I try to shove it back in my handbag before Sam sees it, but it's too late.

Sam reaches for my phone. "This is the brain-dead ex Haley told me about, I'm assuming?"

My heart sinks a little further. "I guess he wants me to know that he's doing just fine without me."

Sam's jaw clenches slightly. "What a gem of a human being."

Jake is determined to finish me off and make certain I understand that I never mattered to him. Which seems to be a recurring theme in my life. All I ever wanted was to matter to someone. Not the invisible millions who watched the TED Talk or read my book, but one person who didn't want to live without me.

"That's cruel," Sam says. Then he presses the phone on again and looks closely at the picture. "Clearly he traded down."

I smile. "That was him calling. I guess he decided a picture was worth a thousand words." I try to muster a laugh. "It seems to be a group text. How kind of him to include me, don't you think?"

"What's your password?" Sam asks.

"4545," I offer without thinking. My mind is still reeling from the humiliation.

Sam taps quickly, opens the photo app, and flips the camera toward us. He presses his handsome face beside mine and lifts the camera up. Instinctively, I offer a big smile, and our beaming faces are snapped into history. I look slightly shell-shocked, but my makeup is fresh. It's obvious I'm wearing my best dress with the lace collar, and then . . . then there's the fact that Sam Wellington is so blasted good-looking. We look uncannily cozy in the photo, comfortable with one another, and I think I actually look prettier beside him simply because he is so handsome. He taps away again, and soon I hear the whooshing sound of our picture off in the universe—the text universe. He places the phone beside me.

Alongside our picture, which I must admit looks like a romance movie advertisement, are the words, "We are ecstatic for you! Us next!"

Sam sits in his sea foam–green chair, and I tell him, "You seem pleased with your handiwork."

"Guy had it coming. I think we should send the next one in a bikini from the beach on the Mexican Riviera."

"Do you now? I hope you brought your bikini."

"Your problem, Dr. Maguire"—he leans back in the chair he dwarfs and crosses his arms over his bulky chest—"is you've spent too much time in the lab studying happiness rather than living it. I find it questionable, and I'd like to see this research of yours put to good use."

"In a bikini. So I heard. It's so forward thinking of you. You wouldn't by chance be on the board for the National Organization for Women?"

"I'm making a legitimate offer for a fantastic day on the beach. I'll bring the picnic and everything." He puts his hand to his chest. "No sexism meant. Come in whatever you feel is appropriate for a day in the sun. A muumuu maybe? Bring your friends along if you're worried about my character."

"I'm not worried about your character or my ability to handle you if necessary."

"Oh, now that is intriguing. A PhD who can defend herself with what, if you don't mind my asking? Karate? Tae kwon do? A knife you carry strapped to your thigh?" He laughs at his own joke.

"Do you want to try me?"

"Heavens no, I was just imagining what that might look like. I trust that you can defend yourself. You made short work of me today in the lobby." He sits up and aims his deep brown eyes at me. "You know that guy isn't right in the head, don't you?"

"Jake?"

"A normal person who breaks up with someone doesn't try to hurt them. He's not right in the head, in my opinion. It's his wedding day supposedly, and if he were in love and not playing a sick game, he'd be concerned with his new wife, not his ex and punishing you. I think you're lucky to be away from him."

"Is that so?" My answer is snarky, but his words warm my heart to the core. I needed someone to remind me that what I went through wasn't a normal breakup.

My mind drifts back to Jake getting Sam's text. Compared to Jake, Sam Wellington is straight off the pages of *GQ*. Only, he clearly isn't all about looks and false flattery.

"I've apologized. So we're good, right?" I ask Sam.

He frowns but seems to relent easily. "As long as my sister gets her book, we're good."

"I told you, my calculations are off. I can't in good conscience set your sister up for a lawsuit with her book launch—"

He cuts me off. "I think your research has proven correct and you're familiar with all facts on happiness. My analysis is that you've confused happiness with euphoria." His hand envelops mine again. "Nothing feels as good as falling in love. That's not happiness, it's ecstasy, and it doesn't last." He picks up my phone again and punches in my code. "This guy . . ." He points to Jake's photo. "You're so out of his league. I want to know what you were thinking. Is there a science behind that?"

I yank my hand from his. "What is it you want from me, Sam Wellington?"

"Me? Not a thing. I'm simply telling you the truth. I don't see what you saw in the guy. I think by now we've both established that neither one of us is great at false flattery. I'm only saying I'd never lend that guy money. He looks shifty."

"Luckily, he won't be asking you for money," I say, thinking Jake probably had enough of my money to last him a good while. "So we're all right? Truce? I can go?"

He sits back again. "I'd never keep you. I'm glad we got a chance to work things out."

"I appreciate your interest in this future book, Sam, and the offer to help me get grant money, but I'll work things out with your sister. I appreciate that you both believe in me, but trust me, I'm not myself right now. Getting out of this contract is the best thing for your sister as well as me."

"You believe that?"

"Yes. I need out of this contract. This isn't where I expected to be in life. I have to recalculate, and it's very hard to do with everyone's expectations on me." I let out a weary sigh. "I'd just rather have my midlife crisis at home in front of the television. After all these years of work, aren't I entitled to that?"

He laughs again, and I'm drawn by the sound of it. It's genuine and from the heart, as if I truly earned his joy. "You're a tad young to have a midlife crisis."

I shrug. "I'm an old soul."

His warm smile emerges and brings with it a small thrill that I can only hope is late-onset seasickness. "That makes two of us. Old souls navigating the hipsters' singles' cruise. Think they might make us walk the plank?"

"One can hope," I grumble.

His eyebrows rise.

"I feel the need to set the record straight. Just so you know, I'm not unhappy because I'm educated. In fact, it's essential that you feel all types of emotions, including sadness, to truly embrace happiness. It has very little to do with intellect."

"So you've said. Can you prove to me statistically that smart women are as happy as women of average intellect?"

"I can, actually. Would it make a difference to you?"

He lifts his wide shoulders in a shrug. "Probably not. Statistics can be manipulated. The truth is, the only truth that matters to most of us is our own experiences. That's why your second-guessing your data means nothing to my sister, who simply wants that next book."

Touché. My experience tells me that men prefer simple women who worship the ground they walk on and keep reality at bay. I doubt that I'd believe any statistics to the contrary either.

"I'm sorry that a smart woman broke your heart."

"I'm sorry that a self-entitled numbskull broke yours. You deserve better. Anyone who would send you that photo knowing that you might still be grieving? He's heartless. Any grieving over him is completely wasted. It was the fantasy he sold you, not reality."

While he's talking, I wonder if he's ever been married. What type of intellectual woman broke his heart? What was his part in the break?

"What do you do for a living, Sam Wellington? You know, when you're not waiting around your suite for apologies from caustic female scientists?"

He shakes his head slowly. "Nope. I'm not going to tell you what I do for a living."

"Why on earth not? That's basic conversation 101."

"Because I think you, Dr. Maguire, put people into categories and sort them like socks. I want to see your eyes light up at the sight of me the way they did when you came up with a plan to escape dinner tonight." He loosens his tie, and it hangs haphazardly around his neck.

"I shouldn't have done that. Haven't we established that already?"

"Maybe sorting people into categories contributes to your current lack of happiness. So I'm going to make you figure me out with as little data as possible. Let's see if you're up to the task."

"You needn't worry yourself," I tell him. "Nor test me."

"It's easier for you to assume that I dislike intelligent women and put them in the bin for Wednesday pickup, isn't it?"

I did assume that, and everything in my heart wants him to deny it, but he seems unable to give me the satisfaction. He'd rather play this cat-and-mouse game.

"Good talk," I say as I rise.

"You're going to write the book?" he asks. "My sister promised that title to her sales team. The company's stock depends upon your delivery, and she's risked everything on this venture."

"I think we're done here, Mr. Wellington." I'm reaching for the main door when the kitchen door to my right opens suddenly, and I'm met by Marcus with a tray hoisted on his shoulder.

"Dinner is served," Sam says casually, and I'm trapped. He knows I'm famished. Haley will ask why I'm back so soon if I head to the room. I'm like a POW at this point, and the enemy who threatens to unravel my career plans and force me to write a book whose data does not exist is at the table. I'd be eating with the wolves.

"I'll just find a buffet. I don't want to keep you."

"Just sit down, Dr. Maguire. Where am I going to go? We're on a boat. You can practice your speech for tomorrow on me."

I look at Marcus with the silver tray and then back to Sam. I'm always running from my problems. Maybe this is God's way of telling me to sit still and deal with them.

"I don't know why you're so suspicious of me, Dr. Maguire. I only want what's best for you and your career. Same as your friends."

He sounds sincere, but then again, so did Jake.

"I'm currently thinking early retirement might be best for my scientific writing career," I tell him. "Resting on my laurels or going out with a bang, as they say." I turn toward the door again when he motions toward the tray that Marcus has just placed on the table. It would be more than rude to leave now, and the only reason I'm here in the first place is to apologize. If I walk out now, I'll have to come right back and apologize again.

He lifts off the silver cover. "Marcus is going to tempt you with some nutritious"—he looks closer at the plate—"turkey?"

"Miss Kathleen told me that Miss Maggie would need the turkey for a good night's sleep," Marcus says.

"I'm starting to feel as if I have a personal nanny." I smile at Sam. I have to admit, he affects me in ways I can't explain. He feels like the antithesis of Jake, and that fascinates me so that I want to go deeper. Jake said all the right things and didn't back it up with his actions. Sam says all the wrong things, but his actions are straight out of one of my movies.

"So Kathleen got a hold of you first and I'm having the healthy blue plate special." I start to laugh. What else can I do?

"I actually ordered dinner before you got here, with Kathleen as my counsel."

"That was your first mistake. She eats a lot of things that come in some form of pressed sawdust."

Sam holds the chair out for me and I sit. "We had a nice dinner. I wish you'd stayed." He takes a breadstick from the basket on the table and crunches the end of it.

I suddenly wish I'd stayed too.

"I know it was uncomfortable, but you're going to have to get tougher in business. Especially if you plan to work for the esteemed Dr. Ernie Hamilton."

My eyes narrow. "How do you know about Dr. Hamilton?"

He ignores my question. "Kathleen ordered you turkey with a side of roasted vegetables because she says you eat too much red meat. So start eating. I'm not taking no for an answer. My sister would have my head if I didn't take care of her best author. Besides, you've already choked tonight, so you can't embarrass yourself further." His face has a hint of mirth, but he doesn't laugh.

The butler covers the meal back up while we bicker, but at Sam's firm tone, he takes the silver cover and whisks it away.

"Really? No mashed potatoes? I'm on a cruise and she still expects me to eat roasted vegetables?"

"Tomorrow night I'll make sure you have your mashed potatoes, and I'll even get you a steak if you're up to it. We'll celebrate your triumph of another great speech here. Say, 8:00?"

I want to be incensed, upset by his obvious harassment, exasperated. What is his endgame exactly—that I agree to write six more books I don't have for his sister? I mean, I could get Jules fired for less. Well, maybe not. Regardless, I decide to threaten all this after I've eaten.

The butler lays a napkin across my lap as though I'm suddenly a fine lady. He sets a warm, moist towel in a bowl in front of me, and I press it to my face and emerge refreshed before wiping my hands.

Sam is beside me, and I can almost feel his gaze upon me. He doesn't seem at home in a suit, yet he looks made for this one. He's rugged by nature with a wide, square jaw. Though he's clean-shaven, he has a day's shadow. He's not a mountain man, but he's probably been a Boy Scout and could survive in the wilderness—maybe a professional snow skier?

Sam certainly isn't hard on the eyes, so I plan to focus on that aspect rather than whatever drivel came out of his mouth earlier. Maybe I'm too hard on people and expect them to be perfect like my parents expected me to be.

The sparse turkey plate with vegetables seems like a meal fit for a king after my day. But it's not what I was expecting after a long day of starving myself and a stealth round of speed dating. So much for the glories of cruise food—Kathleen and her "I hate myself" diet have been here and put their stamp on my evening.

Still, I wolf down everything on my plate, and I'm mortified to see that it looks as though I've licked it clean. When I look up, Sam is leaning on his fist and grinning at me.

"You made short work of that. I had to keep my fingers out of the way."

He's so blasted handsome. I want to drink in his inviting eyes and linger in his expansive suite. Because I'm not in any hurry to leave his side, this is the main reason that I should run out of here without turning back. It's only been two months since Jake and I parted, and Sam is too hot to be anyone's rebound. Not that he'd be interested in me if I didn't work for his sister.

"I guess you were right. I was famished, and I do appreciate you taking care of that." This comes out sounding more condescending than grateful. Maybe I need voice lessons to work on my tone.

"Kathleen may have ordered your dinner, but in my defense, she told me you were on a special diet for focus. I didn't want to screw up my sister's cash cow—I mean, best author."

I give him a side eye. "You believed her? I have a bigger appetite than Kathleen gives me credit for. Trust me, I could have focused after a steak. Just sayin'."

"I believed Kathleen until I saw you eat. How on earth are you so slim?"

"God gave me other issues to contend with, I guess. Weight is not one of them." I knock on the wooden table just for luck. Social etiquette, however . . .

"We had baked Alaska for dessert at the table, and it was delectable. The whole time you were missing it, Kathleen and Haley went on and on about how much you would have enjoyed it."

I pout.

"I didn't think it was fair for you to go without, so I managed to sneak you some dessert in the order." He nods at Marcus, who disappears behind the door again. When he returns, he sets down a banana split with three scoops of ice cream—chocolate, vanilla, and strawberry—and a mountain of whipped cream shaped like a luscious, edible Matterhorn.

"I think I love you!" I say without thinking, and this makes him laugh. His laugh is obviously a rare occurrence and, though I'm loath to admit it, all too precious to me.

11

....

Up to 90 percent of our happiness is based on our inner
thoughts. Knowing oneself intimately, without judgment,
both reduces stress and increases positive emotions.

The Science of Bliss by Dr. Margaret K. Maguire

....

I DON'T SLEEP A WINK WORRYING ABOUT SPEAKING. Granted,
I might have a sugar hangover from the banana split, but I'll never
admit to that. I have a right to be nervous because I haven't had the
proper time to prepare for such an event. Data states that people
are supposedly more afraid of public speaking than dying—which is
stupid. But if you die, someone else has to speak at your funeral and
you're off the hook.

Actually, I'm not afraid of speaking. It's simply not my best form
of communication. My brain works faster than my edit button, and
the results can be horrifying. The TED Talk was perfect because I
had all of my data there to spill and there were no questions from
my colleagues. I knew my audience—other brain nerds like me. No
infernal interruptions by people asking for the definition of a *mirror
neuron*. If I'd known that "normals" would watch it on YouTube while
searching for the secret to happiness, I would have never pulled off

that calm, scientific demeanor. I would have instantly turned into that awkward girl in high school who thought cardigans were the height of teenage fashion and watching *The Bachelor* on Monday nights was the most scandalous thing I could do.

"I miss Jake," I say to Kathleen before I catch my error. You can imagine how this goes over.

"You miss the guy who has tried to steal your research and pawn it off as his own? You miss giving him that opportunity? The slouch who doesn't even have his doctorate? Maggie, when are you going to face the truth? Why are you so naive about people? Sometimes they're no good!"

"Are you finished? Relax. I only meant I miss his effortless way with the crowd and the way he soothed a room with his opening joke. He eased the audience into the scientific data in a way that made them . . . happy. You know, comfortable."

"It was comfortable because you didn't have to do it, that's all." Kathleen's harsh nature gives way to the real her. The soft one she hides most of the time. "You never needed him, Maggie. He robbed you of your self-confidence by telling you lies over and over again until you believed him. All right?"

I nod.

"Shake it off—it's game day, baby!"

I'm speaking in one of the ship's many theaters. This one is normally reserved for comedians and dancing reality stars. The near-capacity audience sits in the plush, navy padded seats, abuzz with happy energy and smiles all around. My job is to keep them that way. It never dawned on me that this many people would be interested in science while on vacation.

From backstage, it seems the audience is sober—as it's only 11:00 a.m. I have to admit, I was counting on a not-fully-cognizant audience. "Don't they know it's five o'clock somewhere?" I ask Kathleen. "This can't be good for me. This crowd needs some beer goggles."

"Not everyone on a cruise is here to drink. These people are looking for love and substance. Isn't that lovely?"

"No. No it isn't. Not when I have to speak." I peek through the curtains again. "Haley is working the room."

Haley is spreading her light, which she does so easily—like the people are flowers and suddenly perk up to face the sun.

Kathleen moves me out of the way and looks through the curtain. "Hmm. All ages. Who knew?" Then she looks toward me. "Does it feel dark in here to you?"

"The lights are supposed to be low until I take the stage."

She shudders. "I suppose you're right. Now, don't be nervous. Think about how you feel when you finish one of your happy movies—remember that high?"

I sigh. "I love escaping to movies."

"I know you do, and if you finish this speech this morning, you can watch all the movies you want. Your new publisher is friends with a producer who works on them for a certain channel you love. She's managed to gather a collection of new Valentine's Day movies for you. They're not even out yet, so you'll be one of the first to screen them."

"You're lying!"

"I'm not. As soon as this speech is over, you can go straight up to see Sam and get a preview."

"Sam?" My high is replaced by a dark low.

"He's got a theater room in his suite. Jules gave him the DVDs because she said you two got on so well last night."

"I wouldn't say we got on. I would say there was lots of ice cream involved."

"That's just as well, because I think Haley might have a crush on your publisher's brother. If you decide to go, you should definitely invite Haley. Wouldn't that be amazing if she met someone on this cruise?"

"Sad Sack?" I shake my head. "Haley definitely does not have a crush on Sad Sack. Have you seen our Haley?"

"Maggie! Maybe your contacts are fogging over, but Sam is hot."

"We're talking about the same guy, right? The hormone-deficient guy you made me apologize to last night?"

"You know exactly who I mean, and stop calling him that. Are you a medical doctor? The guy whose room you had dinner in last night, as if you were some kind of homeless person wandering around a cruise ship. Honestly, Maggie. It's like we don't even know who you are anymore."

"Last night I was going to be a dancer if you'd let me. I feel like you were the dad in *Dirty Dancing* and put Baby in a corner. Or in this case, a suite, making me apologize for something I wasn't even sorry for. Pathetic."

Kathleen hasn't left my side. She's clearly been given handler duties by Haley—as if I'm Lindsay Lohan about to fall off the wagon at any moment now.

"What is it with you and Sam? No one that tall and that buff is hormone deficient. And coming from me, that's a professional opinion." Kathleen places the back of her hand on my forehead. "Are you feeling all right?"

"I'm sorry. He just pushed my buttons, that's all. Haley doesn't need a guy who thinks women must be stupid to be happy. She's not stupid, not even close." I just don't want to watch Haley walk off with Sam. We shared a moment, and while it may have been mostly created in that romantic, dreamy side of my brain, he's one man Haley doesn't need to lay claim to. Though I'd never admit it out loud, I don't really want to see Sam with anyone. He can find love next week, and she can be as simpleminded as he pleases—once he's out of my view for good.

"He didn't say that. Plus Haley always did like her men brilliant, and Sam's sister was selling him pretty hard at dinner. You missed all that, but apparently, aside from being an excellent hero when the Heimlich is necessary, he's also very successful."

The universe is conspiring against me. It's that simple. Now, besides leaving my fantasy world of happily ever after, I'm supposed to play matchmaker for my one friend who has never wanted for male attention in all of her natural-born days.

"You do remember that my fiancé just ran off with an acrobat? I'm not really in matchmaking mode."

"You might fool Haley with the romantic notion of your terrible heartbreak, but I know you better than that. Some part of you wanted Jake gone for a long time before he left. The way you looked at me when you told me you were engaged?" Kathleen rolls her eyes. "You were resigned to it. I'll never believe for a minute you were in love. Addicted maybe, but certainly not in love."

This is one of those conversations that's best to avoid because I know she's right. Heartbreak wasn't the reason for my self-imposed sabbatical, but I'm not ready to admit to the truth that a very big part of me was relieved when the wedding got called off. The genuine reason was I didn't think I could do my job without Jake. If I had to marry for it, so be it. It wasn't like there were other suitors clamoring for my attention. For as much as I live in the fantasy world of romance, my own engagement was probably one of the most practical decisions I'd ever made.

"I'm sure Sam's very successful, Kathleen. I went to his amazing suite, remember? You don't get one of those working at the mart."

"Maggie—"

"I'm about to speak on the science of happiness and bouncing back from failure—which, I might add, I have yet to accomplish—so can we talk about Haley's love life afterward?"

"When is the last time you remember Haley being interested in anyone?"

"It's been a long time," I admit. "But you said yourself, in your prophetess voice, that Sam wasn't for her. Why the sudden surge of interest in making something happen now?"

"If Sam comes to the event, I want you to engage him. Maybe invite him to lunch with us."

"He's sitting at our table. Why would I invite him to sit somewhere he's already sitting? This is all very suspect."

"It wouldn't be if you hadn't spent the last two months isolated and watching romantic movies. Your Spidey sense is way off."

"Touché. But what makes you think he'd come on an invitation I gave him?"

"He's fascinated by you. Haven't you seen the way he looks at you? I think he's really interested in the results of your data, but too proud to give it much credence."

"Can I just ask you, when has Haley ever had trouble getting a man's attention?"

Something doesn't sit right with Kathleen's hasty interest in Haley getting her man. I stare at her intently, hoping to break her and discern her true motive, but she offers me nothing. Stoic as Lot's wife as a salt pillar.

"I just thought you could handle the connecting because, you know, it's awkward that his sister is one of Haley's biggest clients. She doesn't want to jeopardize that."

"Got it. Help Haley flirt with Sad Sack. Can I get back to my notes now?"

"Maggie, I just want you to care. I want you to fight for something. If you won't fight for your career, maybe you'll fight for your friend's love life."

In all seriousness? I'll fight for those new movies. What can I say? They're addictive and I need a fix. Neither of my friends seems to get that I want to care.

"If I could care, I would. I just don't. I need to increase my neuro-transmitters—build me up some serotonin—and uplifting movies are what I need right now. I could probably prove it scientifically."

"I'm sure you could. Are you ready?"

As soon as she asks, the lights cut off and everything goes black. Colored strobe lights start to crisscross the room, and the throbbing, exhilarating beat of AC/DC plays.

"Are they serious?" I shout to Kathleen. "If these people are expecting Britney Spears, they're going to be sorely disappointed. Who could follow this intro?"

A deep male voice booms out of the speakers. "She's a respected neuroscientist, trained at the best schools, and currently researches at UCLAAAAA! Let's give a warm *Empress of the Seas* welcome to Dr. Margaret Maguiiiiire."

Kathleen pushes me forward onto the stage, and the lights and music cut off instantly. I'm standing in the stark silence with all those expectant eyes staring me down. A single light goes on overhead. Seriously, if I could dance like Britney, I would totally start.

"Good morning!" I say too loudly into the mic I'm wearing. It squelches and makes an unholy noise. The audience grabs for their ears. Not a great start. "You've probably heard the old adage that money can't buy you happiness. Statistically, that's not true. The data I've studied actually reveals that money can buy you happiness." I pause for dramatic effect.

There are a few groans and a few cheers.

"But don't lose heart," I say, sticking my forefinger in the air. "Money makes you happier to a point. The good news is that *more* money doesn't necessarily make us happier. Once our needs are met, the data shows we may begin to spend it wrong." I clear my throat. "The good news is that, according to my research, you're spending it correctly. Money probably bought you this cruise, and we are happier when we spend money on life experiences versus stuff."

An eruption of clapping bursts forth, and I decide to tackle the hard stuff next—like how marriage makes you happier if it's a good one, but children don't. People hate hearing that message. I hate telling them that. It's like saying I don't like puppies, and I've learned that it's best to get it over with early on in the speech.

I get lost in my thoughts for a moment. I mean, as a single woman with enough money and no kids, I should be bursting at the seams with happiness—statistically speaking.

There's an older man in the front row. He looks like Santa Claus and seems just as delighted by life. I wonder what makes some people genetically predisposed to optimism and joy, and others human Eeyores. That's definitely a possible study. I make a mental note.

"We want to know what we're doing right! I'm here to tell you that, but I'm also here to tell you how you can improve your capacity for happiness based on the science!"

A scratching noise fills the room and my mic cuts out. A small puff of black smoke bursts forth from the large black speaker in front of me on stage, then a bigger explosion with sparks. There are screams from the crowd, but my eyes are glued to the smoking speaker. I grab the pitcher of water left on a stool for me and throw it on the smoke, but rather than burning itself out, the smoke begins to curl up toward the ceiling. It's followed by a small open flame that starts to rise. The flame gets bigger as I watch for far too long, until the ear-piercing wail of the fire alarm sounds and the audience scatters—no longer questioning if it's part of my act. No, there are no Britney pyrotechnics that accompany my science talk.

I watch as a spark takes hold of some kind of pyrotechnics device in front of the stage, and small bursts of what seem like fireworks pop and sizzle until a black, rubbery rug beneath the stage catches fire. The remaining optimists in the audience, hoping for those dance moves, scramble toward the exits while I stand mesmerized by the activity, studying the data rather than taking action. My throat starts to feel scratchy, and I cover my face with my sleeve. Then I remember Kathleen is backstage. That moves me into action and I dash behind the curtain.

"Kathleen!" I yell over the shouts of the escaping audience and panicked crew members.

She doesn't answer, and I hear another small explosion, followed by the door shutting, seemingly to contain the fire. Now I begin to panic and rush to the back edge of the stage, but my foot catches on something and I tumble forward for what feels like an eternity.

Visibility gets murkier, and I watch as the sprinkler system on the ceiling, the one with no water pouring from it, disappears from my view. My throat burns as I struggle and gasp to capture any remaining oxygen. I hold my breath and army-crawl toward a flashing exit light, but it also disappears in the thick haze before I can reach it. The smoke overtakes the room and I'm confused which way to go—everything feels surreal, as though I must be dreaming. My heart is pounding and I struggle for breath. There is no more air, only dark, stifling smoke.

I can hear my name being called over the shouts of panic. I'm lifted from the ground and carried through the dark, all-encompassing cloud until it miraculously clears and the cool ocean breeze stings my face. My throat is raw, and when I inhale the fresh air, it makes a crackling sound in my ears. I cough and sputter at the first touch of oxygen. The sunlight burns my eyes.

Sam's sturdy arms hold me above the deck, and his dark chocolate eyes are bearing down on me.

"Why didn't you move quicker? When the rug went up?"

I don't know. I stare at him silently.

"You stood there, then you bolted the wrong way and disappeared. I was trying to call to you, but the audience practically knocked me down trying to get out." He sets me down but keeps his arms firmly around me, bracing me as I get my bearings. His jaw is clenched and his tone is upset—as if he's angry and feels some sense of responsibility toward my stupidity.

"I didn't want to cause a panic. I thought of Kathleen and figured everything would be out before I returned with her. It all seemed so surreal. Shouldn't that rug be fireproof?" My voice is hoarse.

"Kathleen was in the back row beside me. Didn't you see her?"

I shook my head. "There were so many people there."

"Next time," he says coolly, "panic. It's okay to panic. What were you thinking?" His tone makes me feel shamed to my core. The question haunts me and hits me in a dark place. I was more upset about upsetting people than in fighting for my life. What if I hadn't thought Kathleen was behind me?

Possibilities emerge while I stand there grappling with my thoughts. I didn't think this through—because really, what possibilities are there if one succumbs to smoke inhalation? I can think of only two: casket or cremation.

That's not what I want.

"You need a vacation," Sam says as though he's read my mind. "A real one. You're burned out, and I'd recognize that look anywhere."

I stare at him, blinking wildly, and nod. "I am? No, I—" But my protests don't come. He seems to know my heart without me speaking a word. How can that be? Maybe Kathleen's prophetic gift rubbed off on him.

Sam keeps me braced steadily with one arm while his hand softly traces my cheek, and I stand entranced by his dark eyes. Chaos is swirling around us, people are in hysterics. There is screaming and the sound of glass breaking. The crew is shouting to each other in a foreign language, and smoke billows from the indoor hallways. But out under the breezy sky on deck, I feel safe. Perhaps safer than I've ever felt. Sam has this soothing way about him. He takes care of things that need to happen without asking, without direction. Somehow he anticipates and reacts before anyone recognizes there's a problem. Usually it's my responsibility to take care of crises. My life thus far has been one big checklist, and it's like Sam has come in and checked everything off.

I try to reason that this means nothing. I'm finding meaning where there is no data to support it. My emotions are just getting the best of me because it's been so long since anyone gave me any affection. Jake wouldn't even kiss me on the cheek until we were engaged. Then, once we were engaged, he told me that we should simply wait until we were married to make it official. How could I have been such an imbecile?

I stare into Sam's eyes earnestly, wondering how he instinctively understood something about me that I didn't have the insight to see. I am burned out. I've been going full speed ahead for my entire life. My self-induced binge-watching coma allowed me to *be still*.

He's so near, and I close my eyes and wait for his lips to press against mine. His breath is soft against my cheek. I feel his lips on mine, and it feels so natural . . . then the slightest butterfly touch on my top lip before he abruptly tears himself away. I shiver and step toward him again, willing him to finish what he's started, but his eyes motion to his left as he moves back. The spell has abruptly broken.

Haley, her emerald eyes wide with shock, is gaping at us. She's nearly standing between us, looking at Sam and back at me, and considering our proximity, this is not easy to do. Her mouth is a long oval. Her perfectly formed, delicate jaw dangles as though she cannot believe what she's witnessing. The slight color she possesses in her porcelain skin has drained from her face, and she mutters a tiny sound, almost like a baby's whimper.

Kathleen stands behind her, arms crossed. Shame heats my body. *This is what happens whenever I follow my feelings. Feelings are for the weak.* As if Sam senses the change in me, he wraps his arm around me again, perhaps to defend me from Kathleen and Haley.

I wrestle myself free of his embrace, but the action goes against every impulse I possess. I want to snuggle into the crook of his neck and for once do exactly what I want, rather than what's right.

That's why I went into science to begin with, to please my parents. As I stand away from Sam and apart from my friends, once again I'm that small child, studying as diligently as I can to please my parents. I'm looking up at them with my report card, begging for their approval.

We're soon joined by Jules, who audibly gasps as her hand flies over her mouth. "Sam?"

Now is probably not the time to mention that my computer was left in the flames.

I know the right thing to do—the "girl code" thing to do—but my heart isn't in it. Sam understands, and he knows how weary I am. I don't know how he could, but he pegged me. This job, the constant treadmill of life. It's killing me day by day, a little at a time. I realize that Jake had taken the pressure off me—he was my life preserver who made life bearable and not, in fact, the love of my life. The love of my life would never purposely try to hurt me and gloat about it.

Sam Wellington, with his dark, brooding eyes and collared shirt, makes me feel like the stupidest girl on the planet, and for once in my life, it's perfectly fine by me.

12

Pessimism is associated with a shortened life span, so it
benefits your lifestyle and life span to seek out joy. Gratitude is just one way to increase your happiness quotient.

The Science of Bliss by Dr. Margaret K. Maguire

IT'S NOT ENOUGH THAT MY SPEECH practically blew up the
ship. I'm now the most hated woman on this barge. Let me add
that a singles' cruise after a bad breakup is not the place to muster
abhorrence in others. Desire and passion, definitely, but not silent
hostility with a side of loathing. Apparently there are three former
Rockettes on board to speak about their life experiences at the Radio
City Music Hall. These women have a larger fan base than one might
think. Since their speaking stage is now a burned-out shell, their
discussion panel has been tabled, and just like in junior high school,
it's the nerdy girl's fault. It shouldn't be. How hard is it to move a set
of dancers to a different venue? Aren't they bendable?

The bigger question in this floating universe is why they chose to
plaster *my* picture all over the ship, rather than that of three women
who were once paid to look enticing. I have to give her credit, Haley
obviously is a better publicist than whomever the ex-Rockettes hired.

126

My speech—or, rather, the few sentences I managed to blurt out before the explosion—is now the scandal of the "New Year, New You" cruise, which might be better than the old scandal of the choking woman in the middle of the elegant dining room. Judging by the looks I've been getting, it's like I'd been found on the lower level of the *Titanic* with a boy from third class. Why did I ever get off my sofa?

As I crash on the couch in our stateroom, I try to avoid the obvious tension after my friends happened upon my supposed heartbroken self kissing Sam Wellington—the guy Haley happened to be interested in for five minutes.

"Why didn't that happen during the Rockettes' talk? And why is my poster all over this ship instead of theirs? Who thought that was a good idea?"

"As your publicist, I did, and I worked very hard for that product placement. The least you could do is appreciate it." Haley frowns. Kathleen stands behind her, like my father always did to back up my mom for a shaming session.

I backpedal. "Right. And you're so good at what you do."

It's no use. I am a disaster. A disaster who belongs in sweatpants with a tub of ice cream on my stomach.

"You were kissing Sam. You're not going to explain that?" Kathleen's brow furrows. That's never a good sign. "You haven't even called your parents yet to tell them there's no wedding to Jake, and you're kissing some random guy on a cruise ship!"

"He's not random," Haley adds. "If only he were random. He's actually her new boss's brother. Way to make an impression, Maggie. Jules rushes to see if you're all right after the fire and finds you desperately in her brother's clutches. What on earth were you thinking?"

One could argue I wasn't thinking, but why should I have to defend myself?

"Listen, Haley, I was happily shoveling ice cream into my mouth and living in a fantasy world through my television set, where everyone is sweet and kind. You bear some responsibility in this fiasco for taking me out in public before I was ready. On a singles' cruise, no less!"

"Quit changing the subject," Kathleen says. "You were kissing Sam on deck. After I told you about Haley. Forget the bad decision making on the part of your career. What about girl code?"

"I was kissing Sam." For a brief moment, I go right back into my television romance world, only this was real. No one in my movies kissed with quite as much passion as I felt with Sam Wellington. I suppose now is not the time to reiterate what a fantastic and amazing kisser he is. Not that I have a lot of experience, but that guy can generate some heat. Imagine if we hadn't been interrupted. I never saw it coming. He looks so innocuous. "Life can really surprise you. Definitely not innocuous."

"What did you say?" Kathleen asks.

"Innocuous. You know, bland . . . innocent."

"I know what it means. What are you talking about?" Kathleen taps her toe, and it feels as if I don't have a friend in the world, probably deservedly so. "There's been nothing bland or innocent about you since you stepped on this ship. You've gone off the rails! Maggie, we're trying to salvage your career, and you don't even seem concerned that your talk got canceled."

Something about the way she says this triggers me. "Because I could have died!" I shout. "Excuse me for not being upset that I didn't make a stupid speech about happiness to people who are happily on a cruise. It was bad enough I had to go to the sick bay. But then afterward I had to run away from an angry old man who wanted to see the Rockettes. He was convinced one of them was his future bride. I can't imagine why that old goat is single."

"You're single too, Maggie. We're all single. There's no shame in that. Is being single the reason you're kissing some dude, because he's the first person to try something on board?" Haley is practically foaming at the mouth. "I thought you were chasing after the bartender. Now you find that your publisher's brother is on board and that seems more inappropriate to you, so why not? Here's a better way to sabotage my future. I can take out my job and my best friend in one small kiss of death. Kiss my single status goodbye, switch out Jake, and no one is the wiser."

For once I'm speechless. I walk around the coffee table until I am calm enough to respond. When my head finally stops pounding, I stand over Haley and Kathleen, who have both sat down on the sofa.

"You think that's why I kissed Sam? That I'm afraid to be single? Haley, I know you've put up with a lot from me in the last couple months, but I would never say something like that to you."

"You were calling him names last night, Maggie! Now you're having a public tryst on deck?"

"Public tryst? Haley, you're jealous!"

"I'm not." She stamps a foot on the carpet.

"One guy doesn't fall under your spell, so immediately you call dibs on him. He asked me to coffee yesterday, Haley. I'm not going to fight with you over a man. Any man. You want him, you're welcome to him." Even as I say this, the pit of my stomach aches. "But don't accuse me of being some kind of floozy."

"Floozy? Is it 1920?" Haley scoffs.

"What's this really about, Haley? I kissed someone briefly. So very briefly." I get lost for a second. "It's not a crime. You make it sound as if it's something I make a habit of."

"Two months ago you were marrying Jake. Now you're kissing some guy you only just met yesterday! What are we supposed to think? Did you forget how we found you a mere two days ago? It sounds like more avoiding of your problems to me. Unfortunately, you're just creating new ones!"

"Maybe I am," I agree.

"What happened to the workaholic we knew who could never leave the lab to so much as grab a coffee? The woman who told us that Jake was perfect for her because he supported her hours? Tell us, Maggie! What's changed?"

I shrug. "I don't really know. At first I couldn't bring myself to go into the lab for fear I'd run into Jake and have to explain to my co-workers that we weren't together. Then one day turned into the next, and that turned into two months. I realize I seem off my rocker, but my body shut down. I guess I really needed the break."

"What does that have to do with Sam?"

I pause as I contemplate Kathleen's question, then draw in a deep breath. "Somehow he made me feel like I didn't have to answer to everyone else any longer. That it was okay to do something simply because I wanted to do it."

"We may be slightly concerned for your mental well-being," Haley says. "We used to hear constant chatter about the prestigious NYU and Dr. Hamilton like he was some kind of god. Now . . . nothing. I haven't heard you speak about your job or forward direction in months. When you do return a phone call, it's to tell us one of the plots of a utopian movie. One of the biggest signs of depression is a lack of interest in your normal activities. Maybe you should talk to someone."

"I'm not depressed. I know it looks that way—escaping to my little apartment and watching endless romantic tales that have probably never happened in this lifetime—but I needed a break. I needed to empty my mind of the endless chatter and start fresh before I could figure out what I really wanted and not what everyone else wanted for me." I mutter a short prayer under my breath. "I love you girls, and I get that I must look completely insane to you, but I've never felt more clearheaded in my life. Haley, I didn't know you were interested in Sam until right before this happened, but I swear, I didn't even have time to think about it, it just happened."

Kathleen and Haley exchange a critical look. They obviously don't understand that I nearly kissed Sam last night over ice cream.

"After hearing the chilling sounds of those explosions and watching the fire grow," I explain. "And there was that adrenaline rush of surviving smoke inhalation that made my lungs crackle, plus the fresh breeze of the ocean air on my skin." They both look unconvinced, so

I continue. "Kissing Sam was the most natural thing I've ever done. For once I didn't overthink something. I didn't analyze it within an inch of my life—I just kissed an incredibly gorgeous man. Because I wanted to kiss him. That's all there is to it."

Haley and Kathleen exchange another inside look. They stand up and surround me. "That's not you," Haley says. "You're our Pollyanna who binges on fairy tales. You don't kiss men you've just met."

"'Just met' may be overstating our situation. We shared a moment last night over ice cream, over the selfie of us that he sent Jake—"

"Wait, what?" Kathleen is triggered once again by the sound of my ex's name.

"That's our Maggie," Haley says. "She's lost in the romance again. She thinks she's Sleeping Beauty and the handsome prince has kissed her awake. It's straight out of a Disney princess movie." She stares at me. "As long as you know this is not a movie."

"The kiss meant nothing." I lie so easily that it scares me. "It was the heat of the moment, like that sailor kissing the nurse after the end of World War II. It was all emotion and adrenaline. Ask Sam, I'm sure he'd say the same thing. We were victims of circumstances."

"It looked more passionate than that to me."

"Really?" I ask with far too much interest.

Haley rolls her eyes and exhales deeply as if to make her point. "Five minutes ago you were obsessed with Jake."

"No she wasn't," Kathleen says in her haunting voice. "She never loved Jake. He was just the next goal to climb over, and he was convenient to her career goals since he had none of his own."

"Kathleen!" Haley exclaims.

"Ask her," Kathleen says.

"I thought I loved him," I say. But now, after kissing Sam and spending time with him, I have to wonder if I ever had. I felt on edge with Jake, as though I was never good enough for him and he was lowering himself to be with me. It was a scenario that felt natural to me. But it was also naturally bad.

"Maggie saw a way to keep moving forward and jump the next hurdle: marriage and family. Her first thought when Jake left was how she'd explain it to her parents." Kathleen lifts her hair off her back and shakes it out. "I'd bet my firstborn on it."

"You don't have a firstborn," Haley says.

"It's a figure of speech, Haley."

"For people who have a firstborn!"

"Stop fighting. You sound like a pair of those *Real Housewives* who don't actually know what it means to be a housewife. I don't know what I want, all right, Haley? But I'm so much closer to it than I was two months ago. I understand that I look crazy to both of you, but I don't know what I want because I've never been allowed to figure it out for myself." I start to pace the length of the suite and shimmy out of my blazer as I walk. "I wanted to kiss Sam Wellington after I emerged from the fire like Shadrach, Meshach, and that third one."

"Sam's a widower," Haley says. Shockingly, I'm instantly jealous that she knows something so personal about him that he never mentioned to me. "You should be careful about treating him casually."

"When have I ever treated anyone casually?"

"I'm only saying don't be cruel." Haley's eyes flash. "Just because he said something similar to Jake doesn't mean he's like him. In fact, I don't think he's anything like him. This trip might be a reset button for you, but a lot of people are here because they're lonely and want to find true love. Don't mock that."

As I lower myself slowly into an armchair, her words hit me like a wayward tugboat. "I'd never mock true love. Romance—or the idea of it, anyway—saved me at a time when I lost the point. I wasn't just escaping in those fairy tales, I was restoring my faith in humanity."

"We're here for you, Maggie. You just have to know that it's okay to reach out and ask for help once in a while." Kathleen's voice is soft. "Even the biggest bodybuilders in my gym, the guys who do the power lifting for Olympic training—they need a spotter. That's why we're here."

The fight within me slithers away, and I feel my body relax as though I've finished a new happily ever after. "I appreciate you and Haley and all you've done to try to help me. I know getting this time off wasn't easy, Kathleen." I turn toward Haley. "And Haley, I'm thankful that you've morphed from the meek little publicist I once knew into this powerhouse who could handle the toughest of clients." I sigh. "I know I seem irrational, the kind of person who could be dismissive of a handsome newcomer's feelings, but that's not me. I'm just a person who has never been allowed to figure out what I wanted. My parents told me to keep dancing, to keep striving, to keep studying. Be an A student, be a doctor, get tenure, be an author, be a speaker. Well, I did all that, but now that Jake's gone and I had a career hiccup, I don't know what's next. I'm lost." I lift my arms up. "I'm lost at sea. Literally."

"Why mess with success? Do you know how many authors would kill to be where you are? With a *New York Times* bestselling science book?" Kathleen asks. "There's no reason you have to stop dreaming about being on Dr. Hamilton's team."

"His field is called *moral psychology*. I hardly qualify at this point to even apply."

"Everyone's entitled to a second chance, Maggie. How can you not appreciate how far you've come in your field? You're so fortunate."

I take in a deep, cleansing breath and ponder her question sincerely. "Yes, I do know. How could I not know, with everyone reminding me every five seconds how fortunate I am? But now that I've been allowed to stop and think, I have to wonder, if it was all so fabulous, why was it so easy to give up? Why didn't I miss the work or the striving?"

"May I suggest that you were too busy obsessing over Jake?" Kathleen shrugs. "That's my take. You do have an obsessive personality, Maggie."

"Maybe." I look down at my feet and drum up the courage to meet their eyes. "I have achieved everything I set out to do, other than get married to Jake. Why does life feel so empty? From my own research, I understand that when a person is living well but without purpose, they're still unfulfilled."

"So what's your dream? Your purpose? To sit in sweatpants and watch syrupy movies forever?" Haley crosses her spindly arms. "Give up all your work for a fantasy?"

It dawns on me now how jealous Haley actually is. I thought that Kathleen was messing with me about Haley having a crush on Sam, but I can see the green-eyed monster in her eye aimed at me. She has nothing to worry about. Sam is only interested in me to prove his theory—that women with half a brain are incapable of happiness. I suppose that makes his single status someone else's fault, and while I'm genuinely sad his wife passed away, he can't continue to make other women pay.

"No, Haley. I'd give it all up for the chance to sit still and *be*. To be still and know that he is God, like the Bible says. To figure out what does make me happy, what my dream is. What does God want from me next?"

"God doesn't want you casually kissing men on board a ship, I know that much." Haley's interest in Sam is even more obvious by her rage. "He seems to frown on temporary relationships."

"I'm sorry it was Sam, Haley. I am."

A tear sparkles in the corner of her eye, and it's a stark reminder that every time I do something for myself, there is an equal and opposite consequence for someone else. *They're right. I need to get back to work.*

"We worry you're not being practical," Kathleen says. "You have to make a living."

Her accusation forces me to laugh, even if it's true. "I've been practical my entire life. I've never done anything but follow the rules to avoid failure. Today I was enveloped by smoke and I kissed someone I've only just met. It seems a tame reaction, comparatively speaking." I slide my blue sweater on, though I should probably change out of my smoke-infested clothing so I don't smell like a campfire.

I stare back at my friends. I want to regret kissing Sam. I mean, it's absolutely out of character when you consider that I never made out with my supposed fiancé, but it simply happened. For anything to happen in my life without a month of planning is nothing short of a miracle. I should feel as if I've broken the girl code, but Haley said she called dibs if I wasn't interested, right? So I guess I was interested. I don't want to be the wanton woman who just dropped one man and fell into the arms of another, but try as I might, I can't muster the false guilt. I can't help but think Haley was only interested in Sam for the sheer reason that he wasn't interested in her. Maybe that's a sign of how pessimistic I've really become. One thing is certain, it's time for the truth. No matter what it costs me.

"I don't regret kissing Sam. That kiss just sort of happened. I didn't mean for it to happen, but quite honestly, it's the only thing I've done that I really wanted to do in a very long time. Other than maybe write my own love story."

"Wait, what?" Haley asks.

"I wanted to kiss Sam Wellington, and if I apologize for it now, it will just be one more people-pleasing lie. For once I followed my heart and not the path laid out for me. I won't do it again, Haley. Does that make you happy?"

"No, the last part. You wrote what? Your own love story?"

I flush. "I wasn't simply watching sweet screenplays on film. I started writing one."

"Maybe you want to be a professional figure skater too?"

"Maybe I do. The point is, I wanted to write an ending that made me happy. No one is coming into my lab to sweep me off my feet, so why not write my own ending? Jane Austen did it."

"Shouldn't you be telling us about what Dr. Hamilton wrote and published? Jane Austen . . . really? Your stupor may have been worse than we imagined."

"Or Elizabeth Gaskell. Or Charlotte Brontë. All women who wrote their happy endings because perhaps life's romance was disappointing for them."

My friends look horrified.

"Don't worry. It's just a hobby. I have no plans to quit science and become the next great Nora Roberts."

They both heave a sigh of relief.

"It's a hobby that makes me happy. Being kissed on deck was great research."

Kathleen and Haley are still on the sofa, their feet stretched out on the coffee table before them and their arms crossed over their chests. Their disappointment in me is like an anchor bound to my ankle, but I cannot stop myself. I must break free of their judgment.

I rush to the door and get into the hallway as if it's my first breath of fresh air after the fire. Apparently it's not enough that I've thrown my career overboard. I need to toss my friends too.

13

I often prescribe a steady dose of play to increase an
adult's happiness quotient.

The Science of Bliss by Dr. Margaret K. Maguire

As I walk toward the elevators, I'm dizzy from the
ship swaying to and fro. Or maybe I'm just overwhelmed at
what kind of terrible, selfish person I've become. Telling Haley and
Kathleen why I kissed Sam felt so freeing and expansive in the moment, but as I walk away I realize I may have acted too much like
Jake and not been concerned about their feelings. I slink down on
the wildly decorated carpet. As I do, I think perhaps that design is
to hide vomit, and I slink back up the wall.

My head is stopped by something solid and I tumble back down.
Again, the hot bartender is standing over me.

"You spend a lot of time on the floor," Brent growls. "You might
want to try shuffleboard. Or maybe the spa on deck." He reaches
out a burly arm, and I grab it to lift myself up. "What's up with you?
How'd your talk go?"

"I set the room on fire. Literally." I brush myself off.

"You're the one! Oh, those Rockettes fans are out for blood, girl.

You better keep a low profile. They were discussing it at my bar, and let me say, I wouldn't want to meet one of them in a dark alley."

"Thanks for the warning. How'd your class go?"

"Great. People left happy and drunk. My work is done here."

I smile halfheartedly. "Everyone needs a purpose—looks like you've found yours."

"Come with me. You need to let go and chill out. You're wound tighter than a drum and you're supposed to be on vacation. There's zip-lining up on the top deck and you'll love it. Get a little adrenaline in that system of yours and the world will look brighter, I promise."

"I actually haven't spent the morning drinking, so your idea of fun may be more adrenaline than I can handle. I think I've had enough. I just survived a fire, so hanging from a piece of string in the air—" I cut myself off. Dangling from a piece of string is exactly what charmed Jake away from me. Maybe this is the answer I've been looking for. "You know, I think that sounds amazing. Why not?"

Maybe because anytime that question comes up—*why not?*—it's a very bad idea indeed. Some people were meant to scale mountains and have grand adventures. Others, myself included, were meant to shake things up by changing the channel.

He shoves the ever-present sunglasses back over his eyes—even though we're still in the hallway—and it gives him a very Channing Tatum appearance. The glasses must be some kind of battle cry for him. "First, though, we need to take care of your clothes. You're not dressed for adrenaline."

"Are you sure I'm not already soaked in it?"

He grabs my hand. "I've got an idea."

"Famous last words. Next only to, 'Here, hold my drink.'"

"Who are you going to listen to about fun? The happiness expert who studies all day? Or the guy who knows how to put a smile on people's faces? While you were in the library in high school, I was planning drag car races on the strip by the quarry and how to outsmart

Peter Schmidt's sheriff father. You may have a doctorate in whatever it is you have a doctorate in, but I have one in fun."

He's got a point.

Brent grins. "I need to get you out of that comfort zone. Shake it up a bit." He rakes his fingers through my hair and tosses it playfully. "You're not ready yet. You're still dressed like you're going to a board meeting, and you smell like barbecue. And not the good kind of barbecue we've got in Texas."

"It's my hair." I shake it loose. "I couldn't totally get the smell out of it."

"You wear seriousness like those grandma sweaters of yours. I've known you two days and I've counted three cardigans. No one your age should have that many cardigans."

"I like cardigans." I fiddle with my sweater.

"You need to loosen up." Brent leads me into the elevator and drops my hand to press the button. "Going up!"

"You pressed the down button."

"I told you, you're not going dressed like my second-grade teacher with eau de grill."

Normally this is where I'd make my exit, but going back to my friends or tempting myself with my publisher's brother is a scarier option. Who needs that kind of temptation?

We take the elevator down to the old-town shopping "street" that my suite looks over. We pass all the interesting stores, like the bookstore, the electronics store, even the perfumery (where I could spritz my burning scent away), but Brent leads me to a child's store. It's brightly colored as if a rainbow has vomited in it. Sparkles on the floor lead to a room filled with costumes.

"Here," he says.

"What are we doing here?" I look at the sign. "This is a costume shop. I have no need of a costume. Why is there a costume shop on board a ship? Let's go get some of those cute shorts with the ship's name emblazoned across them."

"You do have need of a costume. The ball at the end of the cruise."

I laugh. "I'm not going to that."

"Why not? Are you above having a little fun and dressing up?"

"I would have brought a costume had I known." I pause. "I'm always the bride of Frankenstein."

"Of course you are."

"What does that mean? What would you expect me to be, a sexy cat? That's the typical barfly costume, right? A chance to wear your underwear out for an evening and call it a costume?"

"Aren't you the judgmental one."

"So, you had no sexy kittens in your bar this year?"

"No comment."

"Yeah. But I'm the one who's judgmental."

"Just because it's true doesn't make you less judgmental."

"It kinda does. What's wrong with the bride of Frankenstein? It's a cool costume, and I get my hair plastered with hair spray so it goes straight up. I've got that skunk stripe down after all these years."

"The point of dressing up is to get outside the norm. How do you do that if you wear the same costume every year?"

"Now who's judgmental? First it was my cardigans, now it's my costume."

"This is an elegant ball. You need to be thinking more *Phantom of the Opera* and less the sad psych department at your school."

"We're not sad. We study happiness," I tell him.

He grins and the muscle in his cheek flexes, revealing his deep, one-sided dimple. He really is a magnificent-looking man, and he could easily render a simpler woman unconscious to her own thoughts. "The zip line will be closed by then. They have to get ready for the Water Lilies show."

The Water Lilies show is where women like Jake's new wife hang from the rafters by scarves and dive into the pool. Esther Williams meets Cirque du Soleil. Not surprisingly, it's not on my list of things to do.

"You may as well get one of the good costumes early," Brent says.

"Is this a joke? No one said anything about a costume ball."

"It was in your pamphlet. It's most likely in your contract as well. They usually require the entertainment to show up."

"I didn't get a pamphlet. I didn't get a contract. I got dragged, remember?"

He looks me up and down. "Did you even dress up for spirit day when you were a kid?"

I shake my head, wondering how it's so obvious to him that I didn't have a normal upbringing where I got to wear costumes. Do I have some sort of sign on my back? "Freak of nature?"

"What about Halloween?" he asks.

"My parents didn't allow it. They said to put childish things away if I wanted to be a doctor. While the other kids were out trick-or-treating, my mother said I was gaining brain cells and one day I'd see the benefits." I'm still waiting.

"All right, then. You realize that's the saddest thing I've ever heard—it's like homeless-dog sad. No church festival or anything?"

"My parents weren't churchgoing people. They worship at the throne of intellectualism."

"Intell—what? Never mind."

We enter the costume boutique that seems strangely out of place alongside the electronic shops and duty-free jewelry stores. I'm met by a wearable coat of arms and a posh burgundy Victorian dress with an intricate cinched bodice and lace bell sleeves. I pick up the price tag—$1,260. I quickly drop the tag as if it's on fire.

We're met by a tiny woman with dark hair and oversized, doll-like eyes. "May I help you?"

I'm still recovering from the price tag and wondering who on earth has that kind of money to spend on a costume.

"Yes, I'm looking for a princess gown," Brent says.

"A princess—no." I press Brent's animated hands to his sides. "No, we don't want anything. Thank you."

"We do," he says over me. "Who is your favorite princess? Don't give me any sob story about how you never saw any princess movies."

"Duh. Belle. She's the smart one who the entire village thinks is odd."

"Hmm." He nods. "Nicely played."

To my horror, the salesgirl quickly produces a Belle costume, complete with a hoop skirt.

"Oh, she doesn't need the hoop. She needs to be active in it."

"I do?"

"Can we get her size? She'll take a tiara too. Put it on my tab." He hands her his ship card.

"Wait, no. Brent, I can get anything—"

But he won't take no for an answer. He's like Kathleen, only with bigger biceps.

The salesgirl takes me into the dressing room. I want to escape, but I've run enough.

"This costume is lovely. You'll be the Belle of the ball," she says with a smile. As if she hasn't told every other woman and child the exact same thing.

"It's beautiful, but it's too much."

"Your man friend will pay."

My man friend?

"No, no. I'll pay. But I don't think all this is necessary. It's very elaborate."

She ignores me and zips me up. "Beautiful dress. Satin, silk, and crinoline. Very well made. Good quality."

"It's $595!" I exclaim at the sight of the price tag.

"It comes with slippers to match. Beautiful."

"Yes, but—"

"Your man friend will pay. Look, handmade taffeta roses."

How on earth do I get myself into these situations?

"Oh, she's going to be wearing it out," Brent shouts into the dressing room. "Just put her things in a bag. She needs to have them cleaned."

"Yes, you do," she whispers. "I didn't want to say anything. You a smoker?"

"No, I'm not a smoker." I raise my voice. "Brent? This dress is very expensive, and I really have no use for it after this costume party. I think—"

"You think constantly! Yes, I know. Just be quiet and let me see the gown."

"I look ludicrous."

"Don't forget she needs a tiara!" he says.

"Belle doesn't wear a tiara. It's part of the reason I like her. She dresses up to go to the library."

"She needs a tiara," he repeats. "Every princess needs a tiara."

The salesgirl, Madge is her name, opens the door, and there's a pedestal with a three-way mirror in front of it. "Wait here. I need to get you some slippers. Size seven?"

I nod, too weary to battle a cruise-ship sales associate.

Brent gasps. "You look amazing. Absolutely stunning."

"I think the word you're looking for is *ridiculous*."

"It was made for you. You have to have it."

"The gown has pantaloons underneath it, and I feel as if I'm wearing a diaper." By his expression, I know that not everything needs to be said out loud.

I step out of the dressing room in the off-the-shoulder yellow gown as if I'm going to a Civil War ball. Brent places the sparkling tiara on top of my head. "Why am I playing dress-up again?" I ask.

"Because you, Dr. Maguire, need to loosen up."

"Can't I loosen up without looking like I work in a theme park?"

"You do look like that. Isn't it awesome? When we go out on deck, every eye will turn to you. I want you to know what that feels like, because you've been hiding behind that librarian exterior for far too long."

My clothes are already in a bundle at the front desk. "Put these in a bag and save them for her," he says to Madge. He grabs my silver ballet flats and hands them to me. "Let's go. You might want these instead of those canary shoes."

"Wait a minute. You're not going to dress up like the Beast?"

He pounds his chest like a gorilla and grunts, "I am the Beast!"

"We have to pay. The last thing I need is to be thrown into the ship's brig after the day I've had."

He grabs my hand. "We're all good. It's paid. Let's go."

I look back at the counter. "No, I can't let you—"

But he drags me on before Madge can sell us yet another accessory.

We take the elevator to the top deck of the ship. It's open and breezy and sounds like a carnival. We find the snaking line to get secured in—it's like we'll be a sliding, shooting Christmas ornament across the ship's open core.

Little girls are gathering around me like pigs at mealtime and clutching at my legs. "Are you the real Belle?" one little redhead asks.

The children seem to be part of a single parents' group on the ship. They've been segregated, as if they're not real singles but a special sort of single not good enough for the general population. That scenario seems utterly outdated, but I suppose if I had children, I'm not sure I'd want them around the speed dating or bikini contests either.

I'm not sure what to say to the redheaded girl so that I don't break her princess heart. My mother would have staunchly told her there was no such thing as a real Belle. It takes me some time to summon up a proper response so the girl doesn't go crying to her mother and ask if there's really a Santa Claus, or has her entire childhood been a lie?

"No, I'm just dressed like Belle. She's the smart princess." I refrain from telling the girl she too can get her PhD. It seems inappropriate for the moment and frighteningly like something my mother would say.

"You're so pretty! Can I take my picture with you?" Her father is right beside her with a camera ready, so I grin while taking her hand.

"Belle, Belle!" More young'uns start to squeal and attach themselves to me. I'm glad for the distraction and bend down to greet each one and take a picture for their parents.

"You missed your calling. You should have worked at Disneyland," Brent quips. Then he turns his wiles on the little girls. "You will grow up beautiful just like Belle, but we have to let her get on the zip line now. She has to practice her skills for when she gets home to the Beast."

"Her skills?" I arch a brow.

"Listen, do you want to be a Disney princess and pose all night or ride this thing?"

"Is that a trick question? Because I'd rather be a princess."

"You said you wanted to have fun. You're not going to do that being fearful. Let's go." He pushes me forward to the line at the top of the ship. If I felt dizzier early, I'm downright discombobulated now.

We move behind the guarded rails, safely away from my "fans," and it's now patently obvious how far up we are. I start to shake like a leaf, and soon I feel my teeth chattering. The line of people soars above the rest of the ship, and the zip line climbs even higher.

The make-believe downtown feels miles beneath us, and the idea of going splat in front of a faux Banana Republic is not the way I pictured myself going out.

"Wait a minute." I grab the rails on each side of me and anchor myself so that no one can go around me. "This isn't going to work." I turn to Brent, but he's stretched across the rails as well, so I can't escape around him. "I'm wearing a dress. They can't strap me into that contraption in this gown. We should come back tomorrow."

"You'll be fine."

"Maybe they have a clown costume at the shop." Honestly, if a clown costume cost me thousands and I could get out of this harebrained stunt, I'd spend the money twofold. There is nothing like discovering that I don't have an ounce of adventure in me while perched atop a giant cruise ship like a wayward seagull. It's not an accident that I've spent my career cooped up in a lab, studying other people's adventures.

Brent appears fresh out of patience. "Your dress is complete with pantaloons. You couldn't even give a Victorian gent a flash of shin in that getup. Think of the little girls down there waiting to see their heroine fly across the friendly sky. You have minions rooting for you."

"That's what the Water Lilies are for. To dance across the sky and look pretty for their little fans."

Brent hasn't seemed to notice the height. He's too busy shooting the breeze with everyone in line as if they've known each other their whole lives. Brent has the same easy way with people that Jake had, and I do admire that. Covet it. Being left an only child who spent most of her formative years in the library, I'm missing that life skill.

As Brent mingles among the crowd, it reminds me how ill suited I am for a man like Sam Wellington. Why this makes me think of him, I have no idea. But Sam probably expects his wife to host state dinners or the like. It could be easily argued that I'm ill suited for any man at this point, but maybe that's why Sam's kiss felt so magical. He was the forbidden fruit, and so naturally I was tempted.

However, Brent is easy. Brent is fun. Brent will bring out the breezy Maggie, if there is such a person hiding underneath the cardigans. He is exactly what I need before I hit the ground running and try to get my life back. Fear rules me. It's time to have a little faith.

Brent is exchanging Snapchat codes with the guy behind us in line and takes a selfie with the guy's date as if he's some kind of rock star. I'm fixated on his idle chatter when suddenly we're at the front of the line and perched on top of the ship.

Some poor young grunt is trying to wrestle with my gown, and trust me, he doesn't get paid enough for this. He stops and stares at me like, *Does the sanitarium know you've been let out?*

"You go, Brent."

"No, no. Ladies first," Brent says.

My heart is pounding out of my chest. The warning sign says that the attraction is not for all guests. *If you fear heights* . . . I totally fear heights. *If you fear a falling sensation* . . . Who doesn't? *If you fear high speeds* . . . Yeah, not a fan. *If you have claustrophobia, do not participate.* It also says if you have any physical or mental conditions that could be affected by this attraction, *do not participate.* I mean, where do I start?

"I can't do it." I turn around, but the wall of people blocks my exit.

"That five-year-old in front of you did just fine. Risk something for once in your life!" Brent is starting to sound like Kathleen. But he's so right. Every time I'm given a chance to fly, I fold up my wings and hide away.

The small Hispanic man messing with my dress looks confused, and I'm sidetracked by this poor guy and my yards of satin. I'm sure he's wondering why I'm not in yoga shorts like everyone else on this infernal ride. To avoid getting a TSA-type pat down, I fold my dress into a diaper shape and tuck the skirt into the sash so it's sticking out like a pool noodle—a natural barrier of crazy to keep most anyone away.

The guy straps me in while another man in sailor gear gives me convoluted directions. My Belle dress is now a big yellow diaper. The sailor removes my tiara and slides a helmet on me. If I want to blend in, flying across the ship in a canary-yellow princess costume is questionable.

I turn to see Brent with his phone aimed. "Take my picture at your peril!" The last thing I need is a YouTube video further shredding any credibility I have left.

He puts the phone into the safety bin with his wallet. I'm now perched on a platform above the giant canyon of the ship and strapped onto the thin metal rope that is supposed to transport me to safety on the other side of the ship. The obvious question is, Why can't I just walk there? I hang on to the handlebars above me, though I know they're only there for moral support, and then jump before I have a chance to obsess about my own stupidity.

I slide off the perch and a whirlwind of colors passes by. There are shouts of encouragement from less adventurous cruisers, who see me strapped in like a baby in a car seat and hoisted across the open-air cavern of the ship. I squeal like a baby pig as my legs dangle hundreds of feet in the air. And then I'm bouncing around on the other side of the ship like a tetherball. Another poor sailor is charged with unleashing me as I bob up and down.

"Was I supposed to see the ocean?" I ask the female crew member. "I didn't see the ocean." I'm so animated and excited. "I did it. Did you see that?"

"I did," she says, as if she hasn't just unleashed the five-year-old in front of me. She unclasps me and takes a long, judgmental gander at my Belle costume, finished with a side-eye look. "Sorry, Princess. No ocean view."

I don't think she's really sorry.

There's a frenzy of applause from people standing by, and the woman says, "They think you're part of the aqua theater." She turns to the small crowd on the rails. "She's not part of the show, folks. Next show is this evening!" She turns back to me and hoists the safety harness back to its starting point. "The swimmers drop with great big scarves. They think you're part of the show," she says again. I don't bother to correct her.

It is questionable that I'd never heard of anyone hanging from a scarf as a profession, and now I'm being bombarded by the concept. I hope that's not a sign it's my next career.

As I get off the platform and puff out my gown, there are a bevy of little girls waiting for me. They've just watched the princess defeat the ugly dragon of the zip line. It's then that I see Sam standing behind all my fans. I smooth the plantation-style skirt and try to maintain some semblance of dignity, but that ship has sailed. My stomach betrays me and flutters with excitement at the sight of him.

Remember, the kiss simply happened. It meant nothing. Don't analyze it. Remember your promise to Haley.

"Did you kiss a frog and turn into a princess?" he says over my six-year-old fan base.

I kissed a handsome prince, I want to tell him, but by the time I open my mouth, Brent is right behind me, putting an end to what was probably a pathetic attempt at a contraband flirtation. I'm grateful he stopped me from making a fool of myself. Haley planned this entire event to spare my career. The least I can do is not kiss the man she's interested in. My feelings for Sam are nothing more than being on the rebound, and maybe a little rebellion on the side.

"Well?" Brent asks me. "What did you think?"

"Fun," I say, but my eyes are fixed on Sam, who is carrying a box wrapped in a red ribbon. "My stomach did flips as I soared across the boat. Incredible feeling." I'm more enthusiastic than I would be if Sam weren't standing in front of me with a gift. I feel on fire with jealousy, and I'm wondering if I was too quick to make promises I couldn't keep. The adrenaline of the zip line is nothing to his standing there.

"Ice-skating next, you think?" Brent asks. "We've got to get some use out of that costume."

I look at Sam, but he merely shrugs, as if to say, *Do what you want, what do I care?* My heart plummets. He makes me feel the same way that Jake always did: invisible and unworthy of his time. As a researcher, I'm taught to look at patterns. Well, here's a pattern and it's not a healthy one. What is it that makes me crush on a man who couldn't care less if I live and breathe?

"Sure," I say. "The skating rink sounds amazing."

We start to walk away and I stare back at Sam, but he does nothing to stop me. I should never doubt my first instincts. Sam Wellington is definitely Jake 2.0—albeit probably with a better job and definitely a better haircut. The kiss made me imagine someone else, that's all.

Besides, I've learned my "life-size jerk" lesson already. Do I really need to strive for a PhD in it?

14

Savor the good times in life. Studies tell us people who savor happy experiences in life are more likely to be optimistic about their past outcomes and their future.

The Science of Bliss by Dr. Margaret K. Maguire

TRY AS I MIGHT, I can't release Sam's kiss from my memory. It wasn't anything like Jake's kisses, which were perfunctory and chaste. Usually on the cheek like the way you might be introduced to a French stranger. Obviously I hadn't known Jake's kisses were passionless at the time. I thought he simply respected me when he kissed me on the forehead like his aunt Charlotte. I thought he was waiting for marriage to bring out the good stuff. More of my fantasy world at work.

Now that I've felt a man kiss me as if he meant it, I understand that Jake's passions were engaged elsewhere. He didn't want to kiss me. I'm enlightened—it's that feeling I get when all the data comes together and melds into an obvious algorithm and a conclusion is born. Romance wasn't made for people like me. Maybe that's why escaping to movie romance is such a vice for me. It takes me away from who I'm truly meant to be on this earth. A researcher. A scientist who helps other people find happiness in their life. It's such an irony knowing that people with a distinct purpose are the happiest on earth, yet I fought my own purpose so violently and escaped to a dream world.

God, I know I haven't spoken to you much lately, but tell me where I belong. Tell me why I'm here.

As I analyze the last two months, it's simple, really. Jake fulfilled my escape fantasies, and I placed him in the role of Prince Charming—a man without a job until my office hired him. Unemployment is fine for a prince, not so much for a guy in modern times. I could blame Jake for everything, but my role as puppet master has to be addressed. Maybe Jake had been trying to escape my plans for his life all along and I was in too deep to notice.

As I follow Brent down the long corridor toward the ice rink in my Belle costume, I'm suddenly awash with shame, understanding how desperately I've been trying to be someone I'm not, how unnatural it feels to be in satin versus a cashmere cardigan. "I'll have to catch up with you, Brent. I'm really not feeling well. I need to get some work done."

"What do you mean? It's time to play. Besides, didn't you lose your computer in that crazy fire? Remind me never to have you hold any electronics. You're like a bull in a china shop."

"That crazy fire could have taken my life!"

He gives me a side eye to let me know I'm being a drama queen.

"That crazy fire did take my computer and my PowerPoint presentation, so I want to get that back up and running before I speak again. I've already had one princess adventure too many for today." The hedonistic lifestyle isn't all it's cracked up to be.

"I thought you weren't going to redo the speech." Brent actually sounds annoyed that I might be responsible enough to care about my career. The way he makes me sound like a quitter infuriates me. I may have been a quitter for the last two months, but it's hardly who I am.

"People want to hear that talk, and I promised them. Well, Haley promised them, but her word is as good as mine. I'm going to stop by the office and—"

"In that getup?"

I neglect to remind him that he put me in this getup, but I also know if I take the time to change, I'll chicken out. "Yes, in this getup."

Brent stares at me, his crystal-blue eyes trying their earnest best to charm me into doubting my own mind—but I've had enough of those fake rom-com moments on this cruise and I'm only on day two. I need to parcel them out a bit. "I thought you were ready to have fun, get out of the library for once."

"I thought so too. Maybe it's not in me. Thanks for trying."

"Whatever," he grunts, and walks away. I'm tempted to chase after him and prove that I can be the life of the party, but it feels like far too much effort to expel to go ice-skating in a stupid princess outfit. I'll find a way to pay him back for the costume.

To add insult to injury, when I get back to the costume shop, my street clothes are missing. The saleswoman who had an answer for everything when we were buying my puffy costume now has no idea what I'm talking about when I ask for the clothes I left in her care. This day needs a do-over.

When I get back to my stateroom, it sings with color. On the entry table is a large bouquet with sturdy red anthuriums and delicate orchids. A brightly carved watermelon is chiseled into a gorgeous rose with petals of fruit at the base. Then I realize Sam is toward the back of the room, and my pulse quickens. I'm momentarily sidetracked by my swooning, ridiculous desire for romance and a happily-ever-after ending, but I chalk it up to the fruit and Brent's disgust with me.

Sam beside Haley sobers me, so I stand strong. I tried to do the right thing by allowing myself to have fun with Brent, but the truth is, he was probably voted "Most Popular" while I was voted "Most Likely to Be in the Library on a Saturday Night." These things never work out.

Haley is the kind of woman romance was designed for—she's

sweetness and light—and Sam looks amazingly heroic beside her. It's as if the two of them were meant to be idealized in glass figurines standing atop a multi-tiered wedding cake. The visual of them together gives me new resolve for my work. Some women are meant to be rescued and romanced. Others, like me, are meant to take notes.

They both stare at me as if I've lost my mind. I am wearing a princess costume at the ripe old age of thirty-one, so let's not mince words. I have lost my mind.

"I know." I nod. "Let's ignore the obvious, shall we? That would be the kind thing to do."

Haley shrugs. "Sam was just bringing me the DVDs of the new Valentine's Day movies so you could watch them. I thought it would be a nice break after the fire. You deserve some downtime."

I stare at the contraband with cartoonish, heart-filled eyes. "That present was for me?"

He smiles.

I quickly regain my composure at the sight of my silver ballet flats under the tiers of yellow ruffles. "Someone stole my clothes after I put this on."

"It was probably some kids. They like to throw things off the deck to see how far they fall."

"My clothes went the way of the *Titanic*?"

"Probably."

"Somehow this costume made an adventurous spirit possible. I know it's not all that brave to be strapped into a zip line, but I've never done anything like that. I'm shocked I was able to do it."

"It's Tinkerbell who flies." Haley's eyes question me.

"I did the zip line at the top of the ship," I repeat. "Can you believe it?"

"In that?" Haley points at my gown.

My face flushes, but I decide it's best to avoid the question, considering the answer is obvious. *It made sense in the moment.* Although Sam brought me the movies, it feels as if I've stepped into an intimate conversation that I'm not supposed to be part of. I look for any reason to avoid more questions.

"I need to call my parents. Are the cell phones working?"

"They must be—yours has been ringing constantly."

I grab my phone and unplug it from the wall. "It's my boss." I swipe through the missed calls. "She's called me fifteen times." Somehow I don't think she's called to tell me Dr. Hamilton is considering my résumé.

"A phone call will cost a fortune in roaming fees. Can't you wait until we're in port?"

"Fifteen missed calls from my boss. It appears that I can't. Not if I ever hope to go back to work again. I wonder if we got the grant!" The old Maggie wouldn't hesitate a moment. Nor would she think about the cost of the roaming phone call. But this Maggie, the disrupted, questioning Maggie who doesn't trust herself, hesitates at everything.

"I'm glad you care about calling your boss. I was beginning to worry," Haley says softly.

It means the world to me that she cared even when I didn't. That's what friends are for, and she deserves Sam Wellington for that fact alone. "You're probably right about the roaming fees. I need to go find a computer to get my PowerPoint slide show back anyway. I'm sure whatever is happening at the university isn't world-crisis important. My boss is probably just being neurotic. No new data has come in for months, so I'd be regurgitating old numbers if I was there and trying to make new connections."

Now, my boss, Dr. Fleece, is probably the least neurotic woman I will ever meet in this lifetime. If she has any emotions at all, they are kept tightly packed away. Probably in the soles of her ugly, black orthotic shoes.

"Do you think they sell computers on board?" I pray my credit card will still work at this point. I can't remember the last time I paid the bill.

"Sam brought you one." Haley points to the coffee table, where a slim red-ribboned box holds the silver hope of my fledgling career. "He got you a new MacBook."

"That's the gift you had? Not the movies?"

He holds up a palm. "I can't take the credit. It's from your publisher." He clears his throat. "My sister," he says, as though I've forgotten the connection. "I'm just the delivery boy, since she and Kyle are having a couples' massage."

Eew. I didn't need that visual of my publisher.

"You have to pay for internet if your PowerPoint is on the Cloud," Sam says, being the great hired handler he is. I wonder if he even has a real job. Maybe his sister hired him to be my handler and the J.Crew clothes came with the position. If he is unemployed, it would explain his irrational interest in me.

"I can't take a new MacBook from my publisher. You need to let me pay you back. I'm sure my renter's insurance will cover the cost of having it replaced when I get home."

"You'll have to take that up with Jules. This seminar is very important to her, so she wants to make sure you're equipped."

I nod. It's clear arguing with Sam will get me nowhere. "I spoke with the office about my speech. They've rescheduled it for Tuesday in a bigger venue. Apparently the fire brought some much-needed attention to my speech."

"That's awesome!" Haley says. "See? A silver lining. You did that on your own. I'm so proud of you. I only wish you hadn't gone to the office in your costume."

"I guess it's true that there's no such thing as bad publicity, because the Rockette lovers did your publicity work for you, Haley."

"Maggie, are you all right?"

The answer is relative, I'm sure. I'm standing before her in a Belle costume. She can make what she wants of that. "I'm fine. It's me again, if that's what you're wondering. The Belle costume broke something loose and I'm ready to get back to work." I look down at the DVDs still in Sam's hand and meet his eyes. "Thank you for the movie fix, but I'm clean now. It's time I went back to what it is I do."

"You don't seem all right. You seem sad," Haley says.

"I'm fine."

"Sam and I were going to have tea and dessert in the luxury Asian fusion restaurant. It seems the ship is willing to do anything to avoid our suing them over the fire. Go get changed and come sit with us."

"Margaret, do you want to join us?" Sam asks me.

Margaret. His use of my full name feels formal and dismissive. I've imagined our whole invisible connection, and considering my fascination with fantasy romance, I'm sure it's not the first or the last time I'll do that. I shouldn't feel any loss by his chilly behavior, but somehow I do. That must be more Jake residual damage. Sam is a stranger I shared dinner and a kiss with once. Most people would chalk it up to a bad date and forget about it.

"You two go and enjoy your Asian fusion," I say to Sam to let him know I'm not jealous. "I've got work to do anyway." Unfortunately, I don't stop there with my enthusiastic, supportive, and suddenly evolved self. "As you said, Mr. Wellington, smart women are incapable of happiness, so what kind of scientist would I be if I didn't allow you to gather your own data on the intellectual women of the ship?" I yank off my tiara. "Haley will be happy to prove your theory wrong."

For the briefest moment, Sam appears hurt. "I thought we were past all that." They both sit down and it appears that Asian fusion is off the menu.

Haley stares me down to let me know I've changed the happy, brightly charged air and made it hard for the tea party to continue on as anticipated. I wanted to believe that I was fine with Haley and Sam exploring life as a potential couple, but my feelings will not cooperate. In my soul, though I know Sam is everything I don't need in my life, I can't deny he's exactly what I want. He's an intellectual who is not turned off by my incessant curiosity, and while he may not believe my statistics due to his own experiences, I have no doubt he could analyze them in detail. The brain really is the sexiest part of the body. I love how he takes care of things—a meal if you're hungry, a computer if you need to work, a kiss if you need to forget the dark smoke.

It's the fantasy factor, Maggie. Get it together. You're never going to get to Dr. Hamilton's side acting like a love-starved teenager.

Judging by my phone's endless messages from work and my mother, it's obvious that not making a decision *is* making a decision. All I've done with my avoidance is make matters worse, and now all those pressing matters have a vice grip on my life. If I don't get it together, this book deal may be all I'll have in the way of income.

"I've got one bar!" I lift up my phone. Sam and Haley are now cozily sitting on the sofa across the room, and since this bothers me I turn away. She could have any man she wants. Granted, Sam is nothing more than a vacation diversion, and by next Friday he'll be out of both of our lives forever. I try to focus on this fact rather than be sidetracked by petty, unrealistic jealousy.

It's only leftover emotion from Jake. Suck it up, buttercup. Haley hasn't liked a man in eons. She's saved what's left of my career and gotten me out of the house. The least I can do is avoid my feelings for a man who is all wrong for me anyway.

Rather than pay them any more attention, I press the button to dial my mother, and she answers before it has a chance to ring on my end. "Margaret Katherine Maguire, where are you?"

"I'm working, Mother. Haley booked us a cruise for me to speak on."

She lets out a hollow-sounding sigh. "Well, I'm glad to hear that you're working at least. This wedding—"

"Mother . . ." I clear my throat, bracing myself.

I go to the opposite side of the room and try to whisper, but my mother isn't having it.

"For heaven's sake, speak up, Margaret!"

"I don't know how to tell you this. But there's not going to be a wedding. I'm not getting married. At least not yet."

She's silent for a moment. My mother is never silent. "Margaret Katherine, whatever do you mean? The caterer—"

"Jake has married someone else, Mother. So it's most inconvenient to have him as my groom."

"What? Jake was just here last weekend. He returned a power drill to your father."

"He didn't mention that he was marrying someone yesterday? An acrobat?"

"I think I should remember if my daughter's fiancé told me he was getting married to another woman. Is that why you've been avoiding my calls?"

Sam and Haley are both glaring at me. It doesn't appear that either one of them is enjoying their room coffee over the Asian fusion tea as they eavesdrop.

"I imagine you think this comes as a surprise to me," Mother says.

I look behind me, willing Haley and Sam to leave the room, but for some reason they don't take the hint. "No, I do believe that when we announced our engagement, you told me it would never happen. So if you want to hear you were right, well, you were right."

"I don't want to hear I'm right. I want to hear why you didn't bother to tell me. You might have saved me all the effort—not to mention the money." My mother sounds as if she's about to burst into tears, and I feel like the worst human on the planet. Because my mother doesn't cry. Ever.

"I guess I was waiting to process the news for myself."

"The country club didn't take kindly to my canceling at the last moment . . ." Her voice trails off into a shameful place I know I've created.

"You mean they won't take kindly to it? I'll tell them, Mother. I'll be home next Saturday and speak with the catering manager about everything." My stomach feels squeamish. If only the motion of the ship were causing my discomfort.

"You needn't bother." My mother's voice takes on a familiar, icy chill. I lower myself into a nearby stuffed pink chair and avoid eye contact with Haley and Sam. "I wondered how long it would take you to tell me the truth."

"You know about Jake," I say breathlessly. Of course she knows. My mother knows everything about my life before I've even made a decision. Kathleen's soothsayer powers have nothing on my mother's. She simply assumes the worst and it generally comes true.

"I spoke with your father about this a month ago. I knew something must be wrong. A mother's intuition."

"You canceled the wedding before this call?" I recognize her courteous yet hidden-rage tone and brace for the great unleashing.

"I've already told the country club," she says with an eerie calm, and I wonder if someone is listening beside her. I thank God for whomever the innocent bystander happens to be—he or she has spared me a great deal of mama rage. "I realize that you've been having some type of crisis, but I never imagined you'd skirt the truth about an event I was planning. A costly event that would never take place. I'd like to say I'm surprised, but you've always been sneaky when it came to Jake."

I steal a glance at Haley and Sam. They're both avoiding eye contact and have the courtesy to act as if they haven't heard a thing.

I don't want the answer to my next question, which tumbles from my mouth. "How did you find out?"

"You'll never guess." That hard edge when Mother doesn't get her way springs to life.

I wait for her to continue. There is no sense in rushing her. She likes to dole out her punishment slowly for the best effect.

"Because your boss has been calling here. Apparently, if you're going to go on sabbatical without telling your parents, you might first try to change your emergency contacts."

Drat! I bite my lip.

"This prime example of manhood who you decided to marry with your grandmother's wedding ring . . ." Mother has to remind me that Jake didn't even spring for a ring. "I want that ring back."

"The ring is safe, Mother." My intuition had told me I would never see Jake Stone again, and I'd made sure the ring stayed in my possession. Now didn't seem the time to bring that up.

"I'm not finished," she says. "Jake has apparently used your credentials to break into the lab beside yours. Dr. Fleece wouldn't give me details, but from what I can piece together, he's stolen something that seems quite important to the university."

I'm breathless. Shame washes over me like a Gatorade bath after a university football win. I can't even get dumped like a normal person. My sudden dreams where I forget all about romance and restart my career come to a screeching halt. I'll never work for the illustrious Dr. Hamilton at NYU. I'll be lucky enough to get a job scrubbing floors at any university.

"Dr. Fleece needs answers from you. You're the one who recommended him. This is no small thing, Margaret. She used the word *espionage*."

Espionage. Jake was obsessed with James Bond movies. Maybe that's who he thought he was. I'll never know. But I need him to get back to the university and set things straight—that I had nothing to do with whatever scheme he had planned.

"I need to go, Mother."

"My phone has been ringing off the hook. Dr. Fleece is most anxious to reach you. Most anxious," Mother says coldly. "I was tempted to give the university Haley's cell phone number because I knew that *she* would never do anything irresponsible like ignore *her* mother."

"She wouldn't, but her mother has passed."

"I figured that when you weren't in that shabby apartment of yours, you must be with your friends, and I was right, wasn't I?"

"You went to my apartment?"

"Honestly, Margaret, you live like a homeless person. Why not live in a box out on the street if you're not going to decorate properly?"

"I may need the box at this rate."

"Your father and I have sacrificed enough of our lives to get you educated and functioning in the world. It's our turn now. You're going to have to figure this out yourself."

I want to ask her when it's *not* their turn. They were in Barbados for my high school graduation, the Bahamas for my college graduation, and, I believe, Paris when I got my PhD.

I turn away from Sam and Haley. "I'll pay you back every cent for the wedding."

"How? You may not have a job!" she screeches as if she might have predicted my fate all along. "I want that ring back. Find Jake Stone."

"I will, Mother. I don't know how, but I will figure it out." My mind is already calculating how I can make Jake believe he can have his job back with no questions asked. As if I have that power. But if I ever hope to get this espionage baloney figured out, I need to get Jake to the university.

"Jake Stone and his new *wife*"—she says the word with the aura of disgust only my mother can inflict—"are currently being sought for questioning regarding espionage at the university. I'd suggest you worry about that presently."

"Currently sought by my university." I say this more for myself than my mother.

"Yes, Dr. Maguire, *your* university. Jake used your credentials to gain access to the physics building next door. Is there a reason you'd leave your important documents lying about?"

"I didn't leave them lying about. They were in my apartment." That must have been the reason he came to tell me about Anichka in person. I remember thinking it was a brave act on his part.

The physics building. My head spins with questions. What on earth would he need in there? Maybe I'd been played from the start. Had he planned all this before I even got him a job? There's no way to know the truth without asking my boss, and I don't dare call her before my speech is finished and I've kept some credibility in my field.

"I believe your boss is concerned that you may have been an accomplice."

"Well, I hope you told them I'd have nothing to do with anything dishonest."

"How could I tell them such a thing? I've been planning a wedding for months that was never going to take place. A wedding you didn't have the common decency to inform me had been canceled."

She had a point.

"We're concerned with your state of mind. What would propel you to spin this web?" My mother's favorite hobby is to analyze my behavior.

My heart is pounding, and I look over at Haley and Sam. I feel as if they've judged me in the worst possible way, as if I've committed the most heinous of crimes. My only hope is that they didn't hear every ugly word my mother said. I exhale. *What does it matter?* Let them hear the whole truth of Margaret Katherine Maguire, PhD. I stay quiet while my mother continues her expected tirade on society and her travesty of a daughter, who's not the intellectual she and my father had dreamed up in their heads.

Mother's voice continues to blare from my phone, though I've turned it down to the lowest possible setting. "The public education system would have let you fail, but that was not an option. You were not stupid, though you tried mightily to prove it to the world . . ."

I stop listening at this point. I feel the same dejection and hopelessness that I always do after a "discussion" with my mother, and that's sad. Nothing was ever good enough, and sometimes I fail to understand why I ever tried. Trying to make an unhappy person happy is a pointless endeavor. I have the stats to prove it.

"All right, Mother. Well, I should take care of this situation. My new publisher is on board."

Mother isn't done. "Do you have any idea how demeaning it was to go into that country club? Roger—he's the new catering manager and came from New York City. He has a very sophisticated palate. I

162

don't believe you've met him. He was horrified that the wedding had been canceled and did his utmost to keep everything hush-hush. But you know how people talk."

Oh my goodness, poor Roger! It must have been devastating for him.

Now, I've been raised by my mother, so I knew better than to speak my sarcasm aloud.

"I'd been telling him you were too busy to plan the wedding. Imagine my shock when I discover you haven't been at work for nearly two months."

"Oh, you know about that too." I'm really without hope here. It's my own web that I've spun and I'm not proud of it. On a happy note, nearly all the television movies were new during those two months, so it wasn't a total loss.

"Your boss said you'd taken a sabbatical to plan your wedding."

"I never said it was to plan my wedding." Though I'll admit, I got a lot of great ideas from the Hallmark Channel if I ever do plan a wedding.

"When you come home, I'd like you to go and explain to Roger what happened."

"Is Roger single?"

"That is not funny, Margaret Katherine."

"I'm trying to make light, Mother. I'm sure you wouldn't rather I was still getting married to a man who might be arrested on espionage charges."

She huffs and hangs up on me. When I look up, Sam and Haley both look more horrified than Roger the catering manager must have been.

"No," I tell them. "Don't feel sorry for me. I have enough to deal with. And Sam, please." I walk toward him and grasp his muscular arm. "Let me fix this before you tell your sister any of what's happening at the university. I know I don't deserve that, but . . ."

He doesn't meet my eyes. I notice he's no longer wearing his casual linen sports coat but still has a crisp white collar as if he's shedding his formal self slowly. Comfortably. With Haley. The knot in my stomach tells me maybe Sam Wellington means more to me than I care to admit.

Jealousy courses through my veins. I don't have the right to ask a favor of him, but my eyes are silently pleading with him for another day.

"You don't have to worry about me divulging anything to Jules," Sam says as he rises. "I'm the soul of discretion."

"Because of Haley?" I can't help myself. I want to hear it from his mouth. That he's recognized Haley's romantic qualities are far superior to my own.

He gives me the strangest look, and I can't decipher what it's supposed to mean.

"I don't know which is worse," Haley says with her pitying look. "What your mother said to you, or the fact that it no longer bothers you."

I shrug, sidetracked by Sam's handsome self and what's going on in that head of his. Sam's eyes give nothing away, but he's heard all my sins laid bare. Not the least of which is that my own mother doesn't particularly care for me. I force my attention back to my best friend.

"Haley, you know my mother." I shake my head. "She is who she is. She's not going to magically turn into Betty Crocker at this point."

Sam's silence is making me crazy. I wish he'd just tear out of the room with Haley on his arm so I could start grieving already. Another frog kissed. That's all that happened.

I can't take it any longer. "Aren't you going to say anything about what my mother's told me, Sam?"

He takes in a deep breath as he ponders his words. "I don't understand her, perhaps, but I believe people should be loved for who they are. Not what they've accomplished. Let's go find the dessert bar."

"Yes, Maggie," Haley says. "Let's go get some dessert. I think you need a little sweetness in your life after that." It's not lost on me that she's inviting herself along.

Call me cold, but I'd rather have a little sweetness without watching my best friend hit on the guy I kissed this morning. "I should call my boss and see what all this is about," I say. "I'm sure it's a simple mis-understanding, but heaven forbid the FBI is looking for me on deck."

"You should call your boss and explain." Sam's voice has an authority that commands attention, and Haley and I both wait for his verdict. "But first I think you should get dessert to bolster your confidence." He leaves the movies on the table beneath the television. "Sometimes, *Margaret K. Maguire*"—this time the way he says my name quiets my anxious spirit—"we've given all we can give, and we must refuel before we have anything else to offer. I think in your book of rules, that calls for dessert."

I smile. Did this man just make a pious, spiritual statement about the importance of sustenance in the form of ice cream?

Clearly I've been dating the wrong men.

15

Happy people live their truth.

The Science of Bliss by Dr. Margaret K. Maguire

I SHED MY BELLE COSTUME on the bathroom floor and kick it aside. I slide into a pair of white shorts and navy-striped nautical shirt. Rather than fashionable, I look like I should be working the zip line. But it feels right. Casual. Chic. Basically, not sweatpants.

I unzip the invisible pouch inside my makeup bag and remove my former engagement ring from its secret pocket. Just a glimpse. It's a simple design. A brilliant cut diamond in a tasteful size and classic setting. The ring sparkles magnificently under the bright bathroom light, and I twist and turn it, watching the beams of color facets change from red to blue to violet—a full spectrum. My grandmother always wanted me to have the ring. My mother held it hostage until I was officially engaged. I suppose my actions of holding it hostage are no better, but a strange satisfaction comes over me when I remove it from the pocket.

I slide the jewel on my ring finger, and for a brief moment all of this is just a bad dream. Jake loves me enough to marry me, to be my happily ever after, and I haven't misread the signs that perhaps I

166

wanted him more than he wanted me. A pattern I seem to be reliving with Jake 2.0—Sam.

Sam brought me a computer. But reality reminds me that his sister wants me to get to work right away. *He brought me sickly-sweet movies!* Again, a reward for a job well done. He's done nothing for me and everything for his sister. My romantic fantasies need to be grounded before they run off with my senses once again.

I tell myself that with Jake, it was simply cold feet and not another woman's feet that led him away. Everyone gets cold feet. My training didn't fail me, and all the data lines up as it should.

"Maggie?" Haley shouts through the bathroom door, and my reverie is broken. I look at myself in the mirror, reminded that the nightmare continues. My fiancé is gone, my job is in jeopardy, and my best friends are doing their level best to restore my sanity. While I'm in a dream state in the cruise ship loo.

I pull it together and yank the ring from my finger. "Yeah?"

"Kathleen just called. She's up at the main pool with that bartender you met. Brent, is it?"

Seriously? Are there only two men on this so-called singles' cruise? "New Year, New You," my foot. Two men for an entire cruise ship of women? Sounds like the same ol' year to me. Two men, two hot friends, and me. Third-wheeling it through my entire life.

"Yes, Brent's his name," I answer.

"Sam and I are going to go up and meet them, and we'll order dessert at the pool. Do you want us to wait for you? Or do you want to meet us there?"

My first instinct is to ignore the invitation altogether and crash with the new DVDs. But my first notions have been all wrong lately, and I've got serious work to do. Still, I know hiding in the cabin is only going to allow me to obsess over Jake and why he never loved me. Or worse yet, obsess over why another man's kiss touched me in such a profound way, when I know that Haley will have him wrapped around her little finger by nightfall.

I needed to find solace in another Disney princess and follow her advice: let it go.

Being a lab rat, I have no frame of reference for what a fantastic kiss is. I don't understand how this hookup generation takes intimacy so casually, or why I have to find the deeper meaning in everything that ever happens. Most days that feels like a curse. Sometimes things just happen. That old Bible verse that essentially tells us life isn't fair comes to mind: "He sends rain on the just and the unjust." That doesn't mean there's a reason to psychoanalyze every stinkin' weather report as if a fluffy cloud could carry me back in time.

"Maggie, did you hear me?" Haley calls.

"Yes! Go without me. I'll be up in a few minutes. I just want to get changed and refresh a tad."

"Okay, don't be too long." Haley pauses. "Or I'll come back for you."

"I'm almost done," I sing.

When I hear the door slam, I stuff the ring back in its compartment, wipe my eyes with a towel, and straighten myself out. When I emerge from the tiny but luxurious bathroom, the computer Sam brought is out of its box and plugged into the wall. I smile at the notion that I can escape into work anytime I please and all I need to do is make an appearance on deck. If I face Sam, this obsessing will all be over. This brings me solace and a sense of freedom.

I press a button on the computer, and it lights up and welcomes me with a message.

All work and no play makes Maggie dull. Meet us at the pool.

Maggie was dull long before this cruise came along.

I grin at the simple message. Rehashing the past is a waste of my time and energy. Life awaits! I mean, why shouldn't I play wingman for my two best friends? Kathleen and Brent would make a great couple. He can give everyone beer bellies at his restaurant, and she can run one of her boot camps and charge the same people to lose those flat tires.

Haley and Sam are harder for me to picture. He's a tortured soul of some sort and, as such, kryptonite for me, so I can't let a stolen kiss cloud my mind. Sam is the kind of man I should pay no attention to, so naturally, I'm drawn to him like a fish to water. While he and Haley are the picture of the wedding cake couple, Haley is too happy for a brooding, hot mess of a guy. He's been through something. She's the kind of girl that baseball players or firemen date. They want to rescue her. She wants to be rescued.

Of course, I may see all of this through a thin green fog of jealousy.

No. Haley's all wrong for Sam Wellington. For once in my life, I want to believe in Kathleen's prophetic gift. *He's not for you, Haley.*

"It doesn't mean he's for you either, Maggie," I say into the mirror over the sofa table. "Get a grip. A kiss means nothing in the real world."

The main swimming pool is next to the bar where I first met Brent. It is far more active today. It's a dinky pool compared to the magnificence of the rest of the ship. It's a simple rectangular shape surrounded by rings of lounge chairs—all taken. If I'd hoped for relaxing sunbathing by the pool, I've been misled. It's more like the swimsuit competition in a beauty pageant. It might be my imagination, but it seems like every single girl in a bikini is walking the deck with a princess wave, while every single guy seems to be relaxing/drooling with a beer and watching the show. It's like visiting the butcher with a throng of homeless mutts.

"Maggie!" Kathleen with her perfect, streamlined body stands up and waves for my attention. Her svelte, one-piece swimsuit in lifeguard red attracts all the attention at the pool, and I see a few men get smacked for staring at her. She is stunning, though, so you can hardly blame them. They are human.

I wave back as I'm handed a blue beach towel by someone dressed exactly like me in nautical gear. *I'm basically the help.*

"Dr. Maguire?" I turn to see a young woman in a white swimsuit with a sheer white sarong wrapped casually around her tiny hips. She looks clean and put together, as if she repels dirt systematically and her clothes iron themselves. "You're Dr. Maguire, right?"

She pulls my book from her designer straw tote and points to my photo on the back. I'm going to say she's not here as a Rockette booster.

"Yes, I'm Dr. Maguire."

"I was so sorry about what happened during your speech! It was terrifying. You weren't hurt, were you?"

"I'm fine. Thank you so much for your concern."

"We were worried that you'd be too traumatized to speak again, so I was ecstatic when they said they were rescheduling. It's almost like you planned it, since you're speaking on resilience!" She leans in closer, and I take note of her perfect, makeup-free complexion. "You didn't plan it, did you?"

"I can assure you that I did not plan it. If I had, I would have planned a better exit strategy."

"Your book changed my life, and I've watched your TED Talk at least twenty times."

My eyes narrow. "Did Haley put you up to this?" I'm automatically suspicious of Haley because this seems so well-timed.

The girl's gray-green eyes go wide, and she brushes back her silky dark hair with her free hand. "Haley?" she asks. "No. Look, I'm sorry to bother you when you're enjoying yourself, but I was so upset by the fire. I'm glad you're all right, because we'd never be here if it weren't for you telling us to take risks and follow our hearts." She points to her friends sitting in a small circle around the hot tub. "I just wanted to tell you how much your research has meant to me. I grew up in a bad environment. Your book helped me see that I don't have to be a victim of it. Happiness can be a choice."

I should really read my own book.

I'm still not buying the young woman's enthusiasm. It seems

choreographed by a certain redhead I know, but when I look over at her, she's too busy flirting with Sam to notice. I feel my jaw tighten.

"I'm Jeana." The young woman holds out her hand and I shake it. "Before I read your book, I wanted to be a teacher. My parents said they wouldn't pay for my education if I went into"—she puts her long, manicured fingers up in quote signs—"'such a low-paying position,' but after reading your book, I knew that teaching was my purpose. I could either deny it and be miserable or do what made me happy."

"That's impressive," I tell her honestly. "You got all that from my research?"

"Yes. I finished the engineering degree that I'd started for my parents and went back for my teaching degree on my own dime. Now I'm teaching high school algebra and I absolutely love it! I had to meet you and thank you personally."

I get all the reader mail, of course, but seeing this young woman makes it more tangible. My research may not have helped me, but it certainly helped someone else.

"Th-that's amazing!" I finally manage to say.

"This is my friend Elise." She pulls another young woman from the crowd. Her friend stares at me as though I'm some kind of goddess, and I want to tell her, "Girl, you have no idea."

Elise is also young and sophisticated. She's wearing a slinky bikini and looks at me apologetically. "I'm sorry I didn't know who you were until I agreed to come on this cruise." She turns to the elegant brunette. "Jeana, the speed-dating round is about to start, so can we go now? I want to get a spot."

"Okay. Listen, Dr. Maguire, I'm so happy they rescheduled your speech," Jeana says. "So happy because of your research. And now you have a story to tell. You're like the phoenix that rises from the ashes, get it?"

I smile. "I do. Thank you again for saying something."

With that, Jeana is dragged away to speed dating. I watch her and her lithe friend Elise walk away. It makes me wonder if my purpose is actually changing or if there's more to study and share with the world. And if there is, where is my motivation?

"Did you need something, Dr. Maguire?" the young sailor with the towels asks me.

"No, thank you. I see my friends." But I hesitate to go join them. Standing behind the sun chairs, I am not desirous of being the most awkward fifth wheel on a weird double date with Haley and Kathleen.

They both deserve love. Really, nothing is different on board this ship than when we're out at a restaurant on a Saturday night. They may deserve love, but I don't have to watch it blossom, do I? Especially when I met both men first. Whatever happened to dibs? I'm everyone's "friend." Skipper to their Barbie. And just like in real life, there's one Ken doll for all the Barbies to fight over. Or, in this case, two.

It seems like the world naturally goes off in pairs, as though this desperate ship of singles is Noah's ark—with an extra zebra.

16

Express what's in your heart. Those who disclose their deepest feelings are happier and healthier.

The Science of Bliss by Dr. Margaret K. Maguire

RATHER THAN JOIN IN THE "FUN" of the pool games, I turn back toward the elevator and the true love of my life. Ever faithful and dependable, the one who stood by me through the dark times: cable TV films. In that world, life always ends happily and there are no cruel people who get away with their crimes. Life in a romance movie is fair. The real world? Not so much.

The Mexican sun beats down hard while I wait for the elevator, or, as I like to think of it, my glass pumpkin. My body is faint from the heat and all the people. I'm swaying on the deck. Just as the elevator door opens, Sam Wellington stands in front of it.

"Where are you going?"

"It's warm out here. I should get some sunscreen since I don't spend much time outdoors."

"I have sunscreen. Your friends have sunscreen." He waves his hand toward Haley and Kathleen. "Come get something to eat. We saved you a lounge chair, and you can order anything off the menu.

They'll bring it to you in your lounge chair—that should appeal to you and that appetite of yours."

I look again to the five chaises all bunched together. Yeah, that doesn't seem like the best way to prepare for a discussion on happiness. My body actually recoils at the idea of sitting down between them all and making nice. Sam's towel is beside Haley, Kathleen is beside Brent.

"Did Brent actually bring his own Solo cup?"

"I think he did. He does enjoy a cocktail." Sam shakes his head. "He's angry you didn't go ice-skating with him in your princess outfit. Said you were a spoilsport."

"Because I'm too smart to be happy," I say. "Though I realize I've given you ample reason to believe I'm not all that smart."

Sam leans toward my ear. "You're not ignorant enough to believe that."

Brent pops up from his lounge chair like a piece of toast and jumps over a bench without spilling an ounce of his precious cargo. "Hey, happy doctor, come sit down with us! I gave you time to work after you dissed me. Now it's time to play." He lifts his cup to the sky and stands beside Sam. "Come on now, we had to fight a wicked old lady to get this chair. She told us we couldn't save them. I thought she was going to throw her margarita in my face." He cocks his brow and offers a cheeky grin. "Kathleen had to rescue me."

This makes me laugh. Because I have no doubt it's true.

Sam touches me lightly as the breeze whips my hair in my face. The scent of coconut suntan oil is overwhelming. "I think she's had enough sun for the day, Brent. You know these porcelain types. They don't take kindly to the heat."

"You'd never make it in Texas," Brent says.

"I promised her dessert if she ventured out. I guess I best take her to the sundae bar," Sam says.

"I thought that was just a ploy to get me outside and see if I melted."

"You're onto me."

I hand him the beach towel I've been given, thankful to be rid of it. "You're having fun. Your party looks cozy without me. I'll just go back to the room and see you both at dinner."

"Suit yourself, happy doctor!" Brent sails back to his position on the lounge chair.

Sam doesn't budge. "You saw that I got your computer set up."

"I saw that."

"I shouldn't have. I think you need a break, to be honest."

I've taken two months off, but let's not quibble.

"Dr. Maguire!" A young man who looks uncannily like a young Johnny Depp shows up holding my book.

Sam stands in front of him. "I'm sorry. Dr. Maguire isn't feeling well after her traumatic experience. You understand."

Young Johnny Depp does, and he backs away. But then he rushes me and kisses me on the cheek. "I kissed her!" He raises a fist to the sky. "I kissed the doctor of happiness! The world is mine now!" He rouses the crowd to cheers, but they have no idea what they're cheering for. He may as well have said UFOs were landing on the promenade deck.

"Dr. Maguire is speaking again on Tuesday. Highlight Theater!" Sam shouts.

"Well, aren't you a regular P. T. Barnum. What skills don't you possess, Sam Wellington?"

"Social graces, but I thought we'd already established that." He winks one of those delicious chocolate eyes at me.

"I could have handled that myself. I'm used to the throngs of fans who follow me about." I laugh as I start to walk backwards.

Sam follows me. "How ever do you deal with the fame?"

"It's hard being a star, but someone's got to do it." One glance at Haley by the pool and I halt in my tracks. "Sam, I don't need to be handled," I tell him. But I'm not sure it's true. The last time I was left to my own devices, I was wearing a Belle costume and floating across the ship on a skinny wire.

175

"No, you don't, Dr. Maguire. Hold on to that rail for a minute," he orders. "Don't leave until I come back." Sam jogs toward Haley, removes his beach towel, and inserts the two extra lounge chairs back into the throng of reveling singles. He says something to Haley and she gives me a death stare. We have never in our lifetime fought over a man. *This is insanity. But I made her a promise and I need to keep it.*

"You shouldn't leave on account of me. I can find my own way back. Haley will make room for you on her lounge." Just as I say this, some young guy with abs of steel seats himself on the end of Haley's chaise.

"You could accept some help. Maybe you're not up to par after this morning. Did you think of that? I don't know what you were thinking zip-lining across the deck. Wasn't the fire enough excitement for you?"

"It was!" I admit.

"What does happiness science have to say about accepting assistance when you need it?"

"It's good to accept help when you need it. It shows healthy self-care. But I don't actually need help." I don't know what I'm fighting. Help from a handsome bloke who would be out of my life in five days' time? Nothing could happen. In five days' time, we'd be back to our own lives. Just because he wanted to help me back to my room after I'd nearly fainted didn't mean anything more than that he was a gentleman. Haley doesn't seem concerned as she flirts on her lounge chair. *Good for her. She deserves a break from trying to sell herself so hard to Jules.*

"Of course you don't need help." Sam's hulking presence parts the crowds like the Red Sea as he walks resolutely toward the air-conditioned labyrinth of hallways. We take a different elevator and he presses a button to the top floor.

"I'm not on the top deck."

"But I am, remember? And I have a butler."

"Look, Mr. Wellington, I've forgiven you. I honestly believe that you don't hate intelligent women. You have nothing to prove to me any longer. I'll be fine in my suite. I'm used to being alone. I work by myself studying data and algorithms."

"It sounds like you're alone enough. What's wrong with a little dessert between friends?"

I never thought to question where he was taking me until we arrive at his suite. If he were a player, this would seem like standard operating procedure. But he's not a player—I don't think he could be that great of an actor. Not after his verbal vomit in the foyer when we met. Maybe Haley has hired him as my new handler. She may have known I was onto her about Kathleen.

I take a long, leisurely glance his way. His jawline could cut diamonds. So strong and perfectly formed under the shadow of his afternoon stubble. He has the looks to be a player, no doubt.

"It seems to me that you just find ways of getting women into your suite. Am I not supposed to question how we happened upon your suite?"

"You're onto me again." Sam winks. "Not women. Woman. Give me some credit." He unlocks the door and we're met by a new butler, whose name tag reads Arvin.

"Did you wear the other butler out?"

"Marcus works at night, Maggie." Sam shakes his head. "Arvin, we're going to be out on the deck. Would you bring us some iced teas? And maybe something sweet?" He turns to me. "Give me the key to your room."

"Um, no. That's literally how every *Dateline* episode starts. With a dumb decision."

"Fair enough. We'll just have a light snack and get your blood sugar up. You've got time to work."

I turn to Sam. "Are you planning to chain me to the desk until the book is finished? Because I don't even want to write this book. I have nothing to say as of yet. It's on resilience. Considering that I flew across the deck in a princess costume today, I may not be able to speak about that just yet."

"What do you mean? Like a phoenix, you rose from the ashes this morning. Start there."

"It sounds so easy, doesn't it?"

"My sister isn't asking you to bleed onto the page. She's only asking for you to continue to write about the data you've collected. Chain you to your desk? Not unless I need to."

My guilt is running amok with his flirtatious ways—or is he flirting? Maybe I've been in the lab too long to know. Maybe this is simply friendly banter. Haley has made it more than clear that Sam belongs to her, and with all I owe her, it's the least of my sacrifices. What is it about him that makes me feel so at peace? Why am I willing to forgo every rational thought that enters my head?

"I really shouldn't be here." I hadn't meant to say this aloud, but there it is.

"Why not? Arvin is here. He'll chaperone, if that's what you're worried about. I thought it might be nice to finish your PowerPoint presentation on the deck. You know, away from all the distractions of your crowded stateroom or that zoo of a pool. No one expects a book out of you on this cruise. Just a presentation to pave the way for the next book."

Sam looks innocent enough when he says this, but he's like that hot professor everyone had in college. The one who paid no attention whatsoever to his fawning students. But I can't let my guard down and be one of his fawning students. It would be easy enough to fall for his smooth way of taking charge.

"I shouldn't be here," I say again. *Haley*, I think while looking directly into his intense gaze before focusing on the wall of windows. He was Haley's. "Haley—"

"She's such a good friend to you," Sam says. "She really does nothing but sing your praises, but I didn't bring you here because of Haley, if that's what you're thinking."

"Why did you bring me to your room?"

Arvin is gone now, swept away by the errand of grabbing us

something to eat—as if we didn't pass free restaurants on the way to Sam's suite. Sam's presence commands respect without asking for it, and something about that attracts me in a way it shouldn't. This fact alone makes him far more dangerous than my ex. He is obviously used to getting what he wants, without the manipulations of a lesser man like Jake. This is apparent by his easy way with the butler.

Sam Wellington is comfortable giving orders and unused to being told no. The sooner I figure out his strange interest in me, the better.

"The same amount of people are in this suite as in my own—well, when Arvin gets back. It's not really quieter," I say.

"True, but Arvin and I don't talk as much."

That's the truth.

What does Sam Wellington want with me? "I should go back to the pool with my friends. I'm feeling much better, and Haley can't have all the men on this ship," I tell him, hoping to put in a word for her and take my mind off his fascinating, dark chocolate eyes.

"We both should go," he says quietly.

"Just tell me why you want me here. What's in this for you?" I cross my arms and try to look angry while I wait for his answer. I refuse to be intimidated by his commanding presence. In all my born days, no one has tried this intensely to get close to me. The researcher in me wants to know why and what on earth he's up to.

He draws in a deep breath. "I want the chance to redeem myself."

I exhale. "I told you, it's no skin off my nose what you said in the lobby. It's forgotten."

"That's not what I mean," he says.

I steel myself against his charms. "Mr. Wellington, you'll find a simpleton out there in the world, and she will be lighthearted and filled with joy. You'll be happy alongside her and prove yourself correct in your earlier assessment that smart women cannot be happy."

"I'm not looking for a simpleton, Dr. Maguire. I'm looking for the secret to helping smart women be happy."

"I promise to give you my email address so you can personally tell me that your theory held true."

"You think that's what this is about? What I said to you coming on the ship?"

"It's not?"

"From an outsider's view, you're on top of the world, no?"

"I suppose."

"Let's review," Sam says. "You've had a bestselling book, a TED Talk success, a career at a university—"

"I know my credentials, Sam. I'll admit, I look good on paper."

"But you're not content. It's like immediately after I said that, I knew why I was here."

"On earth or this ship? Just to clarify."

"On this ship." He smirks at me. "I'm not certain, but I'm going to guess that very few people find their life purpose on a cruise ship."

"Well, obviously you missed me today zipping across the ship in a Belle costume. I definitely found my calling."

"You're making fun of me."

"I don't mean to. I'm confused. I can assure you that my life isn't perfect and I'm well aware of it."

He pauses. "I read your book last night."

This both thrills and terrifies me. Nothing I love more than a personally delivered book review.

"I was fascinated by how you managed to sneak your faith into a science book on happiness."

"I didn't sneak it in. It's just who I am. Maybe it's who I was, I don't know."

"I was impressed. Very fact based, your book, but your heart as a scientist shines through. Your faith is admirable in a place like that." The Bible he carried when boarding the ship is open on the table. It's filled with highlights and notes and scraps of paper marking certain pages. Clearly he's far more in touch with his faith than I am at the moment.

"Don't be impressed," I tell him. "My faith is on shaky ground."

Case in point: I'm in a man's room and my best friend has a crush on him.

He leans in closer. "I'm curious why a scientist would take a risk to put her faith in a science text but can't seem to defend it in person."

"It's not that I can't defend it. I grew up in an atheist household. Well, that's not really true. My parents left the church after a traumatic experience."

I suppose the whole of my life could be summed up as BA and AA. *Before Amy*, I had a happy, lighthearted childhood. *After Amy*, the clouds seemed to cover our world and the sun never shone quite as brightly.

"Look," I say, "I know my faith, and I can debate the hardest skeptics on why God is real. It's just . . . my church of late has been the romance channel."

"So I've heard. It appears you're also a very devout follower of said channel. Any particular reason why?"

"I have to find a church where I can trust again. It's stupid—I know better. People make mistakes. I'm no better than the next gal, but I can't seem to bring myself to step foot in a church right now."

"You mean a church where you feel safe?" Sam chuckles. "Shouldn't that be all churches?"

"Shouldn't it?" I exclaim. "You know how in a breakup, couple friends have to choose sides? And it's awkward to be friends with both?"

"Not really."

I glare at him, admiring his innocence. "Well, they do. Most of the time you take your friends and he takes his—unless your friends are paired off, then it gets more difficult."

"Wait a minute. Is this statistically factual?"

"I don't know," I say with frustration in my voice. "It's what I've seen over the years, so it's factual to me. Anyway, the church I went to since I was a teenager chose my ex and his new *wife*." I choke over the last word. "So I need to find a new one, but I'm feeling betrayed, so I'm not anxious to go back."

"It's a church. You can't share it? How big is this church?"

"You'd think, right?" I shrug. "I have a hard time with that. It's not that I don't forgive, mind you. It's that he was engaged to me in that congregation and attending marriage classes for our wedding, and yet the pastor didn't have any trouble marrying him off to another woman outside of the church. I mean, was he in two marriage-preparation classes at once with both of us?"

"I'd hope not."

"I suppose I could say that they have a lot of faith in their marriage prep courses. Only half of the new couple needs to attend."

"Are you bitter?"

"Not bitter, disillusioned." I clear my throat. "Look, I believe God will replace what the locusts have eaten. I'm at the point where I know that Jake did me a favor and I dodged a bullet, but I don't get why it's so hard for the church to do what it says it believes."

"You're talking to a pastor's kid here," Sam says. "All I can tell you is that teachers will be judged more harshly than the rest of us. It's all seen by God. There are no secrets from him."

"You're right. You're totally right." It still felt like a betrayal. Maybe the kind of betrayal that Haley is feeling right now.

"I could tell after reading your book that something clicked in you, and I want to know what it is. Where did your passion go for the work?"

"The what?"

"I can see you're not happy, but when I read what you believe, I'm curious as to why."

"Christians aren't always happy. Some of them suffer unimaginable tragedies, you know."

"Trust me, I know."

I remember that Haley said he's a widower. I'm tempted to ask how, but it seems so personal and I back down before I'm given a chance.

"After reading your book, I happen to know that I'm here to show you the truth, you have every reason to be happy, and you'll get your fire back."

"So what, you're like my guardian angel?"

"I'm definitely no angel. I only know from the first moment I saw you and opened my big mouth that I had something more to tell you. I've been around a lot of intelligent women in my life, and I blew it."

"So tell me." I drum my fingers on the table as though I'm in some kind of hurry. But I'm on a cruise ship. Where do I really have to be?

"You don't feel a connection between the two of us? Familiarity. Like I know you—just a little."

Now I'm frustrated. This is exactly the kind of game Jake played, and after I gave him a job and a title and apparently my credentials, he basically absconded with my life. It dawns on me now that I'm not mad at Jake. I'm mad at myself for having no proper boundaries in my world. Sam seems like a noble opportunity to get that issue right.

"Sam, I'm a woman of science. I'm not into this woo-woo stuff. I know Kathleen says she's got some prophetess in her, but we don't believe her. We nod and put up with her." *Don't tease me.*

"Not like that. As in, I've seen your behavior before in someone I loved—the way you work rather than deal—and it legitimately scared me. Today, after the fire, you didn't so much as slow down. The biggest concession you made for what you'd been through is dressing up and taking a zip line ride."

I'm intrigued by his story and what on earth he thinks it has to do with me, but it feels too dangerous to hear—to be responsible for it. "I'm not whoever she was. I'm fine, I assure you."

"Her mother talked to her exactly the way your mother talks to you."

"That's all fascinating, but she has nothing to do with me. I promise you."

Sam nodded as if he was onto me.

"Just another sticking point between the two of us, I suppose. Please, Sam, I know that you want to help. I believe you with my whole heart, but it's not good. It's too dangerous for me. I'm vulnerable right now. You're everything I don't need in my life. No offense, but—"

"Dessert. I'll leave you alone if you have dessert with me."

"Now you're going to bribe me with sugar?"

"It seems to work. I'm a man of action. I do what works."

"Promise that this will be over after dessert?"

"Cross my heart." He makes an X over the left side of his chest and I try not to focus too hard on his pecs. "You don't have to ever see me again if that's what you wish."

"First, tell me what you do for a living," I say, as if it's some kind of test. "If you want me to trust you, the least you can do is provide me with some basic information."

Perhaps Sam inherited handler duties from Haley so the role would be less obvious, and I might be more inclined to listen to him than Kathleen. I've decided not to fight the handler. For now. Maybe I need one. At least this one is easy on the eyes and allows ice cream on his watch.

17

Passion is essential to one's happiness. What makes an individual passionate? That drive holds the key to their happiness.

The Science of Bliss by Dr. Margaret K. Maguire

I'M A VENTURE CAPITALIST. I discover raw talent and invest in it." Sam lifts one rounded, muscular shoulder, and my eyes are captured by the movement. He might give Kathleen a run for her money in the gym.

"A venture capitalist? I've never met one before. So this is what they look like."

"You should come to Menlo Park in California. We're a dime a dozen."

"Somehow I doubt that."

"Creating drama over what I did for a living was a giant letdown, huh? I know you were hoping for something bigger, more fantastical—but there it is. I invest money in other people's ideas." He takes my empty water glass. "So tell me, Dr. Maguire, now that you know my career path, what category would that sort me into in your black book of data?"

"It's questionable. A venture capitalist. You could be in it for the money, and I'm sure most of them are. Big gambles, big payouts." I give him a once-over. "But I don't think so. Money is not your motivating factor. Or you'd dress better."

"Excuse me?" He puts his hands to his chest. "What's wrong with the way I dress?"

"Nothing. I only meant that you dress for the job, but not beyond." My hand glides up and down in front of him. "You could wear Armani, but you're happy with J.Crew. So that tells me money isn't your motivator."

"How do you know I could wear Armani? Maybe I strive for J.Crew and I'm in debt to wear it. Did you ever think of that?"

"No one goes into debt for J.Crew. If they do, they're ridiculous. Target has perfectly good knock-offs, and you're too reasonable to live outside your means."

"Maybe that's just what I want you to believe."

"Living beyond your means would be irresponsible, and you don't strike me as the irresponsible type. Those broad shoulders of yours like responsibility."

"Do they now? Well, you happen to be right about that aspect, but it's all a lucky shot at this point. What else do you have in your bag of cheap party tricks?"

"The data didn't lie. I have no party tricks. If I did, maybe I'd get invited to more parties."

"Maybe if you didn't leave dinner parties in the midst of ordering, you'd get more invitations."

"Do you think so?" I laugh. "Here I thought it made me all the more desirable."

"This is precisely why I didn't tell you what I do for a living. Do you analyze everyone you meet? You know, treat them like a cadaver and you're the coroner?"

"What a disgusting analogy!"

"But it seems appropriate here. Why do I do what I do, Dr. Maguire, queen of all algorithms?" He sits back in his chair and pulls his ankle up over his knee.

I study him further. "You might do it because you're really into technology and want to be a part of what's next out there in the industry."

"That's true. A very admirable reason to be in venture capital."

"But I don't think that's your motivation either."

He raises his brow, obviously impressed. "You're correct. I'm lucky to get a password changed when I need it. Still . . ." He pauses and looks me over. "You could be just lucky. Or some of Kathleen's prophetess abilities have rubbed off on you. Jury's still out."

"Definitely not prophetic. It's all in the data. You've got money or you wouldn't have a suite with a butler. It doesn't take any kind of scientist to figure that much out, and I'm embarrassed by how easy a giveaway that is."

"Maybe I won the trip. A local radio show might have had a call-in contest and I was the right caller, so I won this all-inclusive trip to Mexico, complete with a famous author at my table."

"Have you ever called in to a radio station?"

"Well, no."

"The money is yours. You're too comfortable bossing people around. If you won the trip, the butler would make you uncomfortable and you'd be asking for his permission. But you felt perfectly at ease sending him off to do an errand."

"Very perceptive. So, Dr. Maguire, why do I do what I do? Why do I invest in young talent?"

"I'm getting to that." I stare at him, drinking in his kind but powerful nature. He *would* make a good man for Haley. The longer I gape at him, the more I'm convinced of their compatibility. After an uncomfortable amount of time spent looking in his eyes, I admit the truth. "I have no idea why you do what you do, Mr. Wellington."

"Passion."

"Passion?" It was such a foreign word from his mouth.

"If there are two inventors in front of me, I always choose the one with passion over intellect. They can both get the job done, I have no doubt of that. But the one who is passionate will finish the job no matter what. He sees instances as stepping-stones and jumps over them. Passion makes what he does matter to him, and he has to get it done. So I invest in passion."

"How very romantic of you."

"Meaning, if I were my sister, I wouldn't invest in your next book."

"What if you already did?"

"I'd try to find a way for you to get your passion back."

"What exactly do you think I've been doing for two months?"

"Passion is a double-edged sword, Dr. Maguire. It's very easy to become a victim to your passions if they're not kept in check."

"We are talking about a science book, aren't we?"

"Passion can be taken too far." He gets a faraway look, and it feels as if I've lost him.

I shift in my seat. "You promised me dessert," I say to change the subject.

"And you shall have it. Sugar seems to be something you haven't lost your passion for."

I could give him the stats on how sugar lights up the frontal lobe and the reward centers of the brain, but something tells me he's well aware of my so-called addictive nature.

Sam's eyes don't seem filled with thoughts of my addictive nature. He takes my hand and leads me outside to his expansive deck, where a love seat chaise lounge is placed. A single ottoman is in front of it, and my heart begins to race at the thought of sitting beside him in such a cozy position. I'm far too weak for this right now. Sam says all the right things, does all the right things, and worst of all, looks like a Greek statue. I need this kind of temptation like I need another month of movie marathons.

I break free of him and race to the railing. It's formed in a V like the glass wall in his bedroom. I'm drawn to the curved edge of the

V and feel the need to re-create *Titanic*'s "top of the world" scene. I glance back toward Sam.

He smiles with his dark brown eyes and offers that cocky grin of his. "Go ahead, I won't laugh." Once again, he's reading my mind. "My sister had to do it the minute she saw it."

"I can't do it alone!" I reach the end of the railing where it meets the edge of the ship. Since the suite is on the top level of the ship, I imagine only the captain's chair has a better bird's-eye view. He follows me and grasps my waist at both sides while I step onto the first rail. I glance over my shoulder, and his face is so close I feel the intimacy intensely. His magnetic energy shoots through me and settles in my stomach like the biggest, most exhilarating roller-coaster drop.

His deep voice tickles my ear. "You're on top of the world."

My heart is thumping in my chest, more so than when I was perched on the zip line in a princess skirt. I worry it's audible over the low hum of the ship cutting through the gulf. I can't let him know he's affected me, so I have to follow through. I step forward and lift myself onto the concrete lip of the ship and raise my arms. His grip gets tighter around my waist, and my whole body feels light and high on adrenaline at his touch. His hands send shock waves through my entire system, and I lose all will to launch into my Leonardo DiCaprio impression. I can't even remember what he said, but I don't want to turn around and stare into the depth of those dark eyes. I'm breathless at the very thought and it's obvious I've lost my mind. I step off the rail and lean back against Sam's broad chest. His arms clasp around my waist and I lean my head onto his shoulder.

Haley. I close my eyes against the breeze. *He belongs to Haley.* She'd laid claim to him, and even if he didn't belong to her, one anchoring gaze from her and he'd be secured for good. Did I really need something that precarious in my life? Even for a week? I can get rejection at home. It was time to have some fun.

But try as I might, I fail to pry my head from the crook of his neck. He smells so good, so earthy and fresh, and I fit into the curve of him perfectly. As if I was designed to be there. I rest into him and feel the desire to be nowhere else. My anxiety lifts and I relax. It's such a foreign feeling that I startle myself.

"Why is your sister here with her husband on a singles' cruise?" I shout into the wind without turning to face him. I can't bear to notice again how his well-defined abs show through his fitted, blue-collared shirt. I can't bear to see those deep eyes, full of life and depth, drill through me again.

He leans forward and speaks directly into my ear. "To support her biggest author." The vibration of his voice against my body is almost more than I can bear. I need to get out of here. I clench my fist and dig my nails into my palm. *Don't trust your feelings. Feelings got you into this mess. Think, Maggie, think.*

"Your iced teas, sir." Arvin announces the cozy, colorful scene behind us. On the table are two tall iced teas overflowing with ice, with lemon and a sprig of mint, beside a luscious slice of cake with frothy, pink whipped frosting. My head begins to shake back and forth. The seduction of Dr. Maggie Maguire is far too easy when cake is involved. Add one handsome man with brains and I'm done for.

I still don't understand why Sam is choosing to pursue me rather than Haley, or what his motive could possibly be. He had to have been given the task of handler. There is no other excuse. But the truth is, it doesn't matter. He'd said his truth when we met, and I need to heed that warning. What kind of person have I become? Do I simply do whatever I please now, without thought to the collateral damage? How am I any different from Jake at this point?

I unravel myself from Sam's embrace. "Thank you, Sam. This is really an incredible place to write, but I need to get back to my suite. I prefer to be alone when I write, and I'm sure there are better things for you to do on this ship than babysit me."

"Did I say something wrong?"

"No, no. I'm thinking of Haley. She'll assume I'm back in the room working, and I don't want to let her down again. The truth is, I

KRISTIN BILLERBECK

haven't been myself since . . . well, that's neither here nor there. I've been mercurial of late and that's not my personality."

"No?"

"No. I'm a scheduled person. I do the same things at the same time every day. This has been a fluke."

"But you're back now? The organized you." His voice comes in waves and resonates when he speaks into my ear over the wind.

"I am."

"I'm sorry to hear that. I'll miss the soaring princess."

"You'll be the only one. There are people who were put on this planet to be the life of the party, and then there are those of us who were built to report on it."

"I'd like to think you can have a touch of both."

Sam's expression seems disappointed, and I'm triggered. But this is how I know I've made progress—I let him be disappointed. It's not my job to make him happy.

"Your friends have a big influence over you, don't they?"

"I wouldn't be here if it weren't for my friends. I owe them more effort." I look at the cozy setting with cake and juicy orange slices alongside the iced teas. "I've blown it big-time at my job. I took a long sabbatical to get over the breakup. Not really the breakup. I didn't want to explain to my boss what the new office structure would look like. I didn't know how to handle it. It was unprofessional. It was unprofessional to get him a job in the first place."

"From the sound of it, it might have been healthy. I think it could get depressing reporting on people's happiness when you're feeling miserable and having to face your ex every day. Nothing wrong with taking time to grieve."

"Right?" The iced teas and their buckling ice are calling for my attention. It's something that I would have done for Jake on a hot afternoon, and the thoughtfulness of it touches my heart—even if the butler did it. But then, he had to be told to do it.

"I wasn't trying something," Sam explains. "I sincerely thought

191

this iced tea and dessert break would be relaxing for you, but no more pressure. I can see how badly you want to get out of here, so don't let me stop you."

The last thing I want to do is leave his side. Which is exactly why I have to get out of here quickly. I smile at him and he smiles back. There is so much in his eyes that I want to read as passion for me and not his sister's business. I lift up on my tiptoes to kiss his cheek but can only reach his jawline, so it comes off as more sensual than friendly. He looks at me awkwardly.

"Thank you, Sam. You're a good man to look out for your sister. I'll get the book done because I'm a professional and I'm a woman of faith. And a woman of faith sticks by her word."

Sam rests his elbow on the railing. "I don't think that mercurial girl who changes her mind like the wind is completely gone. I see a little light behind the hazel eyes. It's in the gold flecks." He brushes the backs of his fingers against my cheek.

Instinctively, I press my fingers underneath my eyes. Jake never noticed that my eyes had gold flecks in them. "I have more bad news for you."

"From your book of facts?"

"No, just my personal assessment."

"Hmm?" He juts his strong chin toward me. "What's that?"

"You'll never be happy with a woman who doesn't challenge you intellectually, so whatever gave you that impression that smart women can't be happy? You need to fix it."

"That's why I'm here." He stares past me through the window. "That's why you're here."

"You're not like Jake, my ex. I thought you were at first, but you're far more complicated. And by the way, Haley has her master's degree. Besides being stunning, she's actually brilliant."

"Is she now?" He steps closer to me, and I feel my stomach starting to get tingly.

"Thanks for your hospitality, Sam. I'm just going to follow the butler out." I step back and hit the wall of windows. "Ouch!" I rub the back of my head. "I think you secretly desire an intellectual woman. All of this airhead business is just an excuse to keep you single so you don't have to commit."

"Is it now?"

I follow Arvin back into the suite. "Arvin, I'll get my computer myself." He hands me back my suite card. "Thank you for being so helpful."

"Would you like something other than cake, miss? I'll be happy to get you anything you'd like that's on board."

"Maybe a lobotomy to figure out why I select unavailable men."

"Miss?"

Once I'm out in the hallway, I lean against the wall to recover after the stifling air in Sam's suite. I feel the back of my head, where a lump is forming. Sam wants a smart woman, and considering the show I've put on today, we can surmise that definitely isn't me.

I avoid thinking about the fact that I wasn't in a stifling room. I was out in the fresh, open air with the stretched-out blue of the gulf surrounding me as far as my eye could see. But nothing felt expansive with Sam near me. My world felt small and cozy and . . . safe. I shiver at my romantic notions getting the better of me again. *The last two months have ruined me.*

Sam probably felt nothing I felt, and for all his talk of passion, it was all about work. Sam's a workaholic. I'm a workaholic. People like us don't have storybook endings. People like us are the residual friends who give the lucky couple bad advice, but they ignore it and find their own romantic bliss.

"Did you need help finding something, miss?" a woman in uniform asks me.

"No, thank you." But I don't move from the spot. From the possibility.

Sam is nothing more than a handler sent to get me to behave and get back on track. All romantic similarities are works of fiction

I created to swallow the pain of losing Jake and my credibility in a two-month span.

I have all these residual questions, and I press my knuckles to the door to knock softly, but I can't bring myself to go chasing after someone's attention. *Never again.*

I've been terribly self-absorbed for the last two months. There has to be a balance between being a complete doormat and being a raging narcissist who doesn't bother to show up for work so she can watch romantic movies.

I do wish I'd asked about his wife. I have been so caught up in my own heartache, it never dawned on me that he probably suffered mightily losing a spouse. I wish I understood what he meant about too much passion and how it can harm a person.

My hand is still raised when Arvin opens the door. "Hi."

"Miss. Can I help you? Did you forget something?"

My hand slowly floats to my side. "No, sorry. Wrong suite." I jog down the hallway, suddenly feeling the urge to race around the track with Kathleen and escape in a healthy way with exercise and self-torture and not ice cream. I am making progress.

It has been a long time since I've been to church, where they taught me never to be alone with a man in his private quarters. Maybe that wasn't such archaic advice after all.

18

Altruism, or giving back, is essential in creating sustainable happiness. Compassion toward others releases endorphins in our systems.

The Science of Bliss by Dr. Margaret K. Maguire

AS THE SUN SETS ON OUR SECOND NIGHT on the cruise, my friends and I head to our spa date, which Kathleen has booked to ease the tension and get this vacation away from the stresses that seem to come with me as a passenger. I'm basically the Jonah of this cruise ship. I'll be lucky if they don't toss me overboard in exchange for smooth sailing.

I should have warned my friends that lately I tend to be like a storm of chaos. I can literally do nothing—like sit on my sofa—and there will be a mess of drama surrounding me. I know it isn't biblical, but it's like God seems to test me at every turn to see if I'll believe, even if nothing ever goes right for me. This Job lifestyle is getting old quickly.

Let's recap the cataclysm that is my life currently:

1. I have nothing to write for a book that's due in six months.
2. My "fun" partner for the week is far too adventurous for me and only reminds me how truly librarian-like I am.
3. My job is teetering on a precarious cliff, and I'm hanging by a dangling zip line.
4. The only man who has expressed an interest in me other than Jake feels as if I am holding the secret to happiness for him.

My current romantic attachments are going the way of my career—straight into the toilet—and I should be fine with that. I'm totally good on my own.

Maybe rather than a working vacation, my friends should have done a true intervention and written me nice letters and sent me off to a fat farm, where the biggest treat of the day was fresh carob juice with tree bark sprinkles.

Fresh purple and white orchids line the spa's water feature, which bubbles and trickles gently into the entry. In the middle of the water is a perpetually blooming cherry blossom tree. The essence of essential oils—ylang-ylang, lavender, and citrus—scent the sea-blue room and ooze tranquility. The New Age music makes me feel like I'm in an aquarium watching fish glide through the sea—only I'm one of them. The water tumbling over the round, black spa rocks provides a soothing aesthetic that slows my heartbeat and calls for a nap. The cares of the day dissipate in a fog of olfactory heaven. It would be ideal if it weren't for the silent tension between Haley and me.

"We're here for our seven o'clock appointments," Kathleen tells the young woman at the desk.

We are led into a wide, circular room that surrounds another pink cherry blossom tree, with bamboo stalks containing stuffed rattan lounge chairs. We're handed a leather menu with the spa's offerings and given a glass of water with cucumber and basil floating in it. It's not nearly as inviting as the iced tea on Sam's deck, but I force that comparison from my mind. *Be content in all things, with whatever you have.* I should be satisfied with the cucumber water, and I certainly shouldn't be coveting anything Sam Wellington offers. I'll never know his motive, and rather than unlocking some great mystery, I need to let this one go.

"Your aestheticians should be here shortly," the receptionist says. "Anything on the menu is available during your service—just let your skin-care specialist know. She'll be happy to make recommendations if you're unsure of your needs."

"Does she give career advice?" I ask.

"Pardon me?"

"Maggie!" Kathleen chastises. She turns back to the receptionist. "Nothing. Thank you. We'll be fine in here."

The receptionist leaves the room, and the uncomfortable silence continues. Generally Haley, Kathleen, and I can discuss anything, but Sam Wellington is another matter. He's a subject that isn't sailing away on the floating rose petals dropped in the bubbling waterfall behind us. It's as if his enormous, brawny presence is standing beside us, willing us to acknowledge him.

"This has gone on long enough," Kathleen says. "Haley, you need to forgive Maggie so we can move on. She isn't after Sam Wellington, and she didn't sabotage her speech on purpose. What is wrong with you lately?"

Haley's face is contorted in pre-tantrum mode. "This isn't about Sam! Or the speech."

"Good, because I've already told you he wasn't for you," Kathleen says. "You ignored me at your own risk. It's not like it takes any kind of discernment to see that he's into Maggie."

"He's not into me!" I say too loudly as they both look at me.

"Shh!" a spa attendant says.

"Maggie's not into him, so what's the problem? She is still not over Jake," Haley says. "And a man like Sam isn't going to stay single for long."

Now who's prophetic?

"I am right here, Haley. If you have something to say, you can include me if you want my opinion." My friends seem to have forgotten I can speak for myself about Sam. Not that I have anything to say. "We're on a cruise. In less than a week, Sam Wellington will be gone and back to his own life, and we'll most assuredly never speak of him again. So why is there this tension, Haley?"

"Because Sam is worried about you, and I've tried to tell him you're not like his wife, but he won't listen. He believes you're in danger, and that's why he's practically stalking you."

I knew there was something else going on! Men like Sam Wellington don't suddenly fall for out-of-work librarians.

"Danger? Of what? Overdosing on gelato? Not fitting into my jeans? What exactly am I in danger of? Besides losing my job, that is."

"He's worried you might . . . you might hurt yourself."

I slump into my chair, humiliated at my pride—that I'd mistaken Sam Wellington's pity and his fear of the past repeating itself as his interest in me. "You've said enough, Haley. I get it, and don't worry, Sam Wellington is all yours for the duration of this cruise. You won't see me making a fool out of myself again."

"Maggie!" Kathleen gives me that look as if I should know she's on my team, but seriously, it would be easier to believe in their altruism if they weren't getting a free trip out of my agony.

Haley doesn't know when to shut up and keeps talking. "Sam's wife was an ER doctor. She worked crazy shifts, like forty-eight hours. One night she took something to stay awake for her work, and it turned out to be deadly."

My mouth is agape. "I just met this guy, Haley. Why on earth would he fear for the life of me, someone who's practically a complete stranger? Well, other than being the person his sister is heavily invested in financially. Her company's advance did pay for a lot of gelato, if I'm honest."

She shakes her head. I'd like to shake her scrawny neck at the moment.

"You made people think I wasn't mentally balanced, Haley, and that I needed to be handled for this trip," I say. "That's why he thought I was trying to hurt myself during the fire. That I didn't move because of . . . Okay, yes, I'm depressed. I have been depressed. My life doesn't look anything like it was supposed to and God has abandoned me. The church picked Jake because that's what God really thinks. That women are just chattel and only a man's happiness is important."

"You don't really believe that, Maggie. That's blasphemy."

"Maybe it is, but if it's not true, I need to see some proof. Where are Jake's consequences? He has none. The church acts as if everything he did was righteous and true."

"The church is simply people, Maggie. Flawed and sometimes just plain wrong when they make their own rules. You can't be angry at Sam. He's got such a good heart," Haley says. "When he saw your shell-shocked face getting on the ship, something snapped in him. He said he worried you were struggling like his wife did, trying to be everything to everyone."

Do I really need the humiliation of knowing that Sam's only interest in me was to relieve the unimaginable guilt of his wife being gone? I may not know the details, but I'm wise enough to pick up on the obvious. Sam's wife is gone. He couldn't stop that, but he's got some kind of altruistic theory that he can stop me from my downward spiral.

"People think I'm a victim."

"You've been sitting on a sofa for two months!" Haley sounds like my judge and juror all rolled into one. And for the first time, I wonder if our friendship will survive this. She sounds remarkably like my mother, and I get it, you can't help someone who won't help themselves. The futility of it is maddening.

It's worse that Sam showed any interest in me at all. It would have been better if I had taken his nasty comment at face value and never spoken to him again. Instead, I allowed my heart to leap at the sight of him and imagine myself with a man who was different. But he's no different. He had an alternative agenda just like Jake, wanting to relieve his own guilt by ensuring I'm not ready to jump ship.

"I appreciate your honesty, Haley. I'm sure it was very difficult for you to share my innermost issues with my new publisher and her brother."

"Maggie . . ."

"I get it, okay? I'll be alone forever. I'm too weird for anyone to love me, and Sam is no different. Happy?"

"Why would you want to deny your best friend if you're not into him?"

If I had a pint of gelato at the moment, I would literally shove it into Haley's face. "It doesn't matter *who* he wants. This is a cruise ship, and we're not in a rom-com movie. We're here to have fun and get my career back up and running." Well, we were here for that, until I learned that perhaps my friends were more concerned over my mental state than my career after my self-imposed sabbatical. Nothing like your friends thinking you may be nuts. That's when you must start taking those thoughts seriously—like maybe you are headed for the straitjacket.

Even as I say the words to Haley, the romantic in me isn't dead yet. I wish I could crush that part of me with a hard reality check, but Sam's kiss makes that impossible. I can't stop thinking about the way he looked into my eyes, as if we'd known each other for centuries and crossed through time to get back to one another. It's ridiculous. I know it with every brain cell in my head. Maybe it is euphoria and not happiness. But I want someone who makes me feel the way he makes me feel and is all mine. Not someone I have to share with Haley or any other woman. I'd rather be alone for the rest of my life than compromise again.

"See," Haley says like a temperamental little sister. "She's totally not into him, which means he's free game. I'll be in touch with him after this cruise is over. I'm working closely with his sister." Haley leans in toward us. "She thinks I'd be perfect for him. Just the type of woman to help him move forward after the loss of his wife."

"Like the potluck brigade in my grandmother's bridge groups. I wouldn't be surprised if some of those casseroles are laden with love potion number nine. But you be you, Haley. I won't get in your way."

I feel a certain sense of ownership over Sam, and if this wasn't so unlike Haley, I'd tell her to settle down and focus on being my publicist. The inexplicable crush Haley seems to have on my publisher's brother confounds me. That, coupled with the magnetic chemistry I've felt for this man who said intelligent women can't be happy, has me thinking I may not be out of my gelato-induced stupor just yet.

"This spa date was a good idea, Kathleen," I say, changing the subject. "I wonder if I do that seaweed wrap if it will take some cellulite with it."

"Where were you all afternoon?" Haley asks, her eyes narrowed, and I realize our short truce is exactly that. Short.

"Working on my PowerPoint for Tuesday's speech. It's all finished and I'm ready to rock my talk. I think it's a good thing I had that false alarm so I could really be prepared. I mean, I get that it wasn't great for the cruise ship and we're lucky they didn't send us directly back to port, but overall it gave me time to focus on what's important. There's no reason I can't convince the university that this was just a time to refresh and prove my resilience theories. That should help the grant coming through, and if that happens, I'm applying for that fellowship at NYU."

"Chill. I just asked where you were."

My nervous speech continues. "I'm relaying information already in my head. I don't know what I was so nervous about."

"No, before you were working on your speech. Where were you after you and Sam left the pool area?" Haley seems suspicious. "Where did you go?"

I pretend to be lost in the spa menu. "Are you girls doing a facial?

Massage? This Zen chakra balancing massage with grounding aromatherapy sounds amazing. That would be good before my speech Tuesday, don't you think? Speaking of which, we need to go check out the new venue. It's supposed to be much bigger."

"That Zen thingie sounds like a marketing ploy to charge more money for the same service." Kathleen tosses the menu aside. "I'm having a basic facial. I love when they do the extractions."

"You would," I tell her. "Are you always a glutton for pain? Even in the spa? This is about relaxation. Tranquility. Calm. Not someone stabbing your face with an evil device of Satan."

"You stayed with Sam!" Haley accuses, pointing her finger at me.

I swallow the lump in my throat. I shouldn't feel like "the other woman," but that's exactly how I feel.

"Just for a few minutes," I say. "He wanted to offer me a place to work. He thought his suite would be—"

"His suite?"

"What is with you and Sam?" Kathleen asks her. "Haley, he's not for you. What part of him kissing Maggie did you miss? I mean, I know you believe in the fairy tale like she does, but when Prince Charming is kissing your best friend, it's a sign. And not a good one. Let it go, girl."

"You're not psychic, Kathleen. You don't know everything. Maggie told us that kiss meant nothing. It was about her amped-up emotions after the fire scare. She can't be over Jake yet, no matter what she says. Sam is only worried about her from a professional standpoint."

"Sure he is, Haley. You keep telling yourself that. I know when people are concerned about me, they're constantly making out with me."

"No, no. It was just a little kiss. Chaste," I clarify.

"I know this much," Kathleen says, as if I'm not sitting right here and able to speak for myself. "You're pushing this Sam thing and it's not working for you. He's taking off from the pool with Maggie while you're lounging in a bikini. That's what we in the Christian realm call a sign, and if you're willing to lose your best friend over some guy who is not into you, I guess we don't know you as well as we thought."

Haley, oblivious as ever, goes on. "Jules told me Sam is a Christian, he's mourned for years now, and he says he doesn't want a relationship, but he's solid in his career. She said—"

"You've just rattled off a list. Love doesn't work like that, and Sam isn't going to give you the safety you crave because he's a good businessman. You're doing your own business. Yes, it's scary, but you don't need a man to rescue you. Forget your daddy issues for a minute and look around."

"Maggie is the doctor, Kathleen," Haley says. "If I want relationship advice, I'll go to an expert."

Kathleen shrugs, flips her blonde hair over her shapely shoulder, and leans back in her sleek armchair. "Suit yourself." She says this with divine calmness—her prophetess voice that lets us both know we'll never change her mind with facts. "I'll pray for you to find wisdom."

I groan, and just then my cell phone begins to trill.

"Who brought their cell to the spa?" Haley asks while both of them stare at me. "First you can't be bothered to work for two months, and now you're bringing your cell phone to a spa. Who are you, Maggie Maguire?"

I venture a look at my phone and see Jake's photo on the screen. I hide the picture against my chest. "At the moment? I have no idea, but I'm just going to take this outside."

"Really? Come on, our appointments are coming up," Haley says. "You had two full months to answer phone calls."

Really. "I'll be right back."

I hate that my stomach still flips when I see Jake's picture, and I chalk it up to nervousness—anxiety over his reason for calling. Nothing is how I saw it two months ago. I abhor that as a woman of science, I cannot grasp the truth that this man never loved me and that his presence in my life brings me nothing but pain. Some tiny part of me doesn't want to believe Jake is the man the university is portraying him to be. It's that hope that makes me answer the phone. One could argue it's that hope that's luring me back into a false reality.

All the evidence points to Jake Stone being a manipulative, vile human being who lied to me every time he opened his mouth. But it's a matter of pride. I have a hard time believing I was *that* blind to his deception. It's more about my data-collecting skills than his actual personality flaws. If my people radar is that poor, no wonder I've questioned my occupation for two months.

I answer the phone with a last vestige of hope that the university has misinterpreted some innocent action. "Hello?"

"Maggie, finally. We need to talk. I want you to listen to me very carefully."

His ordering me about makes my stomach clench. Normally I'd do anything to avoid that tone in his voice, and my prior self would wait for further instructions. I would jump at his command. But something is different.

This time I hear his thin, spineless voice, and it doesn't bring that sweet, exhilarating flip of my heart. Instead, it reminds me of Sam's hot vocals . . . his words spoken softly into my ear . . . and the electric spark that shot through my entire being when I was locked in his arms, with the warm breeze spraying me with droplets from the Gulf of Mexico. And while Sam is right—that's not happiness, it's euphoria—I don't want to settle for less than euphoria, and what Jake brings me is nothing like that. It's a fear that tightens my muscles and is familiar to me. It's what I feel whenever I have a conversation with my mother. How could I have missed the obvious Freudian issue within myself?

Maybe Sam is only a mirage, a temporary image of a Coast Guard ship passing by my broken-down skiff—a brief, romantic buoy to get me over Jake and remind me that I don't ever want to feel that way again. I'll never settle for a man who makes me feel anything less than magic. Sam taught me that there is so much more to life and love than a flashing, short-lived beacon like Jake. That must be Sam's purpose, and I can't read any more into it than that. Or maybe it's to show me that when a man is interested in you, even a woman like Haley Adams—everyone's ideal—isn't a temptation. Or so I thought. The truth is, I know what's possible now, and I'm worthy of love.

"Maggie?" Jake says, this time in a gentler, manipulative tone. "I'm sorry about the way this went down."

"What?" I answer curtly.

"The university is trying to railroad us. I need you to go to Dr. Fleece's office and explain to them that—"

"The tanzanite blue of the ocean is mesmerizing," I say in my best far-off voice. The Gulf of Mexico may not be an ocean, but for once I'll let Jake figure out my cryptic half-truths. It's his turn to guess what's going on in my mind.

"What are you talking about?" Jake asks gruffly.

My voice is still dreamy. "I'm on a luxury cruise about to get a seaweed wrap. I'll need one for that bikini tomorrow on the beach. So you see, Jake, whatever is of concern to you right now? It's not a concern for me. I'm over it."

"Maggie, are you listening to me? We're in trouble, and not the kind of trouble your credentials can get you out of. The kind of trouble where the government comes and asks questions and confiscates your computers and data. Are you willing to share that with the world?"

Dang, he's good. Knows how to push every one of my buttons.

"I'm not in trouble," I say lightheartedly. "I didn't do anything wrong, and I'm sure I'll be able to prove it through the university's security system."

"Dr. Fleece doesn't know that at all. In fact—"

"I'm technically still on sabbatical, and since I haven't been on campus, you'll be hard-pressed to pin this one on me, Jake. I'm afraid you'll have to handle that issue yourself."

"Listen, I don't know who that yahoo was in that picture you sent me, but I know you're not with someone already, Maggie. How long did it take you to get a boyfriend in college? I'm supposed to believe that you've moved on in two months? Where would you meet someone?"

"It's really none of your business, is it?"

"You can quit paying this guy to pretend for you—I'm not buying it. You'd have to leave the lab or your apartment to meet someone. You can let this ditzy-blonde act go because I know you don't do a thing without analyzing it on a spreadsheet."

"That's not true, actually. That was the old me. Online dating is amazing for a woman like me. I look *good* on paper. *New York Times* bestselling author, viral TED Talk giver, university professor—I could go on, but you get the gist. I'm a hot commodity out here in the dating world. I should have tried it sooner. Much sooner. And it turns out, this guy actually has a job. Very successful venture capitalist. Do you know what that is, Jake? It's a guy with money."

"Maggie, I know you're not unprofessional enough to ruin my livelihood over petty jealousy. I fell in love—"

"I can assure you, I'm over all that. You two are perfect for each other." *The moral equivalent of two alley cats.*

"I made you, Maggie. Don't forget that. You were too afraid to make a speech before I came along, remember? You dressed like a bad librarian and mumbled every word. Without me—"

"Actually, I remember having a setback after you appeared. You had nothing to do with the TED Talk. Or that amazing contract I signed with my publisher. If Sam taught me anything, it's that working for love is too much . . . work."

"How can you toss aside what we had?" Jake growls, as if he's going to lead with his seductive side. When I say nothing, he goes full desperado. "We were going to be married. Now you're going to leave me in the dust because your career shot off like a bullet? I could only play second fiddle to you for so long, Maggie. I know it's antiquated, but I couldn't handle you making more money than me. It takes a special kind of man to do that, and it wasn't me. I tried. I really tried, but you had no mercy on me. You never let me forget that you were the one with the doctorate."

If I weren't a Christian woman, I'd tell him to prepare himself. At this rate, his flying Rapunzel wife is going to be making more money than him. He'll be trading cigarettes in the pokey.

I stop my obsessive thoughts there. I still don't know that I have a job, so humility is probably my friend.

"It's not enough for you to beat me career-wise. You have to destroy me personally too? I never saw it in you to be so cruel, Maggie. I can't imagine what our pastor would have to say about this."

"*Your* pastor. I haven't been to that church in eons."

I press the off button and shut out Jake's tired, empty whining. Then, with renewed confidence, I block his number. He can't manipulate me or shape the truth if he can't reach me. The new—er—old Maggie is back.

My obsessive thoughts sail to Sam. I relive the low, deep vibration of his voice, which resonated within my soul. Charming, romantic movies will never be quite as satisfying, and the knowledge that he was only trying to save me from myself creates a dull ache in the pit of my stomach.

Even if I have to watch Sam walk down the aisle with my beloved friend Haley—and why wouldn't he want to?—I'll never again settle for a man who doesn't bring my spirit to life. Life is too short.

19

W E'VE SWITCHED TO THE LATE DINNER SEATING to fit
in our spa visits, but Jules, Kyle, and Sam did the same, so
there's no escaping the elephant standing between Haley and me. The
grand dining room is the only source of social stability on this singles'
cruise. While every other venue seems to be some bad icebreaker
with a name tag or a hokey game show reprisal attached, dinner is a
place of respite. The only people we have to interact with are Jules
and Kyle Jensen and . . . Sam.

Since most of the men on board are upwards of forty and the
women are significantly younger and consoling themselves with a
great deal of alcohol, the cruise is decidedly not for me.

"This cruise is like a bad sorority party where only creepy professors are invited," I whisper to Kathleen.

"You haven't been out of your room. How would you know?"

"I'm out now. Brent and Sam are the only two options on board,
it seems."

"And yet you managed to alienate the two of them, so I guess the rest of the cruise should be spent getting your career out of the loo," Haley hisses at me.

I'm about to make a snarky comment when I see my publisher and her equally infatuated husband walking toward us. "Being married on this ship is like floating on water. Look at how regal they are as they pass all the clawing desperados."

"Need I remind you that we fit into that category of 'clawing desperados,' as you so eloquently put it?"

"Not me. I'm on the rebound."

"That makes you more single!" Haley says. "It makes you rejected and single."

"Nice, Haley." Kathleen tells us both to shut up and behave ourselves. Sam is nowhere to be seen.

"Your brother's not here?" Haley asks Jules as she approaches.

She purses her lips and stares directly at me. "He didn't feel much like socializing this evening."

Join the club is my first thought, but I'm anxiously checking the door, hoping that Jules has it wrong. Some part of me doesn't want Sam Wellington to find me mercurial, as he put it. *Criminally insane with stalker tendencies* is how I heard it. I obviously care what he thinks and that needs to stop.

"Sam read your book," Jules says first thing when she sits down. She's wearing a violet business dress with a rectangular neckline and fiddling with a medallion necklace, twisting and turning it nervously.

I take back my first assessment of Jules Jensen. While I'd still take bets that she was a cheerleader in high school, she's got a darker, more manipulative side. This is the part that got her to the top rung of a publishing house at her young age. It's also the part of her that is staring me down like I'm dolphin roadkill.

"Sam told me he read my book," I reply, channeling Jules's inner cheerleader.

"I think for the most part he enjoyed it."

"I hope so." I'm also hoping she'll offer up more information.

"We were very excited at BrainLit about your new venture and the opportunity to present the idea of resilience in happiness science. I read the proposal again yesterday so that I could speak to marketing after getting to know you better."

I literally don't know this woman from the person who empties the trash cans at night in the lab. "You *were* excited?"

"I've spoken with your department head—Dr. Fleece, is it?"

"Oh, how is she?"

"Missing her lead researcher, from the sound of it. She thought maybe you were working on your book."

I pray that Jules knows nothing about the impending investigation. It's bad enough I haven't been to my job. "I needed a sabbatical. Personal time."

"That's what she said, but you see, my publishing company is starting over. You're only as good as your last book in this industry, and if you take a sabbatical on me, we can't afford that."

Haley pretends not to be listening as she smothers butter all over a piece of bread. Haley hasn't eaten bread since gluten became the devil of California.

"No, of course not. I completely understand." I'm betraying myself. I may understand, but I have nothing to offer her. My conscience gets the best of me. "You want out of the contract?"

Haley drops her knife on her plate.

"No. I still believe your book will offer hope to those who keep repeating the same unhealthy cycles in their life."

Like binge-watching chick flicks and eating gelato.

"Maggie has never missed a day of work before this self-imposed sabbatical," Haley says. "She's ready to work. Aren't you, Maggie?"

Luckily for Haley and Jules, my business mind is back. It has to be. Prince Charming left with my white horse—and an acrobat. "Hmm, yes, absolutely." I search the annals of my brain to complete my thoughts. "The new manuscript should resonate with readers searching for happiness and contentment in their lives." I'm the world's biggest hypocrite. But rather than shut my mouth, I keep spewing.

"We've got random samples of the happiest, most contented people from all over the world," I say, knowing full well the studies aren't ready to be accessed and made consumable for normals. But nothing like a little adrenaline to make it happen. I can't stand for Sam to think I let his sister down, especially after I've made such a fool of myself in front of him. Snuggling into the crook of his neck one minute and dashing out his door the next. He says *mercurial*—which is a kind way of saying *crazy*.

"This sounds wonderful," Kyle says, grinning and nodding. "Isn't that great, Jules?"

The cheerleader is gone. The staunch principal in Jules is speaking. "Dr. Fleece said that she's placed numerous phone calls to you and that you haven't returned any of them."

"We're on a cruise ship," I reply, not explaining that I've seen the missed calls. Lying by omission is getting to be a way of life for me. I need to get back to my morning prayers, and quickly.

I'm encouraged by Kyle's enthusiasm. As I glance around the dining tables with sad, middle-aged men jockeying for seats next to women half their age and way out of their league, I add, "I've been studying the power of healthy relationships, self-acceptance, and the need for autonomy. Even in a relationship. Autonomy despite your marital state is important for happiness."

"Autonomy is important for happiness?" she repeats.

"I've written a grant and I'm trying to collect more data before the book is released, but it's very important to personal happiness that people have the ability to make their own decisions and don't heavily rely on others for acceptance."

"If this grant doesn't come through, will it stop production on the manuscript? If so—"

Haley interrupts and starts with her publicity spiel on how fantastic

I am. To be honest, I'm so grateful for the reprieve from defending myself that I have no idea what she's saying. My eyes rest on the empty seat beside me that should contain Jules's brother. I want to be content. I want to overcome this strange emotion that life without a romantic partner is an unworthy life. *Rom-coms, what have you done to me?*

Logically and scientifically, I'm aware that a woman in an unhappy relationship is far less happy than her single counterpart, so why am I struggling? A better question is, why am I so attracted to a man who told me up front I was all wrong for him? By definition, I'm too smart to be happy. Granted, that translates to me that he believes all women are the devil, which makes him even more off-limits. He waved his red flags with vigor—Caltrans doesn't have as many warning signs when they work the 101.

No wonder my friends are worried, the empty tubs of Ben & Jerry's notwithstanding. I realize what everyone must think of me—that first it was Jake, then it was Brent, and now it's Sam. Is there nobody who won't do? I'm the girl who cried wolf, and coyote, and maybe cougar too. No one will ever believe me, but this time the romance feels different. When I find the man who makes me feel like Sam Wellington does . . . and he loves me back . . . and my friend isn't interested, then it's on!

"A happier single person will be part of a happy couple." This does not come out as an intelligent addition to the current conversation. Rather, the entire table is staring at me as if I have Tourette's. I was hoping to add something without it being obvious that I was scanning the doorway every nanosecond for Jules's brother. "I mean, we are wired to search for happiness but not necessarily equipped to strive for it."

"What I think Dr. Maguire—Maggie—is trying to say is that resilience as it pertains to the science of happiness is an understudied field." Haley is clearly hoping to make me appear normal—but aren't we past that at this stage? "It's a study she's trying to get a grant for as we speak. That future study would no doubt be a bestselling third book for her."

I give her a death stare. *Third book?*

Sam never fills the doorway. His presence never graces the crowded dining room, and I know I've run from the wrong man. Everything happens for a reason, and Sam was sent on this cruise to teach me I'm attracted to the wrong sort of man and I miss red flags. But I can't help but wonder what would have happened if I'd thrown caution to the wind.

Haley, meanwhile—the girl who was supposed to have such a desperate crush on our mutual friend—hasn't even seemed to notice his absence. She's overselling me at this point, so I make a slicing motion at my neck. She then shifts into an animated discussion about the beach and tomorrow's excursion into Mexico.

"We're going to karaoke night tonight after dinner!" Kathleen's clearly done with Haley too. "Jules, Kyle, why don't you join us?"

"Singing makes people happy," I spout like an idiot. *Singing makes people happy?* So does dancing the hokey pokey and the chicken dance at weddings. Do I want to share that knowledge with my publisher? I will myself to shut up.

Haley glares at me, and I know my sixth sense is on target. I need to call it a day on the blathering and maybe walk the plank while I'm at it.

"I talk when I get nervous," I whisper. "I wouldn't be casting any judgment my way, motormouth."

"It's my job to talk," she hisses back at me.

"Let's go sing. Other people's words are safer for both of us right now."

After our meal, we rise to leave, but I can't go without asking the question that's really plaguing me. "Where's your brother tonight, Jules?"

Jules, with all her natural perkiness, frowns. She takes me aside, away from Kathleen and Haley. "Did something happen between you two today?"

"What do you mean?"

"Did he do something to upset you?"

I shake my head. "No, of course not. It's *me* he's avoiding tonight at dinner?" I'm instantly offended. "Why do you ask that?"

"Sam is more sensitive than he appears."

"Well, so is a cactus."

"Pardon?"

"Nothing. I don't understand your question."

"My brother thinks it's best to keep a low profile right now. He's worried that his presence may offend you."

"His presence offends me?" I'm not usually offended by hot *GQ* model material with a heart to match. "No, Sam tried to give me a quiet place to write today, and I—I had my reasons for leaving. It had nothing to do with him, it's just the way I work. He didn't do anything to upset me, I promise you."

"I may have pushed him too far with this cruise. When he said that comment to you in the lobby, I knew I'd overstepped my bounds."

"He's very well-spoken. I've really enjoyed his company, barring our initial introduction."

"Have you?" Jules's eyes are wide as she asks, as if she senses what I'm hiding.

"Why don't you invite him to join us tonight?" I try to hint that this isn't about me, that I'm being heroic here and taking a pass on her brother's favors for my gorgeous friend—who has never wanted for male attention in all her born days. "Haley would love to have him along for karaoke."

"Haley?"

"And Kathleen too," I say to take the pressure off my matchmaking ideas. Mostly because I hate myself for making such a promise to Haley. Tonight I thought he could be alone with Haley and their magic would happen. Nature would take its course, and I would find solace in more sweet movies and ice cream. It was the circle of life, Maggie style.

"I don't think he'll be joining you, but I'll let him know if you like. I'd planned to go to his room and check on him anyway."

"He's in his room?" I ask. "I'd hoped he was out meeting new people and eating at one of the more exclusive restaurants."

"Have you met my brother, Maggie?" Jules chuckles. "He doesn't want to make you uncomfortable. I'm sure the mere thought of offending you is enough to keep him away tonight. He was only trying to help you meet your deadline, but he's so strong natured, I can see how it would feel threatening."

"Threatening? No, he was never threatening! On the contrary, I haven't felt that comfortable since my sofa back in California." *Why does everyone think I'm a charity case?*

Jules comes closer. Her cheerleader exterior disappears and an unsettled expression crosses her face. "If you had any idea what he's been through, you'd understand he only has the best of motives. I realize that I'm his sister and naturally inclined to believe the best of him, but in this case, it's true. He wants to change his outlook. I think he may have thought you had the answer on how to do that."

I nod hastily. "I'm sorry that I didn't." It's time for an impulsive exit, which is getting to be my specialty. I can't even remember the *me* who used to overanalyze everything.

20

Happy people live their truth.

The Science of Bliss by Dr. Margaret K. Maguire

M Y QUEST FOR FUN— the one that does not include gelato and extreme avoidance—continues. Tonight's adventure? Karaoke in a disco-lit ballroom with streaming purple, blue, and magenta themes. If Alice had a nightclub in Wonderland, this would be it. It's tacky to the extreme, the kind of vulgar that makes you willing to throw caution to the wind and act like a different person. Which fits my current bill.

When I do the old Maggie, I get sucked into a vortex where I make bad decisions—like answering Jake's call while avoiding my boss's inquiries. When I do the new Maggie, the party girl Maggie, I fail in some way so that my friends—or some people—are fed up with my childish behavior.

There has to be a happy medium. Karaoke seems like that middle ground. The night is full of promise. As long as I don't get caught up in feeling too bad for Sam. I didn't do anything wrong this afternoon. Certainly nothing I should feel guilty for. I mean, he brought me to his luxurious suite—why would there be an innocent motive in that? Whatever Sam's motive is, be it to push me to write, to relieve his guilt, or to seduce me, letting my guard down with him leads me into temptation. The kind of temptation that left me at the altar for a scarf-clinging dingbat.

Statistics don't lie. Love isn't safe for me. *Boundaries, Maggie, boundaries.* I'm a worker bee. A drone.

The nightclub is just wild lights so far. There are no throngs of people and serious clubbing going on. The DJ is playing "Yesterday" by the Beatles, and the lights slow to a sorrowful spin, like a bad sixth grade dance. It's like the party no one showed up for—or the first couple song at the skating rink. The small crowd is waiting for the party to start.

Enter Kathleen.

Kathleen loves to lead in essentially every part of her life, including the fun parts. If there's a conga line, she'll be at the front of it. If there's a marathon, she'll be first out of the starting gate. It's no wonder she can get people to volunteer to be practically drawn and quartered in the name of exercise and health. It's my theory on why she's my friend. Since I'm so difficult as a follower, I think it fills her with a certain purpose in life. If Kathleen can get me to act in my own best interest, she's won.

"I need a partner. Come sing with me," Kathleen says, grabbing me by the hand.

"I think the fluffy canary princess flying across the ship on a zip line is enough entertainment for one day. I want to have some reputation left by the time I speak."

"You're too self-conscious. No one cares." Kathleen waves her hand around the room. "Okay, these ten people care. They're here to have a good time. Let's give the people what they want!"

After some poor kid's harrowing rendition of Def Leppard's "Rock of Ages," Kathleen takes the stage, dragging me up with her. She chooses the rock anthem "Bohemian Rhapsody."

"This is exactly what you need to forget about everything that's going on back home. You just need to breathe deeply and be in the moment." Kathleen puts her hands together in prayer fashion. "Feel the moment. Be present."

It's all very chill until the Queen tune starts.

I know Kathleen has an amazing voice, but I'm still dumbstruck as she starts us off and gives Freddie Mercury a proper tribute. She sings at church, and it's a struggle for the choir director not to play favorites and give her every solo. Kathleen's voice is very soft and full—nothing like her actual presence, except that it's dynamic.

Here's the thing about Queen's "Bohemian Rhapsody." It's the longest song on the planet. It goes on for an eternity. Or it feels like it as I watch the lyrics scroll by. Kathleen is nodding at me relentlessly, as if it's my turn. Thankfully, she keeps singing until we get to the part about killing a man—then suddenly I'm inspired. Go figure.

When we get to the wild rifts and falsetto voices, I'm past caring what I sound like and I'm using the mic as if I were born to entertain. My voice doesn't scare people off or make them scatter, as it's been known to do in church. Rather, as bad as it is, juxtaposed against the beauty of Kathleen's, we attract crowds from the hallway like bees to honey.

As the room starts to fill, Kathleen tries to drown me out. I'm meek, but they have this terrible MC who keeps pushing me to get louder, make more effort. Being the people pleaser that I am, I comply and raise my voice as if I'm Celine Dion and my fans need this for their livelihood. Soon I take over, and Kathleen is standing behind me with her beautiful voice. Drowned out by the ego that I didn't know resided within me but seems desperate to get out and share itself with the world.

The audience is electrified and shouting encouragement. Kathleen is right about one thing. All of my troubles are forgotten. Everyone around me is having so much fun, and it's daunting to think of backing down now. Why should I? I'm on a cruise and I'm having fun. *Fun!* I wonder if I'd ever tried something like this in high school if my world would have looked different. My parents didn't take us on vacations, though, so the chances of karaoke on a cruise ship were nil. Unless it was a museum trip or a library opening, we kept to ourselves in our mausoleum-quiet house.

When we sing the final chorus, the crowd erupts with applause and the line to sing is now huge. I have inspired people—just not in the way I imagined. Apparently there were a lot of bad singers in the audience just waiting for their moment to shine.

When we get back to our seats, Brent has shown up and is beside Haley. It's as if he's the bloodhound of fun, sniffs out a party scenario, and immediately shows up.

I'm still coveting his people skills and wondering what it's like to command a room like him. Karaoke gave me a small taste of life as an extrovert.

"Kathleen, you were awesome. What a voice," Brent says. Then he nods toward me continuously, like one of those bobble-head dolls. "Dr. Maggie. That was . . . an interesting rendition. Freddie Mercury is probably—"

"Rolling over in his grave?" Sam has arrived. While I worried I'd seen the last of him, I'm mortified he chooses to show up at my worst possible moments. Every. Single. Time.

"Well, you can sing," Brent says to Kathleen. "Can you dance? They're having a dance-off in the Legacy Studio. You up for it? It's being judged by someone from *Dancing with the Stars*."

"No way! Love that show." Kathleen is in her element. Constant activity in a competitive state. She was born to rule the seas. "Come with us," she says to me.

"I'm so good at singing, I think I'll stay with my first talent," I say, but the truth is, I want a chance to redeem myself and explain my crazy behavior this afternoon in Sam's suite.

Kathleen is whisked off to the heart-pumping beat of Bon Jovi's "Living on a Prayer." Meanwhile, I can only pray the song itself isn't prophetic. Haley and I are alone with the distinct scent of sandalwood and Grandpa's tobacco room tickling my senses. Sam is now sitting on the wooden stool beside me, and I exhale deeply, calmed by his presence, before remembering how I left him this afternoon. Haley is standing beside him, playing with her hair.

"You didn't come to dinner," I say with as little emotion as I can manage.

"Did you miss me?"

I did, actually. Desperately so. But my analytical, scientific self takes over and I grimace rather than admit the truth.

Haley is pulling out all the stops, and her body language shows she's teetering on the edge of desperation. As she coils her hair around her finger, she brings attention to her voluptuous chest, and her expressions are animated though she's not even speaking. I guess this is what she learned at the parties I was never invited to during college.

When my jealousy dies down and I observe with a scientist's eye, I can see that she'd be a perfect sidekick for Sam. She's educated and filled with a bright outlook on life, and she'd cheer for small heroics like taking the garbage out.

Why can't I be more like Haley?

My mouth betrays me again. "You two should sing something!"

"We should!" Haley picks up the karaoke menu off the counter. "What's your poison? Rock? Pop? Eighties? Country?"

"I guess it would be my musical guilty pleasure," Sam says with a wink.

"Your what?"

"Maggie—Dr. Maguire—has a theory about men and their musical guilty pleasures. I heard her telling Brent about it the day we boarded."

Haley glares at me. "Dare I ask?"

"It's a theory about how forthcoming potential partners can be. Are they willing to admit their bad music taste," I yell over a flat rendition of "Sweet Home Alabama." "Are they willing to admit their embarrassing tastes for the sake of vulnerability."

"Really, Maggie? Do you have to analyze everything?" She rolls her eyes and gives Sam a knowing look as if to say, *Can you believe her?* It's exactly the kind of comment I'd hear in high school, and I'm astonished that Haley could do this to me. Maybe in front of Kathleen, where we're all in on the joke, but this feels like bullying through and through.

"I didn't say it was based on facts. Just a fun game I like to play."

She sighs as if I'm so exasperating. "Maybe Sam wants to sing a song just because he likes it." She grabs his wrist with both of her hands and tugs on him in her cutesy way. "Sing with me, Sam Wellington!"

"I—uh—" Sam tries to protest, but Haley yanks him up to the MC, and before I know it she's riffling through the pages and whispering in Sam's ear. She's animated and attracting all the male attention in the room as she giggles and flirts with Sam.

I was wrong. I'm not okay with watching this process. I'm heading for the exit when Jules and Kyle enter.

"Maggie, did you sing?" Jules asks.

"I did," I say. "Your brother is about to."

"My brother? No way. He would never do karaoke." She turns to Kyle. "Look at my brother! Can you believe it?"

He rubs his chin thoughtfully. "I can't."

They lead me back to the table I just left, and Kyle motions for the waitress. He orders us all club sodas with lime, and I focus on that kindness rather than Haley flirting with Sam as they wait to sing.

When their turn arrives, Haley is giggling and yanking Sam to the stage. The MC asks their names. Haley grasps the mic. "I'm Haley and I'm from Los Angeles, California! And this is Sam from Northern California!"

Haley acts more like she's in a wet T-shirt contest in South Beach than a karaoke show on a cruise ship. What happened to my friend?

"How long have you two known each other?" the MC asks. "Are

221

you here together, or did you meet on this wonderful 'New Year, New You' cruise?"

"We totally met here!" Haley giggles into the microphone. "He was sitting at my dinner table with his sister."

Well, it is a new year and Haley is definitely a "new you" at this point. Gag.

"Those seating arrangements strike again!" The MC gives the audience an inside-joke expression. "All right, ladies and gentlemen, give a big round of encouragement to Haley and Sam!"

The theme song from *Beauty and the Beast* begins, and Haley manages a glimpse at me. The music suddenly stops. I don't know what my expression looked like, but it was clearly not encouraging. Haley is whispering into the DJ's ear, and soon a new tune begins playing: "Endless Love."

When Sam misses his cue, Haley takes over. "My love . . ." she sings while staring longingly into Sam's eyes. Something in me snaps. *She's not exactly subtle, is she?*

When Sam eases into the duet, I feel the same emotion I did when I found out Jake wasn't being straight with me. It's more than simply watching a man like Sam fall prey to Haley's wiles. It's the betrayal that one of my best friends would knowingly pursue a man she saw me kissing. *Who does that?*

When I'd confront Jake, he'd tell me I was imagining things. "You're being paranoid, Maggie, honestly."

We'd be at the movies, and he'd be getting texts and running off to the restroom to answer them. And it was all exactly what I'd feared. Anichka had taken my place, and now Haley is. It's like I'm some kind of starter drug for the men in my life to get serious about another woman.

I drain my club soda and get up from my stool. Brent is now beside me, his hand on my shoulder.

"What are you doing here?" I ask.

"The dance-off doesn't start for fifteen minutes. Kathleen and I were worried about you."

"Worried about me?" *Sheesh. Join the club.* "I'm fine, just watching some sad karaoke."

"I've seen the way you and Sam look at each other."

"Sam?" I stare at his handsome physique as he belts out his endless love for Haley. Whatever I might have felt for him, which I'm sure was only leftover emotion for Jake, has evaporated. "I was only attracted to him because he told me intelligent women can't be truly happy. I wanted to prove him wrong." I shrug. "It's no big deal."

Brent eyes Sam and Haley, then me. "Your friends may buy that story, but I'm a bartender. I could give you a run for your money on your happiness statistics with what I've witnessed over the years. And from what I've seen between you and that guy—well, kingdoms have been built on less."

"Not happy kingdoms, I can assure you." I fiddle with a cocktail napkin. "Why are you really back here?"

"I don't know," he says. "I only know I felt guilty leaving you here with Haley and Sam. When are you going to fight for something you want?"

"I don't know what you mean. I think you're missing your bar. Go dance it off with Kathleen. I'll be fine. I'm resilient, remember? I'm writing a book on that next." I should probably write my next book on how to trap a man. Clearly there's no end to me writing about subjects I haven't a clue about.

As Brent shouts, "Come on, let's blow this Popsicle stand and dance," the music stops abruptly.

The room turns and stares at us, and Brent grabs my hand and leads me from the room.

"Thank you for the drink, Kyle!" I call out behind me as we exit the realm of sorry *American Idol* trials and head toward the poor man's *So You Think You Can Dance.*

Not being able to help myself, I turn and look at Sam and Haley on stage one last time.

"Stop torturing yourself," Brent tells me. "If you want him, go get him."

"Yeah. I don't do that. Haley wants him, Haley can have him. I'm on the rebound, remember?"

"He doesn't want Haley. Shouldn't that matter? For someone advertising the subject of resilience, you sure give up easily."

"I believe if something is meant to be, God will make it happen," I say.

"Like you getting all those degrees? God just cleared a path for you, huh? What about getting your book published? Did you just sail right through that roadblock?"

"Stop psychoanalyzing me."

"Listen, I saw an unhappy woman come on this ship. She fell off my barstool a few times without even drinking, and she hibernates in her room. Then I see her face light up when I'm on deck. Because some dork in a business shirt pays her some attention. You don't have to like it, but I report what I see."

"You need to clean your sunglasses because you aren't seeing clearly at all."

"You're both so darn stubborn. You're going to get off this ship and forget you ever met each other, and that's sad. There could be something there, but you're both so analytical, you'd rather wait for the low-hanging fruit and take what comes to you."

"Are you calling my friend Haley *low-hanging fruit*?"

"Maybe. You can't exactly say she's running the hard-to-get game."

Haley's currently hanging off the shoulder of a very uncomfortable-looking Sam.

"She's able to play hard-to-get until she's interested. Then she comes in like a wrecking ball."

"I've met her type. They have a hard time settling down. Too many options."

"It's a good thing I have so few then."

"That's not what I meant. Besides, if you'd put aside your pride and the illusion that Sam wants your friend there, you'd save yourself a lot of trouble."

"Would I?"

"Let's go dance. You can shake this off—and no, that was not a reference to my secret music crush, Taylor Swift."

"I'd love to see you dance to that song. I may have the DJ play it just for my own entertainment."

"Let's go already. If we don't get there soon, Kathleen will be leading everyone in a round of Zumba and telling them it's the next dance craze."

I want to go dancing. I want to have fun and forget all the dark moments behind me, but I'm having trouble moving forward away from Sam. I owe him an explanation. At the same time, I know it's fine. I did the right thing. My feelings for him will dissipate and I'll go back to what I do best: gather data and make it palatable for the real world.

Brent puts his hand on the small of my back. "Dancing is a good way to get you ready to jump out of a plane tomorrow."

My mouth drops.

"Don't worry. I knew when you ditched me at swing dancing that jumping out of a plane was out of the question. Kathleen's going with me parasailing. She doesn't trust the planes either."

"My next book is supposed to be on resilience. Imagine if I didn't survive jumping out of a plane. Imagine the irony."

Brent stops in the middle of the hallway and turns his blazing blue eyes on me. "You'd better figure out what you really want, Dr. Maguire, because I'll tell you one thing, it's not to put out another bestseller."

Sam and Haley exit the stage together, once again looking like that cake-topper couple. With clarity and utter humiliation, I realize what I truly want. What my passion is.

"I want to be someone's person," I say out loud.

"What did you say?" Brent asks.

"When I grew up, I saw the other parents in the audience watch their kids sing at the holiday show." I move Brent into a small shop so that Sam and Haley don't see us. "Prepare for my sob story. It's a sad one."

"I feel honored," he quips.

"The parents would have their video cameras out, and their faces were so filled with anticipation and joy as they watched their children sing. Or not sing. Occasionally their kids would just stand up there and cry. But not me. Never me. I would perform perfectly as if getting my dinner depended on it."

"Maybe it did," Brent says.

"Those other parents at the Christmas show looked at their children the way I look at gelato. As though they could do no wrong. My parents sat in the same audience, stoic and unmoved. Generally only one would come. The other one was too busy with work."

"That's sad."

I shrug. "It is. But we all have our cross to bear, I suppose. I had serious parents. I guess it's not the worst thing in the world that they considered themselves above a school children's program. They believed in me, so they considered me too advanced to take part in a song and dance show. But I'd beg them to let me because I just wanted to be like the other kids. I wanted my parents to think I was brilliant, and maybe they'd sign me up for dancing or singing lessons, and like DJ on *Full House* I'd have my own fan club. Then my parents would light up when they saw me."

"DJ had a fan club?"

"Keep up. Of course she had a fan club!"

I pull Brent in closer as Haley and Sam pass. She's laughing and clinging to his arm.

"It's going to be rough going back to your room tonight," Brent says.

"It's fine, really it is."

"So how did you get in the show if your parents didn't want you to be in it?"

226

"The teacher would tell them nonparticipation could affect my grade, so they'd allow me to stand up beside the other children on the stage. I wouldn't have a homemade tree costume or hand-sewn dress, but I was a part of it and not alone during that time. I'd be in my street clothes and keep my eyes off my mother, who was scowling in the audience, embarrassed to be part of the charade of childhood."

Brent crosses his arms. "So I'll ask you again. What is it you want? Only you have the power to change things."

"I'm starting to figure that out, but I think I want to have someone on my team, you know? Someone who has my back."

"Since I met you, I've heard a lot of excuses that don't seem to mesh with the Maggie Maguire that I met here. Look in the mirror and see who you are in the world. You've accomplished more than most people will in a lifetime. So I'll ask you again. What are you going to do about it?" Brent cups my face, kisses me on the cheek, and promptly leaves me alone to ponder his question. And why I'm telling my sob story to this poor bartender on a singles' cruise.

There's a man sitting in a chair at the store's entryway. It's obvious he's heard our entire conversation. He's maybe in his early forties, with hair graying at the temples. He's handsome and seems kind, but it hurts me that he's on this cruise alone. He deserves love, doesn't he? *Don't I?*

With clarity, I realize that I don't just want to find someone who looks at me like I look at gelato, and I don't just want a team member. I could get that by working at Target. No, I want the fairy tale, the whole shebang. That kind of pie-in-the-sky, romanticized thinking was never allowed in my household. And it's utterly ridiculous when I can provide easily for myself—but it's my truth, plain and simple. I'm embarrassed by my truth and how basic it is.

"I want the fairy tale," I say to the man.

"The fairy tale doesn't exist," he barks. "You see this place with the pathetic singles and watered-down drinks? That's the future."

"Actually, the data says that it does. It might be rare and only for a special few. I'll have to look into the numbers, but the fairy tale definitely exists."

"All right, lady. Whatever you say."

"I'm a scientist."

"Is that so?" he asks as he drains his drink and puts the empty glass on the store's countertop.

"Yes, that's so. And the fairy tale exists. I'm going to make it happen."

"You do that, darlin'. I'm going to have another drink." He taps his glass.

As I walk out the door, I'm met by Sam in all his J.Crew glory. "Sam!" My mind searches for something meaningful to say so that I don't spout off my own sad-sack story and scare him away—as I've just done to Brent. "I thought you went dancing with Haley."

"This may surprise you, Dr. Maguire, but I'm not much of a dancer."

"It does surprise me. I picture you putting Derek Hough to shame, and I'm sure you have some sequined pants somewhere in your suite."

"Who?"

"Never mind."

He leads me into the breezy hallway. "I need to tell you something. This doesn't excuse my behavior when I first met you, but I hope it will at least offer some insight." He takes my hands in his own. "My wife was an emergency room doctor."

I focus solely on him and the information he's trying to parcel out as soberly as possible. "She was smart." I nod, finally understanding. *And you lost her.* Even though Sam is a completely rational human being, his emotions associate smart women with his life's biggest loss. The human brain is so vastly complicated.

"She passed away after a forty-eight-hour shift. She took something at the hospital to stay awake when they had an influx of patients after a bad highway accident."

I nod slowly.

"Apparently she had an underlying heart condition that was unknown to us, and she went into shock from the medication."

"I'm so sorry, Sam." I grasp his hands tightly, and our eyes lock. There's so much pain in his beautiful gaze, and I want to kiss him tenderly until the pain goes to the far recesses of his thoughts. My own eyes fill with tears as his relate the depth of loss. I've been there. I understand, and I want to tell him so. When Amy died, all I wanted to do was take her place. Being left alone on the planet felt like a huge mistake on God's part. Is that why Sam and I seemed to sense each other's innermost feelings so early after meeting? The pain of my own loss bubbles up and I want to tell him the truth. The whole truth. Not the mask that I've worn for so many years.

"Nothing was ever good enough for my wife," Sam goes on. "It was what I loved about her and also what drove me crazy. She couldn't leave her patients. No matter what her body told her, she kept forcing herself to go harder and faster. I couldn't fix that in her and get her to live with margins. I couldn't make it better. I guess that's when faith became real to me. When I discovered any control I had was nothing but a mirage."

My heart grieves with him. I can't make things better either, and I know the kind of powerlessness he feels. It's a despair straight to the depths of one's soul, and yet God expects us to go on. "We don't see trying to make things better as pride, but I suppose that's what it is. We're not God. We can't fix everything."

He stares off into the distance. "The day I met you in the lobby was the two-year anniversary of the day I lost her. My sister wanted me out of the house so that I wouldn't ruminate. Something about you struck me the minute I saw you—well, your author picture, actually. Some similarity that I can't pinpoint. It's not looks. You don't look anything like Isabella."

"Isabella." I say the beautiful name carefully and with the utmost respect. I don't know what comes over me, but I wrap my arms around him and rest my ear against his chest. I listen to the steady beat of his heart. His arms embrace me tightly, and the music and chattering surrounding us fall away. I want to stay here forever, where the world is slow and steady and nothing comes between us.

He whispers in my ear, "I don't know why you're not motivated anymore to finish this contract, but I can't fix that either."

I pull back. "I don't expect you to fix it. You're not responsible for someone else's happiness."

"That"—he points at me—"is what I came to tell you. I didn't know why I was dragged on this barge until I saw you. You be you, Dr. Maggie Maguire. Whatever that is. If it's dangling in a princess costume, you do it. Life is short and this is the only one you've got. Jake was a fool, and it's about time you realized that and let it go."

"I do realize that." I realized it the moment Sam kissed me and I felt passion like I'd never known in this lifetime—from a simple kiss.

"Your mother is diabolical, and none of that should matter to you making your dreams come true."

"My mother wasn't always like that, she—" For the first time in decades, I'm tempted to tell someone about my sister. About Amy. The name I couldn't mention in my home any longer. The mere mention of her existence would destroy my parents, and I'd learned this truth early. I couldn't bear to cause them any more pain, so I'd buckled and done what was expected of me. But I'm broken now. The secret is getting harder and harder to keep. It keeps rising up like a bobber in the water.

"Write the book, don't write the book. I came to tell you that I expect nothing of you, other than you making yourself happy so you know the joy you write about. It's not against the rules to make yourself happy. Fix your eyes on Jesus, the author and perfecter of your faith."

Even without the Bible, I can tell Sam is a man of God. He has that assurance and kindness about him, even when speaking words that aren't necessarily sprinkled with grace.

I suppose that's why Sam confounds me. He's lost what he loved too, but he hasn't walked away from God or hidden his pain away like I have. Everything about Sam feels so authentic.

"No one is asking you to be a martyr. Anyway, I'm sorry I made you feel nervous or judged this afternoon. That wasn't my intention. This is your life. Go and live it abundantly." Sam turns on his heel.

"Wait, where are you going?"

But Sam just keeps walking away from me with that long, concentrated stride of his. How could he share such an intimate moment with me and express so eloquently what I felt in my heart, then simply walk away?

The data is starting to suggest that I repel people—especially if they're of the male variety.

21

Happy people don't tell everyone their dreams. They make them happen.

The Science of Bliss by Dr. Margaret K. Maguire

THE SUITE IS COMPLETELY EMPTY when I return from a busted night of fun. Haley and Kathleen are making the most of their free cruise and clearly dancing the night away, and I'm grateful for the alone time. Brent's question, "What are you going to do about it?" haunts me. I pick up the brand-new MacBook and see my future as clearly as if Kathleen had made a prophecy. I'm going to finish what I started in these two months of my blissful sabbatical.

I want my happily ever after. And if God isn't going to give it to me, I'm going to write it myself. The only thing that got more disdain than the television in my household when I was growing up was the forbidden romance novel. There's a wee bit of rebellion in my latest idea.

As my fingers touch the keyboard and I look over my PowerPoint for my speech, my mind flutters back to Sam's kiss, his embrace, and his departure for the bluer waters of Haley Adams. In my story, the nerd girl wins, not the pretty girl who bats her eyelashes at a fella. That is so cliché, *so easy*. But a hero who sweeps a girl out of the lab and off her feet, who whisks her past her condescending parents? That's the real hero. That's what future happily ever afters need on their channels: proof that occasionally the intellectual girl meets her hero and the pretty girl runs along and waits for the next ship to come by.

I only have this one life. I've given enough of it to my parents' dream for me and I've succeeded. Or have I? I've made someone else's fantasy come to life while I remain wholly unfulfilled.

I open Dropbox to find my screenplay I've been working on for the last two months. Now that I've met Sam Wellington and Brent Spoils, I know exactly what's missing from it.

No one can write my story but me. And it's time to write my happy ending. Sure, I'm a weirdo. What data jockey isn't? But Anichka is a weirdo too. She hangs from scarves for a living. I could argue that isn't even a real job and that her weirdness factor is off the charts. The only way she gets away with her brand of oddball is by being beautiful. In today's age, that seems wrong, harkening back to a time when a husband gave more cows for a gorgeous wife.

Beauty wipes out a lot of oddball, and it seems wholly unfair. Like life is stacked against you. I try to reason that Anichka's life isn't actually such a blessing. I mean, after all, I'd escaped Jake. She's stuck with him. Who really won in that scenario?

The program I wrote my books in has an option for screenplays. I refresh my Dropbox account and open it to the beginning of my story. The happy ending I've always wanted feels something like being alone on a deck in the sea breeze with a man who makes me feel like Sam does. Valued, cherished, and worth listening to, not because of my intellect or data, but because I exist. Now I know what to write.

THE SCIENCE OF LOVE

Maggie K. Maguire, PhD
Draft

FADE IN

INT. UNIVERSITY LAB—DAY
Seven rows of white tables, each with a
computer, are featured with a shaft of
morning sunlight streaming through the wall
of windows. Several people in lab coats are
reading from their computers.

DRIFT OVER to white room with focus group
answering questions. DRIFT to a scuffed-up
desk separated from the rest, where a kitten
calendar and several binders are lined up
haphazardly against the wall. PAN to a mess of
scribbled notes on the desk. The desk cannot
be seen under the mess.

Groans emerge and hands riffle through the
papers on the desk.

CLEMENTINE
Where is it? It has to be here!

She swipes her arm across the desk and clears
everything onto the floor. DRIFT to floor and
loose papers surrounding the desk. Hushed
lab comes alive as people begin to chatter
nervously.

INT. LAB MANAGER'S OFFICE
Strange sounds emerge from under the desk, then
two hands appear, plastered to the carpet. Out
crawls Clementine, her makeup askew, her shirt
wrinkled, and her overall look disheveled.

CLEMENTINE
I thought I'd met someone and this would be
my last submission to the *Psych Journal*. But
the love of my life has left and everything is
gone! Gone! My work . . .

As I read over my screenplay and say the dialogue out loud, I'm annoyed by the trill of my cell phone. The work emboldens me. When I see it's my boss, I don't panic or ignore the call. I answer it as though I'm back to being an actual adult. "Dr. Maggie Maguire speaking."

"Dr. Maguire, it's Dr. Fleece. It's so nice of you to pick up the phone."

I don't bother to give an excuse.

"I suppose you know why I'm calling."

"I've heard rumors."

"All of the department heads are here with me now. So you're on speakerphone. This was a good day for you to pick up our call. I've been holding off on a decision until we reached you. If we didn't today, we were going to have to take steps toward your removal."

"Hello, everyone. I miss you."

There are a few unintelligible murmurs, as if no one wants to claim to miss me—in case I'm on the chopping block.

Dr. Fleece continues in her lecture mode, void of any human feelings. "As you know, Dr. Maguire, Jake Stone has been suspended from our department pending a police investigation into why he used your credentials to gain access to the physics department."

I have no idea what Jake would want with the physics department. Does he even know what physics is? Other than the invisible law of motion that keeps his new wife twirling in the air?

"It's come to our attention that your sabbatical, which was very ill timed indeed, may be part of this illegal scenario. The department suggests that you too be suspended from your position until the investigation is complete. I had defended you until your recent lack of concern over this matter."

"In my defense, I'm on a cruise ship." As soon as I say it, I realize how dumb it sounds. *I'm sunning myself on the deck of a singles' cruise—you get the picture.*

"Now is not the time, Dr. Maguire."

"I understand." But I don't. I've never failed at anything in my life, and I'm being let go. Temporarily or permanently, it hardly matters. I hadn't done my best and I deserve this, but some part of me must have wanted it, because I can't bring myself to see it as anything but God's will.

It's appropriate that I'm at sea. My life is literally floating without a destination. Surprisingly, I don't care as much as I probably should. I want to work on my screenplay. I want to finish something that has nothing to do with reading through data and reporting on other people's happiness rather than finding my own.

"Please call me when you return to California so that we can discuss the investigation. I'm quite certain you'll have phone calls waiting for you from the campus police department."

"Thank you, Dr. Fleece. I know this has burdened you, and I'm sorry for that. When—" I stop and correct myself. "*If* you choose for me to return, I'll do my utmost to finalize the grant and get the department the money it deserves."

"Yes, Dr. Maguire, we are looking forward to your next book being as successful as the last. I'm sure your publicist passed that on for us."

"Just in case you were wondering, there was a fire on board the ship, so my talk about the last book has been rescheduled. The ship seems genuinely excited to hear me speak, so I'll be sure to put in a plug for the university."

"Please don't."

I hear a few groans in the background and wonder which of my colleagues has turned on me without ample proof. You'd think a science department would look to the data rather than believe the first rumor of my career demise. Okay, maybe it's the second rumor. I don't think I got many brownie points for bringing Jake into the department.

"Like I said." Dr. Fleece gives an exasperated sigh. "Call us when you return. We'll look forward to discussing your future here at the university." She clicks off the line.

There's a flurry of chaos as the stateroom door opens to Haley and Kathleen giggling and shouting wildly. Both of them are carrying their shoes in their hands and dance into the room as if they've had too much to drink.

I slam my laptop shut. "Wow, sounds like a fun night. Have you two been drinking?"

"Of course not. This is what fun sounds like, Maggie. You should have some!" Kathleen shouts.

"Shh. You two must have blown your ears out in the dance hall."

"You were working?" Haley runs over to me and slams herself onto the couch. "If you're not going to take advantage of the cruise, that's the best thing you could be doing. This speech is going to go so well, you're going to—"

"Wait a minute." Kathleen, ever the buzzkill, walks over to my computer. "Let me see what you're doing."

"I'm an adult, Kathleen. Are you really going to check my work like my mother used to do with my homework?"

"Listen, I know that people say they did fifteen reps with a weight set when they really did only five or so. People lie to protect themselves all the time. No judgment, I just want to see that you've got the files open to your data. Of if you're scanning the Kardashians' every move."

"Yeah, I care what the Kardashians are up to." I yank my computer tightly to my chest. "No. I don't need to prove myself."

"You spent two months on a couch," Haley says. "I agree with Kathleen. I think you need to prove yourself."

"You girls are my best friends. You don't trust me?"

"In a word, no." Kathleen wrestles the computer out of my hands and opens it. Unfortunately for me, it hasn't been off long enough to need a password, and my screenplay in all its glory is open to page 83. "What is this?"

"Is that a screenplay?" Haley looks at me as if I've betrayed her last vestige of faith in me. "You're writing a screenplay now? What's next? Giving up real work for your art?"

"I'm not giving up anything. Give me my computer back." I take it from Kathleen. "I've been dismissed from my position at the university until the investigation into Jake is over. You both told me I needed a hobby. Well, I found one on my sofa."

"What did Jake steal?"

"I don't know. They wouldn't tell me, but I'd guess he was stealing the copper wire they use for conductivity and selling it on the black market."

"Take a picture of your sorry apartment. They'll know you had nothing to do with it," Kathleen says.

"I'm lucky they don't put me on a sea plane and send me back tomorrow to answer questions. They did ask me not to mention the university in my speech."

Kathleen and Haley exchange a glance.

"It will be fine," I assure them.

"This is what you've been doing?" Haley asks. "Working on a screenplay? I knew you couldn't just be watching those movies the whole time. I've never seen you sit still for longer than five minutes."

"I watched a lot of movies. It was research. All those dog-eared novels I read as a kid came back to haunt me. I never knew screenwriting was an ambition until I stopped striving for five minutes."

"If this is what you're going to work on, I'm confiscating this computer."

"Don't be childish." I feel my anxiety starting to rise as I think of my manuscript in the hands of others.

"This is a fine hobby. I'm glad you found yourself a hobby besides borrowing cats. This is a step in the right direction, but why can't you work on the outline for your new book? Is it too much to ask that you actually do something for the jobs that pay you?"

"Hey, first of all, Neon loves me. I feed him fresh salmon. His owner buys that stuff off the highest grocery store shelves. Cheapest stuff you can buy. Then she leaves it outside for the raccoons to eat. Vile woman. The raccoons could attack Neon!"

"Well, we can be happy Maggie hasn't started feeding the neighborhood raccoons," Kathleen says sarcastically.

"Yet," Haley adds. "You're welcome to work on this screenplay when you get home, but no more escapism into false worlds and false realities."

I love how she says this, like she hasn't created my terrible reality that I'm currently trying to escape from on this crazy ship. "Did you have a nice time with Sam?"

Her mood instantly lightens. "Oh my goodness, we had a blast. Didn't we, Kathleen?"

Kathleen gets my question on a deeper level and stares mournfully at me. "We did have a good time, but we missed you," she answers without emotion.

"You wouldn't think so, but Sam can really dance when he gets going," Haley says, still in her own fog of romantic bliss. "I thought he'd have that whole white-man shuffle going on—you know, where he bites his bottom lip?" She slaps her knee like we're all sharing in her joke. "But he has the moves!"

Kathleen shakes her head. "He really can't dance. I think you were blinded by the out-of-body experience you seemed to have in trying to teach the dab to us. The guy has white-boy disease to the nth degree—he was like an arthritic monkey. I almost felt sorry for him. You wouldn't have enjoyed yourself, Maggie."

I smile at Kathleen. *It's okay*, I mouth, but the concept of Sam as an arthritic monkey dancing to hip-hop makes me laugh out loud.

"Brent was too stiff as well. He can't get around those monstrous muscles of his to move well. His arms are so big, they'll barely go down to his sides, so he looked like he was doing the sprinkler the entire time." Kathleen imitates Brent's dance moves. "I'm telling you, they were horrific, and we got the best dancers on the ship. If this is the state of the singles' club scene, we are all doomed. The human race is doomed."

"It's the state of the singles' scene on a cruise ship. It's a small sample. I have faith there are soul mates out there for each of us, and I don't really care if mine can dance. It would probably be better if he didn't."

"Okay, princess," Kathleen says. "That's enough romance writing for the day. Put that computer away."

"You told me to get a hobby and I got one."

"A hobby that gets you outside that head of yours. Not this. This is just more escapism."

"I don't know what to tell you. It seems like you can't be happy no matter what I do, so I'm going to take Sam's advice and make myself happy. First I work too hard, then I don't work enough. I mean, do you want my Google calendar to make me a schedule?"

"Sam's advice?" Haley's ears perk up. "When did Sam give you advice?"

"We talked." I don't give her any further information. It feels like it would be breaking an intimate confidence.

The idea of Sam dancing with Haley after the moment we shared in each other's arms on the breezy deck—well, Sam dancing with anyone, really—turns my stomach into a ball of knots. I have to remind myself what the Bible says about jealousy and envy, because I've got them in spades. Pretty sure that isn't God's ideal, and if I ever want to get back to church, I need to start being who I used to be.

22

Other people cannot be responsible for your happiness, and vice versa. Own your own life and take responsibility for what makes you happy in this lifetime.

The Science of Bliss by Dr. Margaret K. Maguire

WHERE DOES ONE GO WHEN FAILURE invades every aspect of her life? If I follow my own advice, well, there's nowhere to go but up, and I've gone my own way long enough. Jake checked off all the boxes. He wasn't religious when we first met, nor did he believe in any higher power, which my parents loved. And I told myself it didn't matter. We both believed in science. Wasn't that enough? I'll never know if he truly believed, but he'd marked the territory of our church and taken that from me. There's no one to blame in this scenario but me, and that's painful. It's so much more pleasurable to blame other people and be a victim—but even my best friends have tired of that routine.

Okay, God, have at it. I've done nothing to improve my situation, no matter how much escape I've tried. It's all you now. All you. No one can save me but you. Not a job, not a man, not my friends. It's all you.

It's a pathetic prayer, but I suppose God knows that my brain

241

isn't running at full capacity. Failure feels better at the beach, where one can look out across the distance and know that there has to be more. I simply have to put one foot in front of the other until I find the path again.

Getting off the ship for our beach excursion feels like getting out of prison. I'm not great at forced imprisonment, even with fantastic food and a fancy ball at the end of it. I'm still huddled with the masses with nowhere to get away and recharge. Our little gathering of awkward acquaintances includes Jules (for all intents and purposes, my only boss at the moment), her husband Kyle, Brent and Kathleen—who are leaving us for the parasailing excursion—and Haley and Sam.

Let me paraphrase. That's Kyle and Jules, Brent and Kathleen, Haley and Sam, and me. Well, there's Arvin the butler. So one could argue that my apparent date, Arvin, is the best dressed of this crew. Except Sam looks incredible in his navy shorts with white ship wheels. They don't look like something he'd pick himself, so I'm assuming that when his sister kidnapped him, she also made some fashion choices. He's got deck shoes on and a marl-gray, long-sleeve linen sweater pushed up to the elbows. He looks like he's running crew for an elitist East Coast university, if I'm honest. It's a look that works on him though, and he pulls it off as manly and sexy.

It's daunting to be on the beautiful, romantic coastline as an extra, but I grip my notebook containing my rom-com screenplay and remind myself this is the perfect place to finish my story. While the girls may have confiscated my computer this fine day in the dry heat of the Mexican sun, they can't take my notebook from me. I wrote "Travel Journal" on the cover so they have no reason to read anything I've written within the pages. As far as they're concerned, my screenplay is a simple play-by-play of my cruise journey thus far.

As I follow the trail of my group, the white-sand beach sizzles the bottom of my toes, even with flip-flops on. The water is a tranquil aqua and clear all the way to the floor of the sea. Unlike California, the tide is subtle, lapping gently toward the shore like a clear glass lake.

Sam hasn't spoken to me since he told me what happened to his wife—what seemingly made him avoid intellectuals. Who can blame him? I overanalyze everything, like why the sand here is white and slick under my feet, while at home it's much more gravelly and brown.

I mean, who cares, right?

Meanwhile, Haley and Kathleen have tossed their cover-ups with abandon and run into the ocean, where they are laughing and trying to dunk each other. Kyle and Jules are staring into each other's eyes like newlyweds. And I have my screenplay, the sum total of romance in my life presently.

Arvin places all of the beach chairs out for our group. He lays a towel over each chair and provides a few bottles of sunscreen. Someone else pours a metal tub full of ice and puts in bottles of drinking water. It's the perfect setup for a beach-read day.

While Kathleen and Haley frolic in the ocean, Sam comes and sits beside me. "Is this seat taken?"

"There wouldn't be a seat if it weren't for your butler. Feel free. It seems as though I'm invading your party, not the other way around."

"There would be no party were it not for the great Dr. Maggie Maguire speaking tour."

"Are you making fun of me?"

"Again with the suspicion!" he says. "I wonder what would have happened had we met under better circumstances. You wouldn't question everything I said in jest, for one thing."

"I might. It's a bad habit I've developed. Nothing to do with you, really."

"So what if we *had* met under better circumstances?"

"Better circumstances than a singles' cruise to a paradise beach, you mean? What would that look like? The perfect meeting."

"A man and a woman without so much baggage on one small trip, I imagine. You see me across a crowded room, I see you. I don't say anything stupid and we enjoy one another's company."

"That's so normal! Shockingly so." I'm thinking I should write that down in my notebook. "I suppose it would have helped if my best friend wasn't a gorgeous redhead with a crush."

"I didn't kiss the redhead." Sam sounds irritated. "I kissed *you*."

"That was the emotion talking. We were both frightened after the fire, and there was so much at stake with your sister being the first female president at BrainLit."

"You're such a know-it-all, Maggie. You claim to know why I kissed you?"

"It was a crazy day. So much chaos, the smoke, the darkness—"

"That's why you think I kissed you?" He shakes his head and looks off over the water before turning back to me. "My kiss didn't tell you there was more to it than getting caught up in a situation? I like to think I brought my A-game to that kiss because it meant something to me. You're the first woman I've kissed since—well, you know . . ."

"Really, that's an honor, Sam. I don't take that lightly, but it's all right if you were testing the waters." I shrug.

Sam's kiss had so much passion in it, I felt utterly destroyed by it, like I'd never settle for anything less in my lifetime. I hadn't known I could feel such peace and explosive energy simultaneously in a mere kiss. But so much passed between us—a surge of emotions and connections—and I knew one thing, standing beneath the shadow of Sam Wellington. I wanted him to kiss me again. More than I wanted a fellowship at NYU under Dr. Hamilton, more than I wanted my screenplay made into a movie, more than I wanted to go home and prove my innocence at the university.

How did I, this left-brain, rational-thinking scientist, turn into the teenage girl of my youth who dog-eared pages in my forbidden romance novels? It was the one vice my parents never caught wind of, and I embraced my rebellion wholeheartedly. The same way I do everything else in life. I just never expected it to happen in real life. Sam makes me want to believe anything is possible.

"You should strip down and go in the ocean with your friends," Sam says.

I narrow my eyes.

"That didn't come out right. I meant, you should go have fun. You don't want to sit on the beach with me and my boring self."

I do. I really do. "I don't go in the water."

"What do you mean? It's like a clear Caribbean bathtub out there."

"I don't do water."

"Do you swim?"

"Not very well."

"I'll spot you. Let's go." He reaches for my hand.

"No, really. I don't like the water." My pulse starts to quicken, and I can feel the beads of sweat gathering on my forehead.

"All right. No pressure. I thought you might like to cool off, is all." Sam kicks off his Sperrys so his bare feet are next to mine. He touches my toes with his own until I meet his eyes again. He continues to play footsie with me in the sand, and his skin against mine sends a surge of electricity through my veins.

It's chemistry. Simple pheromones and chemistry. It means nothing.

"Did you know pheromones are species-specific? An iguana pheromone will only stir another iguana." *Just shut up now.*

Sam offers that confused look that I'm used to by now. "Is that so?" I nod.

"The redhead—Haley—is sweet. She's smart, she's fun, and she's beautiful."

Oh my heart.

"But she's not you, Maggie Maguire. I find myself wanting to know everything about you. What kind of food you like to eat. What you want to do on the weekends. If you wear socks to bed. If you ever trade gelato for popcorn during a movie. Why you bring up the pheromones of iguanas in normal conversation."

My head begins to spin and I'm weak at his words. "Don't tease me, Sam. I've always been a sucker for words, and if this is some kind of test, I've failed." I run my hands through the silky curls at the nape of his neck. "Haley never wanted to be me, that much I can say with certainty." I crack a joke rather than face him and look directly at those brown, soulful eyes. Time has passed while I was lost in conversation, mostly the invisible communication that passed silently between us. "Haley can have any man she wants, and she appears to have chosen."

"Has this man been rendered helpless under Haley's spell, or does he have a choice in the matter?"

"No one has a choice with Haley. She gets what she wants."

"You must find me awfully weak to think I don't know my own mind."

When I finally look around me again, Brent and Kathleen are on the dock in the distance, getting strapped into parasailing gear and ready to take to the skies. Jules and Kyle are walking hand in hand up the crowded stretch of public beach. And Haley . . . Haley is missing.

While I can't see Haley, I know she must be on her way back, and I'm panicked as I check around for her. She'll accuse me once again of trying to steal her man. As if I could do that. She'll know that I didn't keep my promise and that my desire for Sam has taken on a life of its own. Sam makes me weak in the knees and soft in the brain, but not in the same way Jake did. It's not the debilitating, blindsided, ignorant way I acted toward a man who couldn't love anyone but himself.

I give myself a little grace in that Jake Stone felt natural to me. He felt like my parents. *I'll love you if . . . I'll love you when . . .*

In contrast, Sam's presence pacifies me. It offers me the notion that I don't have to dance for his affection or win at everything to be worthy of attention. I simply have to *be*, and that feels so overwhelmingly amazing and . . . violently uncomfortable. I want to run from it, but the peace I have is like what I felt in church when worshipping. I feel connected, cherished, and wholly me—that I am enough. If I never see Sam again, he's gifted me with that knowledge that love doesn't have to hurt.

"Maggie, did you hear me?"

"I didn't," I say, frantically searching the beach for Haley. "Is Haley all right? She got out of the water, right?"

"Forget about Haley for a minute. I don't want to end what's between us. I want to see you after this cruise."

I shake my head. "That's not possible."

"I knew the moment I saw you that you were the one for me. I've only ever felt that one other time in my life."

"No, I'm not. You're just moved because you felt something for someone else after your wife. I'm just the first, the bad pancake. You throw this one out and then the next one is the good pancake. She's your forever pancake."

"I know what I feel, Maggie. It irritated me that I'd fall for a woman smarter than me again, and when you stirred me in the lobby, that's what came out." Sam brushed his hand along my cheek. "You moved me in a way I haven't felt since the first time I laid eyes on Isabella. My anger came out because I was repeating history. It annoyed me that I couldn't fall for a nice, unsuspecting, cookie-making, casserole-carrying woman from church."

"What makes you think I can't make a casserole?" I cross my arms and stand to run away from him. He gets up and chases me. I turn back. "Does anyone actually like casseroles? I can grill a mean steak."

"I'll bet you can." He wraps his arms around me and lifts me off the ground. He cradles me as though I weigh nothing, the same way he'd done after the fire. He looks me straight in the eyes, and the emotions I feel melt my heart. If I died this very moment, I'd have lived a full life. Nothing Jake has done, nothing my parents have said to me, nothing matters. For that brief moment, I feel the unconditional love I've craved, no matter how short-lived and impossible it is.

Haley is standing beside us, her lithe body dripping with ocean water. My screenplay is in her wet hand. She pulls her hair back and squeezes the excess drops from it. She stands waiting, as if I'm holding her place in line and I can move on now. I put my legs down and release my hold on Sam.

She points to a place in my so-called travel journal. "'Haley, I'm sorry. It's Maggie. It's always been Maggie,'" she reads.

I shake with terror as I hear my utterly ridiculous words read back to me.

"What is this?" Haley shakes the notebook. I realize now that she must have taken it when Sam and I were talking.

"It's nothing."

"'It's always been Maggie'? Are you smoking something on this beach? Why are you writing this drivel? I thought this was your travel journal. You've got a science book to write and you're still living in that fantasy world of yours."

Sam's mouth is agape, and I'm mortified to be back in reality. The beach no longer has the tranquil sheen that I planned in my screenplay.

"Don't read any more, Haley. Please don't. It's just a hobby. I'm not good with names, so I used ours."

Haley's face is drained of color, and she looks at Sam and then back at me.

"Please," I mutter. "It's just a story. Fiction."

"Did this really happen?" She shakes the notebook at me.

"No, I told you, I'm writing a screenplay. That's just the end that I created. I was going to finish it while you and Kathleen were in the water. You took my computer, so I brought that notepad and thought I'd finish it here on the beach."

"You came to the beach to write this and not the book for Jules? Have you missed everything Kathleen and I have done for you to get your career back up and running?"

"I can't write that book without all the data in front of me. I need two screens and my algorithms. This was simply for fun."

"I give up, Maggie. You're like an addict. I can't help you if you don't want to help yourself, and you clearly don't want to help yourself."

"What else was I supposed to do while my best friends were on a

248

double date with the only people I know on this ship? You don't think that was difficult, to be the odd woman out yet again?"

"I thought you enjoyed being the odd woman out. You seem to relish the title." She opens the notebook again. "You used my name. You used Sam's name!" She keeps reading, though I try desperately to grab the notebook from her grip.

"Haley, please. That's like reading my diary. It's not ready for public consumption. I'm going to get it edited by a professional. And, of course, change the names."

"My name is in it, seems like I'm entitled to read it. As is Sam."

I'm horrified and my expression must show it. "I was going to change the names. Sam . . ." My eyes plead with him not to look. "They're just markers so I can remember to find and replace them. That's all. I needed an ending, and it was just easier with the two of you here to write your names until I got back to my computer and input everything in the screenplay."

"Sam is your hero?"

"Just his name." This is more mortifying than anything I've gone through with Jake or the university, because I realize that Sam matters to me. What he thinks about me matters. It's his unconditional acceptance of me when everyone else is pushing me to go back to the life I had. Sure, his words said that he didn't want another intellectual in his life, but his actions were completely different. His actions pursued me, coddled me, took care of and protected me.

"This is how you feel?" Haley asks. "You think I'm flirtatious with everyone? You like Sam and think he's off-limits because I forced you to make a demented promise?"

Didn't I though? "It's fiction, I've told you. Now give me my notebook. I want to go back to the ship."

"It's fiction? Where your man-eating, redheaded best friend is surreptitiously dumped by a six-foot-two hero and the science professor runs off with him? Oh, that's fiction all right."

"Sam is taller than six foot two. Haley, please. I'm not that creative.

I used what was in front of me, and yes, I wrote myself a happily ever after. Is that so wrong? Jane Austen did it!"

"You are no Jane Austen. You realize your fictional story is exactly what happened to my mother," Haley accuses. "She was left for a younger PhD candidate to live out her golden years alone while my dad raised someone else's kid."

"None of that is in there. You're projecting."

"Don't use your fancy psychology words with me."

"I swear, I didn't even think about your mother and father."

"Does this make you feel good about yourself?"

"Of course not, but it's not about your mother. It's a story."

"This is why everything in your life has gone bad, Maggie. I don't even know who you are anymore. But I know that my former best friend would not take what matters to me and plot it out as you've so brilliantly done here. My Maggie wouldn't hurt anyone she loved by using their story for romance fodder."

For the first time, I'm angry. Truly angry that my friends have hijacked my life under the guise of helping me. Maybe I didn't want their help—did that ever occur to them?

"No!" I shout. "Because that Maggie always did what was right for other people, no matter how much it cost me. I gave everyone what they wanted to the point where it destroyed the person I was created to be. I didn't even know what I wanted anymore. It was so convoluted with what other people said. 'This is best for you, Maggie.' 'No, over here. This is the path to take.'" I raise my hands in the air. "But I've had time to think. God doesn't want that for me. God doesn't ask me to be a martyr for everyone else. He did that. He died on the cross so that I don't have to. Do you know why I'm not happy, Haley? Do you know why I've found the answer for everyone else's happiness, but I've been miserable?"

"Because you didn't steal what you wanted?"

"No, because I didn't even know what I wanted."

"And now you do? It just happens to be a guy who said you were exactly the type of woman he avoided? That's not a red flag to you? Or is that why you're interested? Because he's a challenge?"

"I never said that, actually," Sam tells Haley.

"You did. You said that intelligent women are incapable of true happiness. I heard you, Sam."

"That was my own wounded pride speaking. Obviously I didn't mean it. Maggie knows I didn't mean it." He takes my hand, and it's as if Haley disappears from my view. "You know I didn't mean it, right?"

I nod. "I know."

"That doesn't explain this." Haley waves my notebook in the wind. "You have real work due. Your job is gone, at least temporarily, and no hero on a white horse is coming to rescue you. Do you get that? Do you get that Kathleen and I have given up our week to try to get you back on track? I sent your work to Dr. Hamilton and an application to NYU while you sat around and watched television."

"You did that?" I feel the sting of tears starting. "You sent Dr. Hamilton my stuff?"

"Maggie, I love you. We love you. I'm sorry you felt like you didn't know what you wanted and we were forcing you into something that may have been wrong for you. I only did those things because I thought that was what you wanted, and I wanted you to be happy again. You were always such a beacon of light, always up, always the happy one. We didn't recognize you and it scared us."

"I thought it was what I wanted too. I can't blame you for that. But somewhere along the line, the work stopped being fulfilling, and I needed a break to figure it all out."

"I get it. Maybe I thought too much about my publicity business and my motives weren't pure."

"Incidentally, I never thought that Prince Charming was coming to rescue me. I'm perfectly capable of rescuing myself." I rake my fingers through my tangled beach hair. "Is it so wrong that I might want to share my life with someone else?"

Haley turns toward Sam and then smiles coyly at me. "So you're angry with me for grabbing you off that sofa like the larva you'd become?"

Then it dawns on me. Haley doesn't get that life isn't about being the prettiest, flirtiest princess who can choose from among her suitors like she's starring in her own season of *The Bachelorette*.

My own journey has been a little more rugged. It's been peppered with people who want to tell me what's best for me without actually asking for my input. The only common denominator between all those controlling people is me. And they no longer get a vote. I may be single, unemployed, and on my mother's spite list, but I know now what I *don't* want in my life—and I suppose when you're starting over, that's half the battle in creating a new life.

23

KATHLEEN AND BRENT ARE STILL flying behind a motorboat when I get back onto the ship and onto the deck. I can hear them screaming and waving at the passengers on the ship and having the time of their life. I smile at Kathleen's love of adrenaline—if it weren't for her, I'd never have half my life experiences. She made me try ice climbing (um, no), Rollerblading (not bad), fly-fishing, and horse dressage—and what I learned from the sum of those experiences is that some people are born outdoorsmen and some aren't.

The idea of Haley reading my notebook has me obsessing. Did she show Sam? Did they flip through the pages together? I try to account for how much time they had together before he came back to me. I picture them laughing at my sophomoric Cinderella dreams that I had scribbled in the pages. The ridiculous scenario I wrote . . . Sam literally sweeping me off my feet in the sand. The smallest detail of his swirled-chocolate brown eyes, the freckle on his lip, the tiny scar across the bridge of his nose.

There's no denying Sam's identification in the story. It's as though I painted him in oil. I could just die of mortification at the thought of the two of them standing huddled together, sharing a laugh over my teenage diary–like imagination. I clamp my eyes shut, praying for the plaguing thoughts to disappear. I did all the right things when it came to Sam and Haley, but my heart didn't follow suit.

I plot out my remaining days on board the ship so that I never have to face Sam Wellington again. I could skip dinner for the rest of the cruise. I figure he'll have enough decency not to attend my speech, and at the costume ball I can trade in my Belle costume and go as something that requires a mask. Or a paper bag. Secretly, I hope he attends the costume ball in all his finery. I don't know why I relish seeing him one last time, but I want his handsome face solidified in my memory bank. If for no other reason than because he taught me to feel again.

The only thing that haunts me now is a future where he and Haley continue to have a romantic relationship. If this isn't a fly-by-night shipboard romance, my entire plot will have to change. Then I'll have to throw myself on the mercy of Dr. Hamilton at NYU and get to the other side of the country as soon as possible. Maybe even settle for some junior college in North Dakota if necessary.

I don't believe Haley can make a man like Sam happy. I'm biased. I'm jealous. But I stand by my data. Sam needs more than a pretty face. Haley could be what he needs, if she'd let a man see her true character, but I have yet to see that happen. She plays a role and men fall at her feet. That's the way it works. Sam needs more.

Hours pass before Haley and Kathleen enter the room, as somberly as if they're attending a wake. The silence is overwhelmingly awkward, and the room is sucked dry of its peaceful feeling. Three best friends since college and no one has a thing to say to one another.

Haley finally tosses my notebook on the sofa. "There's your notebook."

I can't even reply. A single tear drops from my eye.

"Don't give me those puppy-dog eyes. I thought this was what you wanted, Maggie. To be a successful author again. I didn't know that your youthful days of fanciful romance were filling up your head. I mean, how much money is there in writing screenplays these days? You couldn't even feed that borrowed cat of yours, most likely."

"It doesn't matter how much money is in it. It was something I wanted to do, and I don't understand why you can't support my dreams for once."

"I did support your dream. Kathleen and I both did, but we didn't know this was your dream. You sprang it on us like a bad check."

"You don't understand, Haley. You think you do, but you have no idea."

"I know that you've known me for years but you sided with some random guy—like I wasn't good enough for him."

I swallow the lump in my throat.

"That's what you thought, isn't it? That Sam was too good for me?"

"No. I thought he was wrong for you. There's a difference."

"Is there?" Haley's green eyes are narrowed like a crouching feline's.

It's never occurred to me how utterly spoiled Haley can be when she doesn't get her way. I suppose she's gotten her way most of the time since I've known her, but when she doesn't, she turns into a screaming toddler.

"I didn't think you understood what Sam has been through."

"But you do, I suppose."

"I'm not going to argue over a man, Haley. You want him? He's yours. I'm only trying to explain why I bonded with him, why I felt a connection that neither of you can understand."

"I'm listening."

"I bonded with Sam because we both felt responsible for someone and lost them. Do you have any idea of the burden that leaves on a heart? It's imprinted like a tattoo that never fades."

"Losing a job and Jake isn't like losing a wife, Maggie. You've been in that lab too long if you think your losses equal his."

"Not my job, Haley. My *sister*." I feel a whoosh of relief mentioning her, as if something dynamic and supernatural has been released from underneath me and I can fly again.

"You don't have a sister," Kathleen says.

"I do. I *did*. I did have a sister." I shake my head wildly. "No more secrets. No more lies. I had a sister. Amy was her name. I lost her when she was eight and I was ten." I hold back tears. "My little sister." *My responsibility.*

Kathleen and Haley both stare at me, waiting for me to tell them I'm joking.

"Why didn't you ever tell us?" Haley asks.

"I wasn't allowed." I correct myself. "I didn't *think* I was allowed. We didn't speak of her after she left us. That's how we handled Amy's loss as a family. We tried to forget that she existed, but it never worked. It only made things ten times worse."

"Your mom never got you counseling after you lost a sister?"

My first instinct is to protect my mother and offer up an explanation for her actions, but for some reason I don't. "My mother didn't want us airing our dirty laundry. My sister died in the backyard pool, and they were already questioned by CPS. Any mention of Amy reminded my mother of her failure as a mother."

"That's why you're afraid to go in the water," Haley says. "Maggie, accidents happen. That was your mother's to deal with, not a ten-year-old's responsibility."

"My mom didn't always try to control the world. That started when Amy left us. We left the church. We left our neighborhood. We just acted like it never happened. There was a short time, honestly, when I did forget that it happened—like I wondered if I'd dreamed it all.

I had to go back and look at the photos, and I promised myself I'd never forget, no matter what my parents said."

"You kept all this to yourself?" Kathleen asks. "I thought we shared everything."

"I can't believe your parents took you from everything you knew," Haley says.

"We didn't mention Amy in our house, but I never forgot her. She was part of my soul. I went forward, powering through everything in front of me. Until Jake left me and I couldn't keep pretending anymore. I'm not Amy. She was the smart one. She was the pretty one. She was the happy, sparkly one that everyone wanted to be around. I tried as hard as I could to mimic her so my parents wouldn't miss her anymore, but then I forgot why I was here. I didn't know what Amy would do next because Jake wouldn't have left her."

"So you only became a doctor because that's what Amy would have done?"

"I don't know. I became a doctor because it made my parents happy. That was the least I could do, wasn't it?"

My mind went back to Amy's empty bed in my room. My loneliness felt all-encompassing, and it left a God-sized hole that nothing seemed to fill. *Maybe*, I'd thought back then, *my parents were right to leave the church. What kind of God would take my sister away from me? Why leave me, the unlovable one, and take Amy, everyone's favorite?*

"Things are all making so much more sense now." Haley appears as if she might cry. "Trauma. I should have known. Why didn't we know?" she asks Kathleen.

"It felt like a sin to say what happened out loud. That's how we dealt with it. Or didn't deal with it, I suppose."

"You told Sam this, but not us?" Haley twists her hair around her finger like she does when she gets nervous.

I shake my head. "I never told him, but I think he sensed something in me. Maybe it's what drew me to him, but we had this connection I can't explain."

"What *drew* you to him?" Haley asks as her empathy dies. "You're living in your head again! He was drawn to rescue you from a smoky death because he's that kind of person. He didn't want to watch someone die!"

"Stop!" Kathleen shouts so loud we're both stunned into silence. "This is not working. You two." She shakes her finger at both of us. "Working together doesn't work. At all! Haley, I tried to help you get Maggie back to work, but that's enough. We have to let her decide when she's done with her pity party. Maggie, you need to stop denying your true feelings. You're going to give up Sam because of Haley—why? What makes her more important than you? Why is everyone always first and you're last? If you want Sam, girl, you go get him. Haley will recover and you know it. She was flirting because she was bored!"

"I was not!" But Haley's resolve dies on the last word.

"That's why her chasing Sam bothered you to begin with," Kathleen says to me. "You're not responsible for everyone's happiness, do you know that?" She turns back to Haley. "And I told you he wasn't for you, so this is your own fault. You just wanted to prove me wrong."

We all go our separate ways on the ship at this point. Sometimes friendships need a vacation so they can heal. This one might need a sabbatical. But I know we'll forgive each other. We always do.

After my speech on Tuesday morning, which goes off without a hitch or a natural disaster, I get a message that I'm to call Dr. Fleece immediately. This must be where my job goes away for good and I call Taco Bell for employment opportunities while I wait for my screenplay to sell. And all I can think is, *Jake has won.* Like always. Evil triumphs. He was better at the game, mostly because I didn't know we were playing. It looks as if he'll leave me with nothing.

Where is God in this scenario? When evil continues to win? Where is the happiness in that?

As soon as I ask the questions, I feel guilty. My faith has waned in trying to make Jake the center of my world. I deserve to be forgotten. Or like Jonah, thrown off this ship for my unbelief. I should be grateful all I did was lose my job.

I enter my suite to make the phone call. It's eight dollars an hour, but how long can it take to fire me? I imagine Dr. Fleece will be expedient. She generally is.

"Dr. Fleece, this is Maggie. I'm returning your call."

"Maggie." She sighs heavily. "I'm so glad you called."

"You said it was urgent."

"It is. Your grant for the resilience study has been approved!" Actual emotion is coming from Dr. Fleece. The world has turned on its axis.

The inner rush I feel is fleeting as I realize I still may be out of a job. My grant may go to the next doctor of happiness to take my place. "Dr. Fleece, do I still have a job at the university?"

"Naturally," she says, as if our last conversation never took place.

"I thought I needed to be questioned by the university police."

"Jake has been arrested and bail was not set. He's a flight risk, it seems."

"He's not on his honeymoon?" I stammer.

"He is definitely not on his honeymoon, unless his new bride is named Bruiser and shares a cell with him."

This makes me giggle. Dr. Fleece is not exactly known for her humor. "How did you know I wasn't involved in his deception?"

"Because his name isn't Jake."

I allow that to sink in for a minute. "His name isn't Jake?"

"He's not married either. He's a professional grifter, a con man. His girlfriend is with him, along for the ride. They con people out of money, steal identities, and move on to the next university. Apparently he's very brilliant, and that's how he's gotten away with it for so long."

"We're not the first?"

"We're definitely not the first. We checked his references and found out that wasn't him. Jake Stone is also known as Travis Kitt."

"And Anichka?"

"Tammy."

Somehow this made me feel worse, not better. The only real romance I'd had that went the distance was with a con artist who needed the time he spent with me to meet and take down his mark.

"Who were they targeting?"

"Dr. Yamoto."

My stomach flip-flops. The doctor had won a Nobel Prize for harnessing blue light into energy-efficient light bulbs.

"I told him about Dr. Yamoto," I admitted.

"He may have made you believe that, but trust me, he knew who he was after."

How Jake—or Anichka for that matter—planned to pass for a Japanese physicist couple was beyond me. But understanding that he was a professional at conning people made me feel better about falling for his shtick. Clearly Sam didn't need to avoid me for my intellect. I apparently lost it a long time ago.

"Where did the grant money come from?"

"Does it matter?" Dr. Fleece asks.

"I just want to know, that's all. I don't want to be tricked again. I've made enough of a fool out of myself, and it's hard to be the resident expert on happiness when you're feeling like a tool."

"No one blames you, Maggie. Don't be ridiculous. The grant money is anonymous, but it's from a corporate source."

"We're not indebted to some corporation, are we? The results don't need to prove a certain outcome, correct?"

"The money is ours, free and clear."

She said everything I needed to hear, so why don't I want to go back? Why does it feel like I'm walking in wet cement? "I'm not sure that I'll be back, Dr. Fleece."

"You're part of the deal, Maggie. If there's no Dr. Maguire, there's no grant."

"What on earth? Who would make that a requirement?"

"I need a date from you, Maggie." Dr. Fleece is back in her typical form. "When can I expect you back at your desk?"

My heart pounds as I think of alternatives, but coming up with none, I relent easily. "I'll be back a week from today, Dr. Fleece."

"Thank you. The department has missed you terribly. Let's put this entire ugly chapter in our history. Hire your friend to get a new TED Talk and let's start over."

It all sounds so easy. *Go back to what you know. Get out of your dream world and your head and get back to work.* This is the job God gave me. It's time to humble myself and get back to work.

I lift my notebook and think about my screenplay. It was a dream. I was entitled to a dream.

I'm not giving up on my screenplay, but I loved my research at one point, and I'll find my joy in it again. Every road points straight back to the university, and this time I'll take the path marked out for me.

24

Resilience is at the core of happiness science. Neuro-plasticity allows the brain to reorder itself after trauma. This is known as post-traumatic growth, and it means that struggles can actually improve us as human beings.

The Science of Resilience by Dr. Margaret K. Maguire

THE COSTUME BALL IS THE CLIMACTIC EVENT on the "New Year, New You" cruise. The flyer, which I never received, says that costumes are to be symbolic of the person you want to become. If that's the case, then I really should have had a Scarlett O'Hara costume, because for once I want to be the woman men notice. It probably would be more fitting that I'm the harlot Scarlett, who has to show up at Melanie's in the vivacious red dress. Desiring the same man my best friend has captured—that seems appropriate.

Our suite is a disaster, as we've all pulled out every bottle, stick, and palette of makeup that we own to prepare for this party. Kathleen and Haley flank me at the mirror.

I brush powder over my makeup. "Am I the only person who didn't get the memo that I was supposed to bring a grand costume?"

"We brought you one," Haley says, leaving the bathroom mirror.

"We knew there would be a costume night. It's nothing as grand as the Belle costume Brent bought for you, but definitely you. We'll let you decide which one to wear." She trails off into the other room and returns holding up my bikini. The one that I bought in college and never wore. I'm not the bikini type. I'm more the Victorian swimming costume type.

"You didn't!"

"Of course not," Haley says. "Just messing with you." She leaves the bathroom and returns again with a pink, Victorian-styled cotton prairie dress dappled with primroses. "We always did think you belonged in another era with your old soul. This is the one we selected for you—because of that show you like on the Hallmark Channel."

"*When Calls the Heart*," I tell them.

"The heart calls now. I'm so hungry!" Kathleen claps her hands. "Let's go, let's go, let's go! Before all the shrimp appetizers are gone and we're stuck with stuffed mushrooms. Nasty."

"I'll stick with Belle."

"Wise choice. We shouldn't have encouraged 1850s fashion—as if you don't have enough trouble in that arena." Kathleen is wearing an elaborate Wonder Woman costume, which consists of a ribbed red leotard with blue-and-white starred shorts, gold cuffs on her arms, and a fanned, red sequined cape. She's got a gold crown with a red star that matches her lipstick perfectly. It's the red thigh-high boots that make the outfit though. She always manages to look strong and not sleazy. How she does it, I'll never know.

Haley is wearing a sequined green mermaid costume, complete with clamshell bra. Her stockinged, green feet stick out of the bottom, and a fanned, sparkling fish tail follows her. I've already stepped on it twice. She can only take tiny steps with her legs plastered together, so it will take us an eon to get to the ballroom.

"How come you both got sultry costumes and I got a gunnysack?"

"You never cared about fashion," Haley says.

"I know I never cared about fashion. That was your job."

"You're wearing the best costume in the room. Brent was so cool to do that. I can't believe he had your number so quickly."

"You really like him, don't you, Kathleen?"

"I do. He's adventurous and fun. He eats like a complete teenager, but I can fix that."

I raise my brow. "Leave the man alone. He has taste buds."

When we're ready and standing at the mirror, I realize just how lucky I am to have such friends. "I never should have been upset about coming here. This is what I needed—a vacation from my thoughts. A chance to speak about Amy and figure out what I needed to be happy."

"And that is?" Kathleen asks.

"To be grateful. For the sister I lost. For the sisters I gained. And for the fact that God has already written the best story for my life. I simply need to be grateful for it."

"Will you tell your parents you're going to celebrate Amy from here on out?"

"They have to deal with Amy's loss in their own way. I only know that I feel so much better talking about her, remembering her and what it was like to have someone love me unconditionally like she did. No wonder no one else could replace that. We were like one." I hug my two best friends. "I'm going home to find Amy's pictures. I'm going to plaster them around my apartment, and I'm never going to be silent about her again. She is why I am who I am. You all are."

"Hurry up! The shrimp is going to be gone!"

"Relax, Kathleen, we're in the Gulf of Mexico. There are more shrimp to be had."

But as it takes us about a million baby (mermaid) steps to get to the ballroom, Kathleen is fresh out of patience and leaves us behind as she makes her way to her sixth small meal of the day.

Everyone has gone all out for the costume ball. The ballroom is elegant and filled with characters worthy of any final scene in the Paris opera. The room is strewn with sparkle lights, and they surround the rails to the dance floor.

I search the room, hoping, praying that Sam will make an appearance. He doesn't seem like the dancing sort, and he's managed to avoid me thus far since the beach excursion. I just want one last glimpse of him to store in my memory banks. I want to remember the connection between us, how his warmth and kindness reminded me of Amy. He made me feel loved and cherished, whether he meant to or not. That wasn't the point. The point was, love was all around me. I no longer want to forget Amy or feeling the pain of losing her. Something about Sam Wellington made me feel again. I'm not numb to the world around me any longer. Life is in color again.

Kathleen stuffs a shrimp in my mouth, and the spicy creole flavors burst on my tongue. "Kathleen!" I giggle while I slide it the rest of the way into my mouth and swallow.

"Well, there's little romance to be had on this boat, so we may as well make the most of the delicious delicacies on board." She strides back to the table where she left poor Haley, who cannot move without great difficulty.

"You're looking for Sam." The Phantom of the Opera removes his mask to reveal Brent's extraordinary blue eyes. I smile at the sight of them.

"I'm not," I tell him. "You make quite a handsome phantom."

"You're beautiful tonight, mademoiselle. **Magnificent.**"

"The phantom costume suits you."

"Does it?" He looks down and brushes his chest off. "I planned to be the Beast—after his transformation into a handsome prince, of course. No one wants to look at that ghastly buffalo head at a party." He winks and places his phantom mask back on his face. "But I lent my costume to someone without one. It seemed fitting."

"That sounds like you, always willing to lend a helping hand." I lift both sides of my skirt and curtsy. "I'm mailing you a check for this gown."

"What else do I have to spend my money on? I saw a beautiful woman in desperate need of a lift so that she'd believe she was as beautiful on the outside as she is on the inside. I obliged, that's all. I can't think of a better investment."

"Brent, you're too good to be true. The first moment I laid eyes on you I saw you had such an incredible heart."

"If only the belles of Texas believed that, my life might look different. But I get friend-zoned pretty quickly. *You* friend-zoned me."

"I didn't!"

"One look at that Sam character and your attention was somewhere else."

I gasp. "It was not."

"Ah, it's water under the ship." He extends his hand toward me. "Would you like to dance, my dear?"

I take his proffered arm. "I would love to." I figure a dance is the least I can do for a man who still manages to see me as a good person after my week of mishaps.

We twirl about the dance floor, and I really do feel like Belle in the great library. The music is lovely, the buzz of the room exciting and light. "Brent, I'm really grateful for you pulling me out of my rut. I don't know why you did it, but I had fun on this cruise. Truly, I did. Despite my attempts to destroy any hope of it. I learned there's a great big world outside of my lab."

"There's also one outside of Sam Wellington."

My smile flattens. "Don't mention his name to me. He had quite a good laugh at my expense on the beach, yet I'll forever be in his debt. Because he taught me one thing."

"What's that?"

"May I cut in?"

Our dancing comes to an abrupt halt as the man in question appears. My stomach twirls about as if it's filled with tiny butterflies in happy, lighthearted flight, but my mind goes back to the notebook . . . Haley and Sam huddled together on the beach with my innermost thoughts and dreams scribbled in front of them. *Haley and Sam.* I just wanted to see Sam one last time. I didn't mean for him to ever see me again—until it was on a book jacket at his sister's home.

I hold Brent closer and shake my head ever so slightly. *No. Don't leave me with him.* I will my eyes to speak for me, but Brent and I don't share the same connection that Sam and I did when we were alone. Brent lets go of me easily and twists me into Sam's waiting embrace. I don't have much fight in me, as it is so natural to be in his arms. My anger dissipates and gives way to the warmth and tenderness I feel being near him. The power of our connection cannot be undone, no matter how inconvenient it is. I understand Sam on a level that seems timeless.

I tuck my head into his shoulder as he dances us about the floor. Because I know looking into his eyes will be my undoing. I'll have no power to resist him if I meet that gaze, and I need to resist him. Sam will sail away from my life forever—just like so many I've loved. It's hard to write about resilience when life is forever forcing your head under the water.

"I wanted your last night on the cruise to be special," he whispers into my ear, and I shiver at his words.

"Thank you for the dance." I pull away from him and stare at my bright, Big-Bird-yellow shoes rather than his dangerous eyes. Dangerous because if he stares into my own, he'll know everything I feel for him. It's imprinted on my soul.

"Haley is near the shrimp table," I murmur to my feet. "She'll probably be waiting for you." It's then that I notice his costume. "You're the Beast!"

He slaps a palm to his chest. "I am the Beast. Brent lent me his costume."

"Why would you dress like my partner?"

"I'll let you guess the reason for that. It seems as if you're quite bright, so I imagine you'll come up with the answer." He winks at me.

"Everything I felt for you is simply my broken heart trying to heal. I imagine that's the case for you too. We were convenient for each other."

"Why don't you ask me what I feel rather than tell me?" His expression is nearly menacing as he asks the question.

"You and Haley read my screenplay," I accuse. "Naturally, I feel you're saying all this so you can make my screenplay come true and have a good chuckle over it. You get to be the hero, and come Monday, I'll never hear from you again."

His hard look softens. "Do you believe I'd do that, Maggie?"

"You'll go back to your venture capitalizing, or whatever you call it, and I'll go back to studying other people's happiness. This is what they call a vacation fling."

"Is it? Did something happen that I don't remember? Because I think vacation flings actually have to involve some kind of fling. I never read about one that included iced tea on a patio with a butler as chaperone. But I could be wrong. You seem to be the expert." A hint of a smile appears.

"You're making fun of me. Haven't you and Haley done enough of that by reading my screenplay?"

"Do you really think I'd make fun of you, Maggie?" He moves closer. "Why do you think my reading your screenplay would make you look ridiculous?"

"That's what people say when they're guilty. They ask a question rather than answer one." I leave the dance floor and he follows me into the silent hallway. The scent of cotton candy fills the room, and my attention is sidelined by the nearby popcorn shop.

"Haley is lovely," Sam says.

"She is." I stare at the popcorn bubbling out of its kettle rather than fall victim to his eyes and gentle words again.

"But Haley is not the one who stirred my heart."

"She's not?" I turn toward him.

"It appears that I must say things plainly—and not because you're less than brilliant, but because you refuse to believe me. Haley is not who I want."

"Everyone wants Haley," I remind him.

Sam shakes his head. "Not everyone wants Haley, Maggie. Regardless of what your research asserts." He touches my arm with his fingertips and I shiver. "I only went to the beach that day so I could see you and find out why you were avoiding me. I was supposed to be avoiding you so I could deny all those crazy feelings that I hadn't felt in ages. The kind of feelings that I never thought I'd have again." He rakes his hand through his dark curls. "When you wouldn't give me the time of day, I realized what meeting you meant to me."

I snicker. He said almost verbatim what I'd written in my screenplay. "Don't tease me, Sam. It isn't kind. Look, I know I'm a pushover from hours spent in front of my movies, but don't be cruel. Everyone has an Achilles' heel. This is mine. When I watch a sweet romance, it makes me remember that love wins and that there is good in the world. Love never dies. Not even when someone you love dies."

"I know that. Who knows that better than me?"

"I'm only saying that you've proven your point, Sam. Maybe I'm not as intellectual as I think I am, so perhaps that means I'm capable of happiness. Do you think?"

"I think you're the smartest woman I've known."

I laugh. "So incapable of happiness?"

"Maggie, please forgive me for my ignorant words. I was protecting myself from what I felt when I saw you—"

"Don't be ridiculous. After this cruise is over, I'll never see you again."

"I can't think of a fate much worse than that," he says, and I will myself to hold his gaze. I'm locked there as so much passes between us without a word. But then I remember his betrayal.

"You and Haley read my private words. Still, it was just a screenplay. I wanted to write an ending that was worthy of a romance movie like all the ones I'd watched on television. I know you're right about one thing. Men don't fall head over heels in love with science researchers. We're the quirky sidekick friend, that's all."

He braces my chin in his hand. "I'd never read your words unless you asked me to."

"You didn't read—" My eyes widen. "How did you—"

"Haley was angry, but she loves you, Maggie. She'd never make fun of you to others. I may not know your friends well, but I know they're thoroughly on your team. Haley wants you to do the work on resilience because she wants her friend back." He lets go of my jaw and takes my hand in his. "She told me how much she hated seeing you alone in that apartment, grieving for a man who never deserved you in the first place. Those were her words."

"My friends really did bring me on this cruise to help me." The thought is almost too much because I know all they sacrificed to get me here. I certainly didn't come willingly.

"I can't stand to think of you alone, questioning your data. It breaks what's left of my heart. You *know* resilience. You're here. After your sister, after Jake, even after the way your mother speaks to you. You're still standing and that proves your strength. You may have lost a lot, but you haven't lost God. He went before you."

"They told you about my sister."

He nods.

"I got the grant for the work on resilience," I say sheepishly. I never thought it would come through after the disaster at the university.

"You did? Maggie, that's incredible. Good for you." His voice changes and shakes a bit, and he looks toward the doors.

My excitement dies at his strange reaction. "I didn't really get the money, did I?" I let out a haggard breath. "You gave the grant money for the study, didn't you?"

"Me?"

"No one else I know has that kind of money, and the government hasn't had my submission long enough. I should have known." I feel betrayed all over again. "It's a pity grant. So your sister will have her book."

"Maggie, I didn't do anything for my sister. I did it for the woman who reminded my heart to start beating again." He lifts my hand and presses a kiss to my fingers. I feel faint at his touch.

"You're a rock star in the happiness-science world. I told you, I can use that information for the companies I fund. I'm not in the business of philanthropy, Dr. Maguire. I don't back anything if it's not a sure thing."

"You think I'm a sure thing?"

"Not only do I think you're the fastest horse in the race, but if you want to take time off and write a screenplay, why shouldn't you? We never know how long we have. God gave you the dream for a reason." Sam starts walking toward the exit doors and pulls me along with him. The surge of adrenaline warms me as we make our break from the masses. "Anyway, I'm honored you'd use my name in the story—even if I was only a place marker."

"Your loss reminded me of my own."

He kisses me softly on the temple. "Your sister."

"Once I remembered her and felt the pain again, it was replaced by joy. That's when I knew I could write the book on resilience. Forgetting the pain isn't the answer—feeling the love we had is."

"Love is always the answer." He grins. "I have a surprise for you." He leads me out the double doors and toward the stern of the ship until we reach the open outdoor theater. Stars dot the sky, and floor deck lights lead us to a pair of chaise lounges. They are pushed together and covered with a white, furry blanket and two pillows.

Arvin is there in his tuxedo with a white towel draped over his wrist. "Dr. Maguire. We've been waiting for you." He holds his arm out and motions for me to sit. The entire area has been cordoned off for the two of us—and Arvin.

I lift my skirt and gingerly climb onto the chaise, and Sam places another fluffy blanket over my legs. He pulls the other chaise even closer to mine and cuddles up under the throw beside me. I can feel his warmth beside me, and no gelato on earth ever tasted as good as being next to him feels. It begins to dawn on me that this isn't the end of Sam Wellington in my life, and I have my pushy, controlling, bossy friends to thank for him.

"This is your movie date," Sam whispers. "Remember the new movies I brought as your reward?"

"We're going to watch them out here?" I ask over the lump in my throat. "Under the stars?"

"We're going to have dinner and a movie, just you and me. No interruptions."

"You're going to watch with me?"

"I've heard there's no actual shooting or explosions in this movie, so I may fall asleep, but I'll be here."

"So no costume ball?"

"Didn't you have enough of the costume ball?"

"I don't think I've had enough Sam Wellington."

"I hope you'll never have enough of me, Maggie."

"For being so supposedly intellectual, I'm a slow learner, aren't I?"

He nods slowly.

I spot Haley and Kathleen on the deck above, waving at me in their ridiculous costumes. "We love you," they shout in unison before running off and giggling like two little girls.

"Maybe I'm not as smart as I think I am."

"Maybe you're not, but I'd love to find out anyway."

"What if I'm only the bad pancake? The rebound girl?" I ask.

"Impossible. I'm reaching for the stars with you, Maggie." He puts his arm around me and pulls me close. He presses his lips to mine and the sky bursts with fireworks. Suddenly I don't want to watch a romantic movie. I never want to wake up from the one I'm living. That's the thing about resilience. You have to know pain to feel the incredible high of coming back from the darkness.

My overactive brain starts up again. "You live in Northern California, I'm in Southern. The logistics of long-distance relationships—"

"We're smart enough. We'll figure that out. I know you love your sappy movies, but I want our story to end slightly more satisfyingly. We'll write our own ending."

I laugh, and he tosses off the blanket and leans in to kiss me. "Mr. Wellington . . ."

The vacation in paradise will end soon. I'll be back at the university scrutinizing the data on happy people. My parents will continue not to allow me to mention my beloved sister, Amy. My friends will continue to make fun of me for my librarian fashion. Sam will live on one side of the state, while I dwell on the other.

Nothing has really changed, except everything is different, covered in the overwhelming wave of love.

The data shows that Dr. Maggie Maguire is finally happy.

ACKNOWLEDGMENTS

I'M SO GRATEFUL TO MY EDITOR Lonnie Hull DuPont, who is such a blessing to me. Thank you for taking a chance on this book and for making it better. Thank you to the entire team at Revell and especially Hannah Brinks Korns for keeping me on task. Finally, to Jessica English, who went beyond the call of duty with her edits. Writing is a team effort, and it's amazing to have an awesome team.

KRISTIN BILLERBECK is a bestselling, award-winning author of over forty-five novels. Her work has been featured in the *New York Times* and on *Today*. Kristin is a proud mother of four and a lifelong resident of Silicon Valley, California. When not writing, she enjoys good handbags, bad reality television, and annoying her children on social media.

THE PROM COUNTDOWN
HAS BEGUN . . .

Perfectly Dateless is hilarious, shocking, and totally real. You'll fall in love with Daisy's sharp wit and resourcefulness as she navigates the world of boys, fashion, family, and friendship.

LIFE AFTER HIGH SCHOOL IS SO CLOSE .... AND YET SO VERY FAR AWAY.

It's Daisy Crispin's final semester of high school, and she plans to make it count. Her long-awaited freedom is mere months away, and her big plans for college loom in the future. Everything is under control.

OR IS IT?

DAISY'S READY FOR SUMMER FUN— BUT IT SEEMS SUMMER HAS
SOMETHING ELSE IN STORE.

A Universally Misunderstood Novel

perfectly ridiculous

kristin billerbeck

Bestselling author of *What a Girl Wants*

When Daisy discovers she needs to do missions work to fulfill the requirements of her scholarship, what was supposed to be a relaxing summer vacation turns into hard work, sleeping on a cot, avoiding scorpions, and stressing about where she stands with her boyfriend Max. Daisy wonders if anything in her life will ever go according to plan . . .

Revell
a division of Baker Publishing Group
www.RevellBooks.com

Available wherever books and ebooks are sold.